ARTIFICIAL AGENT

J.W. JARVIS

BIG DEE
BOOKS

REWARD

As this manuscript's author, I offer you, the opportunity to redeem a cash award for introducing this work to any producer that offers an acceptable contract [to the author] for this work. The reward offered is 10% of any exercised option contract for a film or streaming series up to a maximum of $20,000.00 USD.

Why am I offering a cash reward to readers?

Dream: Since childhood, I've yearned to see my ideas materialize on the big screen. Writing is my outlet, transporting readers' minds to unexplored places. Media venues allow me to reach others who are not avid readers but would still enjoy my stories.

Volume: Writing is an inherently solitary endeavor and, as an author, I struggle to network, mingle and promote my work. Offering readers a reward to do it not only augments my lack of proficiency but also multiplies the effort as each volume in the hands of the reader starts diverse chains of discussion and introduction, one of which will lead to success.

Collaboration: Reading is unique among all entertainment vehicles because it requires effort from the reader: the author and reader collaborate to tell the story. Hearing what readers enjoy is exciting for any author. The collaboration of this reward program offers the reader a chance to help jumpstart the career of an author who entertains them. Besides, producers are much more interested in readers' likes vs. authors' offerings.

Suggestions:
Via this reward, our mutual goal is to introduce this work to a movie or streaming service (Netflix, Prime Video, Max, Apple, Hulu, etc.) producer. You might be familiar with the term "six degrees of separation." This is the theory that anyone on the planet can be connected to any other person on the planet through a chain of acquaintances that have no more than five intermediaries. This is what l aim to accomplish here with your help.

- Think about who you know in the entertainment industry (agents, actors, producers, directors, executives, etc.) and pass this book on to them.
- Think about who you know and who they might know in the entertainment industry.
- Think about those you know who like to read and would enjoy this book.

Send any leads, or opportunities, or introductions via the email link below.

Thank you in advance for your help.
J.W. Jarvis

https://www.authorjwjarvis.com/contact

JOIN MY VIP READER CLUB

J.W. Jarvis' VIP Reader Club members get free books, access to discounts, and other unique items to accompany the books.

Members are always the first to hear about J.W. Jarvis' new books and publications.

If you haven't read **Book 1** in the **First Responder Series, The Phantom Firefighter**, there are details in the back of the book on how to get it for **FREE** by signing up for my **VIP Reader Club**.

PROLOGUE

The room was completely absent of light. Small flashing LED lights provided brief illumination and appeared to be coming from electronic equipment left in standby mode. During the brief half-seconds of red light, he gathered he was in a makeshift medical clinic room. In the corner was a utility sink with dark stained towels hanging from its edges. His initial thought was blood stains, but hard to tell with the limited light spectrum. The faucet dripped once every nine seconds, the calculations one engages in during idle contemplation. A chill filled the room, accompanied by a damp and musty smell. Airflow was non-existent, which caused the floors to feel moist under his bare feet. To increase blood flow for warmth, the man's naked body stiffened as he flexed his muscles. This offered respite from the cold, but pain as the thick, scratchy sisal ropes around his legs and chest dug into his skin more. He was grateful they kept his underwear on, which shielded his backside from the cold metal chair. They bolted the chair to the concrete floor, preventing movement or escape. This was not his first precarious position, but it felt different this time.

Despite the pounding in his head, his memory remained clear about the betrayal during this mission, putting his team and himself in danger. It hurt to think, but he had to contemplate the future. Keeping him alive had a purpose - extracting information. He considered they would try to use sodium thiopental for an interrogation technique, but little did they know that his training helped him build up a tolerance to the "truth serum." They would give up and use other methods before hitting his tolerance level to be effective. Perhaps they would then move to waterboarding, a type of interrogation that caused a sensation of drowning. Even that would be fruitless, as they had drowned him purposely during training countless times, one of which had resulted in his heart stopping for eight minutes and requiring defibrillation. Anything after ten minutes can be fatal.

He hoped that he would have enough strength to over-power his captors while they set him up for one of their torture tests. Most "frogmen" had received training in Krav Maga, but the commander had also received training in Systema. The Russian military used Systema, a martial art, since the 10th century. He knew his opponents would counter his moves with their local combat training, giving him the advantage of anticipating it. Blood seeped from his head to his neck as the door unlocked and echoed in the room. A single-bulbed fluorescent light above him turned on and started flickering from its aged ballast. As the door opened, the dim yellow glow cast over the two figures entering the room, one with a large silver metal briefcase.

They were men of Eastern European descent wearing white and tan camouflage uniforms; the type worn to conceal a trooper in a snow-laden forest. With a weight easily pushing almost three bills, the bigger of the two men had a muscular build, except for his midsection, where he had some extra weight. The type of growth men past their prime have difficulty losing, especially on a steady diet of starchy potatoes. Both men had full beards, the larger man's was mixed with gray hairs. The thinner man was apprehensive to make a move without a cue from the bigger man. Apparently, the larger man was in charge.

The last person to enter the room was a younger woman in a long silver-gray fur coat. The garment would have caused an uproar with PETA for at least three wolves lost their lives in its construction. With the coat hood over her head concealing most of her wavy, blonde hair, she wore bright red lipstick that stood out from her shadowed face. She looked entirely out of place from the other two military figures. There was a scowl on her face as her green eyes locked on the captive. She scanned his muscular body up and down without changing her emotion.

"Are you sure this is him?" The woman had either a Russian or Ukrainian accent.

"Da," says the large man in his native tongue.

"Shame," as the woman gave the commander another look up and down, now clearly interested in his masculine form despite the scars, dirt, and dried blood scattered over his torso.

She moved closer to within a foot from the seated man's knees, still holding her coat together with perfectly manicured hands. The oversized fur coat obscured most of the view of the men behind her. She released the coat and crouched to touch the commander's shoulders with both hands. Beneath the coat was her athletic body, completely naked, with silky white skin and large fake breasts. She straddled the captive and started gyrating on his lap. The warm skin-to-cold-skin contact, and flowery perfume was welcoming to the commander, but he also knew she was trying to get a sexual reaction out of him. It was difficult to resist, but he forced his mind to focus elsewhere. After a minute, she realized her intentions were not working. She pulled off his lap forcefully while slapping him so hard across the face that her nails left three bloody lines on his right cheek. Seconds later, she stormed out of the room, slamming the door.

The more senior officer sighed, then responded in broken English with a heavy Russian accent. "I see you have upset my daughter again. That'll be the last time you do."

"What now, GIP?" says the younger military man.

"Open the briefcase."

The commander thought it was odd that they skipped asking questions and were eager to move on to the torture part. This was not a military operation; it was personal. That probably meant they would not hold back. Despite being in information-extracting hostage situations several times, this new vendetta scenario made the commander uneasy. He had also heard the term "GIP" before in his study of the Eastern European military, but his bruised head and ringing in his ears still present from the hard slap was fogging his recollection. The "G" definitely stood for general, as in the military rank, that he was certain.

"You Americans are all about fireworks, aren't you?" GIP says with an evil grin.

"Here you are, sir," the cadet handed him a red paper-wrapped pack with a Black Cat logo on the front.

"You Americans even think you do firecrackers better than everyone else. I got these shipped from the States. Decided you were too good for those Chinese versions. Their dud ratio is like 50%."

GIP pulled apart a handful of the one-and-a-half-inch firecrackers and lit them at the commander's feet. A loud noise echoed in the small room as they went off. This forced the commander to dance while sitting.

"Did you see that, Cadet? Not one dud out of 10. Maybe Americans are better than the Chinese."

The commander spoke up to find out his bargaining power. "What do you want?"

"It's not what I want; it's what Irina wants. You know, the blonde woman that you just insulted? Only, you can't bring her fiancé back now, can you?" says GIP.

The captive discreetly scanned the room for a weapon. "I'm not following." A ballpoint pen would've been a godsend.

"You're a man that's good with your hands, right? Let's see."

GIP motioned to his helper, who held the commander's hands while he duct-taped a bunch of firecrackers to his fingers on each hand. Before the commander could plead, the wicks were lit, and the Russians held up their palms to cover their ears. The commander watched in horror as his hands ignited with tiny explosions that sent an intense pain through his fingers, as if he put his hands directly on an open fire for five seconds. All ten fingers had a mix of deep red to charred black skin with open sores at the points where the firecracker was in direct contact with the finger. The throbbing reached a level that would make most men faint.

"Jesus, man, what the hell is this about? I should know why I'm here." The commander tried to take his mind off the pain.

"Show him the picture, Cadet, while I prep phase 2," says GIP as his eyes lit up with anticipation.

The cadet pulled a black-and-white photograph out of the suitcase and showed it to the commander. Even in the dim lighting, it was clear why he was under attack. Sometimes, a past mission success catches up in unforeseen ways with soldiers. As the clarity came, Commander Cooling observed GIP pull much larger firecrackers from the silver case. The labels on the firecrackers were M-150 and M-250. The little ATF training he had grimly reminded him that even a smaller M-80 can remove fingers or parts of hands.

CHAPTER
ONE

THE WHITE HOUSE

Dignitaries, the press, and various ranks of the Navy filled the East Room. This included some members of the Royal Navy on holiday. Participants filled up nearly every foot of the oak wood floors, yet the 18-foot gold drapes adorning the windows and massive electric chandeliers made of cut glass and gilded brass were still highly visible. These touches of grandeur fitted a room with such historical significance. Many years ago, this room hosted the funeral of President Lincoln. Today, it would provide the backdrop for awarding the highest military award for valor in the United States.

Since the unit was officially formed in 1962, only seven Navy Seals have received the Medal of Honor. It had also been seven years since a Seal received the award. The last award was for bravery during a hostage rescue in Afghanistan. Today, they would award the eighth medal for preventing a world leader's assassination by neutralizing three Russian paramilitary men.

Michael Cooling disliked the attention he was receiving. He felt the satisfaction of doing his job was enough for that ominous evening in Kyiv. The Ukrainian president had already given the Medal "For Military Service of Ukraine" to him in another opulent ceremony before Michael returned to the States a few weeks back. This stateside ceremony felt more for the American politicians than for him. They were feeding off his bravery to show that the States was an excellent ally of Ukraine. Unsurprisingly, the media was present, vying for the finest image or video. His cheeks were aching from the many fake smiles he performed while some politicians put their arm around his shoulders like they were best buddies. Most people photographed with Michael were unknown to him. The only one that mattered to him was the picture with his commanding officer, Chase, a Navy captain, and his mentor. Chase was the officer who recommended Michael to the DEVGRU unit.

Michael was a man just over six feet tall, with short brown hair and azure eyes. Since youth, his aspiration was to become a military officer. Perhaps his fascination started with his first G.I. Joe toy collection, or maybe it was because he heard his father was an officer in the Air Force. He knew little about his father except what his mother told him. He knew they shared the same first name and that his mother was hopelessly in love with him, but she wouldn't share any more. When Michael had asked why they weren't together, his mother responded that his father's career was more important to him than his family. Michael considered finding his dad through a DNA test but decided against it after joining the Navy. Anonymity is essential, especially when working on secret missions. DNA strands, if leaked, can tell the enemy a lot about a person's weaknesses, such as personality traits or mental health. An operative needs the advantage in the event they become a direct target of the enemy. Michael chose instead to reach the highest rank he could in the Navy while still being useful tactically. His callsign became "Ghostwalker" for his unique ability to sneak up on a threat and neutralize them while remaining completely undetected. Someday, if he ever met his dad, he would have something for his dad to be proud of. His promotion last year to commander of the Navy SEAL's Silver Squadron felt like the pinnacle of his career, even higher than his honoring tonight.

After receiving his medal from the President and taking more pictures, they set up the podium for Michael's acceptance speech. Michael dreaded this part. Instead of addressing nearly 300 people, he would rather dive into an enemy's bunker. As he gingerly approached the steps to the stage, Captain Chase Donnelly intercepted him.

"Commander, sorry, but we have an urgent situation."

Michael felt relief and instant excitement. *Now we're talking.* "How can I help, sir?"

"I need to take you to the briefing room." Chase turned to the White House press secretary, who approached from the front row. "Sorry, Ma'am, duty calls. Can you please make an announcement? We won't be back." The secretary frowned but nodded.

Walking with the captain, Michael observed the crowd's confused expressions. Little did they know how perfect this ending was for his evening. He smiled and waved back to address their collective concern.

"We're heading to the helipad; we have an MH-60 waiting for us."

"Little Creek?" says Michael.

"Yep, then Eastern Europe."

The maritime gray Black Hawk helicopter stood out against the orange and yellow background of the evening dusk as they approached the south lawn. It was a perfect mixture of natural and technological beauty. The military engineering marvels always caught Michael's attention. He would have chosen mechanical engineering if he hadn't majored in strategic intelligence. The helicopter's stealth technology made it almost silent. The blades were whisper-quiet from afar by leveraging modulated spacing configurations, significantly reducing rotor noise and vibration. Michael loved learning and would read the chopper's manual while traveling on missions.

"Good evening, Commander; sorry to ruin your festivities." The vice admiral reached out his hand to help Michael into the helicopter. "We're about 60 mikes out. Let's get you up to speed on the particulars. This is Tier Three Top Secret, but it could escalate."

"Mikes" was slang for minutes in the military. Michael was glad the trip would be short, and it wasn't Tier 5, the highest security level. He wasn't even sure he had clearance to hear it if it was.

"Problems in Kyiv, again, Admiral Jackson?"

"It started there, but we're not going there. At zero-three hundred hours Moscow time, two Ukrainian generals were taken hostage from their homes in a concerted effort.

Both of their wives and one child were killed during the capture. We believe they took them somewhere in Belarus, one of their airfield bases. As you know, this leaves Ukraine with very little military leadership. At least until the president returns. We think this is a military distraction to mount a new strike in the capital."

"Jesus … how old was the kid?" says Michael.

"We believe she was only five years old. These people are ruthless."

"What time is wheels up? Is my platoon there already?"

"Yes, we assembled a team of four, but we don't want you going in. You will run this from the Kyiv command post."

Michael grumbled, "Why? My guys need me there. I have experience with these Russkies; I know how they move."

"You're a celebrity now, whether you like it or not. Your face is all over the news. If they capture you, they will know it was the Americans. We're not supposed to be fighting this war, only helping to supply it."

"So, just like that, I'm stuck behind a desk?"

"For now, you are. Commander, this work is too sensitive to the reputation of the United States. Don't argue with me. Here is the file. Please memorize these airfield schematics. We have narrowed it down to two sites where they are holding the generals."

CHAPTER
TWO

NORTHERN BELARUS

The captured generals were held in the underground storage facility at Orsha Airfield in Belarus. Its strategic location made it ideal in the current conflict. The facility was used to store military equipment, but primarily for jet fuel. The airstrip had at least 40 feet of earth between it and the stored fuel, which protected it from enemy airstrikes. Overseeing the entire operation was General Ivan Petrovsky, a former officer in the FSB for nearly 15 years before forming his own private military organization. His plan was both simple and brutal. Should a multi-national rescue attempt happen, he would have a fallback plan to incinerate the fuel and the generals with it. The airstrip would suffer a giant crater, blamed on a faulty military exercise.

Petrovsky's unit, called The Red Army, was both a nod to their loyalty to the Russian government and its president. His independence, however, meant Petrovsky could operate more effectively on his own. The government funded his paramilitary start-up, and his fighter strength grew yearly. Some of his group came from the country's special forces. Others were men and women recruited in exchange for no or reduced jail times for their crimes. Petrovsky didn't care who his followers were as long as they shared his long-term vision, the Red Union, a resurrection of the once glorious Soviet Union. The Ukraine was one of the 15 states that were part of the original Soviet Union before it dissolved in late 1991. Since then, Petrovsky made it his duty to re-unionize the states, even if it meant killing or torturing comrades that got in his way. As a paramilitary, his group used whatever means necessary, many of which were illegal. Keeping the generals hostage for his current mission was not about his personal goals, but about fulfilling an obligation to a family member.

The general completed his fingerprint scan to get into the tank room containing the Ukrainian captives. Three militiamen guarded the prisoners, each armed with AK-74 assault rifles and Makarov PM handguns holstered on their belts. A thick chain secured the prisoners to a cement cylinder building column. Dark circles around their wrists matched the width of the chain. They didn't even look like generals. Being violently ripped from their beds in the middle of the night, both were wearing full-length thermal undergarments. One's hair was sticking up in wild directions, while the other was unshaven. The men sat on the cold floor with their heads between their knees. A fourth militiaman was dividing up three white potatoes and some sauerkraut between two tin plates.

"What the hell are you doing, Lieutenant?" says Petrovsky.

"Sir? Preparing their dinner, sir."

The general got behind Cadet Anton, one of the prisoner guards, and spoke gently near his ear. "Is that what we do here, Cadet?"

Cadet Anton shook his head in disagreement without answering verbally. As he did, Petrovsky pulled the cadet's 9mm sidearm from his holster and shot the lieutenant through the side of his neck. Dark red blood gushed out of the large hole and spattered all over the two plates of food. The general dropped the gun at Cadet Anton's feet. He walked over to the man flailing on the floor and shook his head. Petrovsky picked up the two plates of blood-soaked food and slid them in front of the prisoners.

"Bon appétit!" The general then turned toward the guards. "One meal a day for our guests unless you want them at full strength like this idiot over there. Since this is their second meal, they get nothing tomorrow."

The guards nodded in agreement and stopped sweating. Even if they wanted to help their comrade, he was nearly dead. They knew better than to move. All militia actions required a direct order from Petrovsky. The Russian general had earned a reputation of being ruthless and unpredictable. Red Army recruits received nearly double the salary and officer rankings, depending on their experience, to join the paramilitary group compared to staying in the Russian Ground Forces. The risk was worth the reward. Men serving under the general sought a quick way to get ahead. Many had gotten into bad debt from poor life decisions or just exited prison and needed to make money fast. Petrovsky only wanted militia in their prime so they could be agile and undistracted by family commitments. He had a strict rule that his men would be no older than 35. If a militiaman reached that age, Petrovsky included a two-year severance with their discharge papers. This assumed that the officer didn't end up dead before then. Either way, the lure to younger men was strong enough to join.

"General Petrovsky, why are we here?" asks one of the Ukrainian generals.

"That's an excellent question, General Kuzma, but please call me 'GIP.' I've built an evil reputation with that nickname, and I would like to keep it." GIP grinned.

"Are you the GIP that blew up a grade school in Kazan?" the other Ukrainian general asks.

"There's only one GIP in Mother Russia. Yes, that was me. Before you accuse me of being a terrorist, know they were teaching American English at that school. Besides, almost everyone got out safely. Everyone knows 8th graders are the biggest bullies," GIP says.

"You have taken everything from us; why do you think we would talk?" says Kuzma.

"Oh, you're not here to talk; you're here as bait. Think of yourselves as two herrings on a line to catch a bluefin tuna. Only this tuna is *red, white, and blue*!"

General Kuzma looked at his captive partner with furrowed eyebrows. His shoulders slumped and his fists clenched. What happens to them after the general gets the desired response from the States? GIP photographed each of the prisoners in case he needed proof of life. He nodded to the guards, who saluted him as he left the room.

He walked down the wide, dimly lit hallway of the facility. Cinder block walls, void of any decorations, went on forever. The underground space was purely for functional purposes and not for long-term occupation. He entered a kitchen area with a small refrigerator, a two-burner stovetop, and a small aluminum sink. Luckily, it also had a small coffee maker as well. He turned the faucet on to fill the coffeepot. The stream had a reddish-brown tinge. He waited for ten seconds till the water looked semi-translucent.

As he waited for the coffee, he glanced at the cardboard boxes brought down from the surface. They contained potatoes, cabbage, bottled water and some grapes. He hoped they had enough food. Including the sausage in the refrigerator, the supplies should last them a week. The enemy would watch the airfield for movement. He didn't want to risk any of his men getting captured to get additional supplies.

His team had left a Tigr vehicle, similar to the American Humvee, under some trees near the storage facility entrance. He hoped that was enough to incite suspicion by the rescue team. Since the airfield primarily served as a refueling depot for aircraft, it was mainly abandoned. There were only two ways to enter or exit the underground facility. The exits had reinforced steel doors. GIP had his team monitoring both, expecting a hostage rescue. The facility had three 50,000-gallon tanks, two filled with jet fuel. Any needs to refill or extract the fuel happened from the surface, but occasionally, the tanks needed maintenance from below.

As the general poured a shot of vodka into his steaming cup of coffee, his phone rang and vibrated.

"Irina, I don't have an update for you yet."

"I know, but I have an additional request."

"You know I'm supposed to be working on a mission for the Kremlin right now. Am I not doing enough for you right now? I'm risking the lives of eight of my best men."

"I'm not asking you to do more; I just have a simple request," says Irina. "I want to meet him."

"Who? The American soldier? No way, way too dangerous."

"I want to look into the eyes of the animal that killed my fiancé."

"You saw him on TV, and besides, I can't guarantee he will show up."

"In person is much different. Please, Father, I'll accept all risks. I'm staying at a hotel nearby, in Polatsk. Just call me if you get him; I'll only come then."

"I promised your mother I would protect you, but she is dead, so I guess it doesn't matter. It's your funeral, and don't expect me to be there in the public eye. The things I do for you, *fuck*!"

"I love you and thank you."

"Da, my little one."

When the call ended, Petrovsky flung his ceramic coffee cup at the concrete wall, smashing it into a dozen pieces.

CHAPTER
THREE

"They are at Orsha," Michael says, as the chopper slowed down to land at the Naval base in Virginia.

"How do you know?" The admiral's eyes narrowed.

"When I was in Kyiv, one of their spies told me about Vitebsk airfield. It's on the east side of Belarus. It is a bustling jump point for the fighters and some convoys heading to the Ukrainian border to fight. Bringing hostages there would be too risky. The militia doesn't like to mix in with the Russian ground forces."

"Affirmative. We'll focus our satellites on the south."

As Michael jogged away from the Black Hawk, he smiled proudly, watching the C-5 Galaxy being loaded up by his Triple-S team. This nickname for his Silver Squadron SEALs stuck after he gave it to the team during a mission a few years ago. The idea came to Michael while watching a movie starring Vin Diesel during a long flight to Budapest.

From a distance, it looked like four real-life snowmen scurrying around the asphalted runway, as the team had already changed into their arctic camouflage gear. The white and gray cover would be perfect for the wintery backdrop that surrounded the airfield. The transport size looked ridiculous for a HALO jump at 30,000 feet with only four SEALs. Michael knew they needed to airdrop a crate of weapons. However, it was only the size of a refrigerator. A C-5 is big enough to carry five military helicopters. This transport was probably the only one available in the area to meet the mission start time.

Not her! Michael was close enough to recognize which team members were going on the mission.

Jasmine Pham had gone through Officer Candidate School (OCS) to earn a commission as an Ensign in the U.S. Navy before applying to become a SEAL. A bachelor's degree was necessary to become a commissioned officer, which she had. Remarkably, she accomplished something no one in history had ever done. Jasmine was the first woman to pass the highly competitive, physical, and mentally challenging process of becoming a Navy SEAL that washed out 70-85% of each class.

Jasmine outranked most of the members of the Silver Squadron. It was humbling for them but frustrating as she was absolutely gorgeous. Her mother had represented the Philippines twice in the Miss Universe pageant and won one of those times. Her father was a retired officer in the Vietnamese Navy. Michael's team admitted it was difficult to treat her like one of the guys. They all wanted to date her. Michael had the demanding job of managing a highly skilled tactical team that took on impossible missions from the United States government and dealing with this new team dynamic.

Michael thought Jasmine was beautiful but had always put his duty to the country ahead of his interests. His last date with a woman felt like a distant memory. Jasmine looked up to him, which made him feel like he needed to protect her at all costs. She was a born leader with a powerful ambition and a bright future in the Navy. She would be the ground lead for this mission, and it irritated Michael that he wouldn't be there physically to support her.

"I heard the admiral thinks you're too fat and slow to help us on this one," jokes Jasmine.

"I didn't know you got a degree in comedy; I thought it was psychology." Michael picked up one of the HALO suits to inspect it.

"Sir, we're just about done loading the supply crate; one of our night-vision goggles went belly-up, so we only have three. White House wants wheels up in thirty minutes. I figured you missed your fancy award dinner with gold-plated forks, so I brought you the next best thing, a banh mi from Pho La La."

"Honestly, I would prefer that any day over a gourmet meal sitting next to fake dignitaries. You're always looking out for me; thanks, Hoanh." Michael liked to call Jasmine by her Vietnamese name, which was pronounced "One."

"Commander, how are you? May I have a word?" says Petty Officer Stinson.

"Sure, what's on your mind?"

"I want to go over the drop calculations with you. If I miscalculate, the winds will take us into Russia for an early breakfast. I figured we might want to avoid that."

Michael put his arm around Stinson, smiling. "Let's head to the control room. Show me what you got."

Ensign Pham handed the paper-wrapped sandwich to Michael as he walked toward the inside of the transport. Michael's olfactory sensors took in the smell of the perfectly seasoned pork tenderloin wrapped in a fresh-baked baguette. His hunger couldn't wait, so he tore a portion of the paper away and took a few crunchy bites as they walked through the cargo section of the C-5. The sandwich hit the spot, but a cold beer would have made it even better.

Petty Officer Sam Stinson was in his third year as a SEAL and second with the Triple-S team. While SEALs have versatile skills in air, land, or sea missions, Officer Stinson specialized in free-fall parachuting and was an excellent marksman. Sam would never admit it, but Michael was confident in his officer's skills. If Sam wanted to, he could calculate a jump landing the entire team on a location the size of a baseball pitcher's mound, even in the most inclement weather. Michael knew his officer was asking him to review his plans out of respect, but maybe that extra confidence was what he needed to be so precise.

"Sir, do we have any idea who did this?" Stinson says.

"We don't have intel confirmation, but I would bet my Desert Eagle handgun that it's the Russian paramilitaries. They do all of Mother Russia's dirty work." Michael licked the last of the sandwich sauce from his fingers.

Minutes later, the long whining sound signified the visor closing. This closed the nose of the plane for take-off. It was about 4600 miles to Belarus. Luckily, the transport was nearly empty and could reach top speeds, allowing the team to arrive in less than eight hours. Michael checked in with the other two petty officers and settled into the cargo-hold seat. The chair was rigid, and it didn't recline. It was the opposite of first class. He tried to rest his eyes. A long couple of days were ahead of them.

Jasmine awoke to the team clamoring around the cargo area, checking their gear and testing their oxygen masks. At 30,000 feet, the team would need supplemental oxygen until they reached an altitude under 20,000, where humans can breathe without aid.

"Why didn't you wake me earlier?" Jasmine's eyes furrowed, looking at Stinson.

"The boys and I thought you wanted your beauty sleep." Stinson winked.

The rest of the team smiled without distracting their focus from continuing to prep their gear. Jasmine knew there was a slight power trip between her team and her, given her superior ranking, but she also knew they had her back no matter what.

"We're 300 miles from the drop. I had to move us to an earlier time with the prevailing tailwinds. Good news though, we will land in a winter wonderland. The airstrip has already received an inch of powder. This should help with our cover," says Stinson.

"Team, make sure you check your mask adhesion. A mask flying off before 20K means hypoxia is nearly certain. We don't have time to clean up SEAL splatter," says Michael.

"If that happens to me, can you at least delete my phone browser history?" says Petty Officer Chapman.

"Why is that?" says Petty Officer Turner.

"I finally found some pageant swimsuit pics of Ensign's mom's glory days." Chapman smiled as he put on his oxygen mask.

Jasmine swiftly made a roundhouse kick, knocking Chapman's mask clearly off his face. It was so precise that his head didn't even move. "Still too loose!"

Everyone but Chapman let out a hearty laugh.

The pilot signaled the drop point was near, and the team, including Michael, breathed through their masks. They completed a final round of sound checks, as the mask also had microphones to communicate with each other. After matching the air pressure outside, Michael opened the aft ramp of the C-5, and the air in the cargo bay swirled around with a bitter chill.

The team focused their vision on the red jump light near the exit. As it turned green, the first two pushed the large metal crate carrying their supplies off the ramp, which activated an automatic timer for its parachute. They subsequently jumped one after another. Stinson was the last one, after which Michael activated the ramp closure switch.

The sudden acceleration of Jasmine's body through the thin air was exhilarating. That was one reason she aspired to become a SEAL. The HALO jumps never got old, no matter how many times you did them. Even though the night obscured the view, Jasmine found the sensation of air resistance on her body and the speed of her fall exciting. The only awareness of her team being near her was her night vision goggles picking up the flashing green lights emitting from their helmets in the distance. Despite the helmets' ability to enable verbal communication, they avoided it at the risk of an enemy eavesdropping. They also had to concentrate on their altitude. To avoid detection, they could only open their parachute at 3000 feet. They would have to trust their wrist altimeters since visibility was tricky at night, not to mention the snowstorm they were entering. Given the whole jump would take less than three minutes, missing the chute release mark could mean death seconds later.

After hearing the distinctive *whoosh* made by the deployment of her life-saving nylon fabric, Jasmine felt her body jerk toward the heavens. The sudden pressure on her torso subsided as she sailed through the air in a more controlled fashion. Her night vision goggles made out some building structures near the airstrip. Jasmine figured they were about a mile away. The airfield was dormant. A handful of small flashing lights sat atop what resembled a control tower. The snow powder exploded upward in front of her as she made her landing. When the white dust cleared, she looked around to see her other teammates disengaging their chutes and beginning to wrap them up. Their next task was to locate their supply crate, probably already covered in white because of the constant snowfall.

CHAPTER
FOUR

Bila Tserkva air base was expecting the sizeable American transport. They arrived late at night. A welcoming party of two HMMWVs was already waiting on the tarmac. HMMWVs were short for high-mobility multipurpose wheeled vehicles, also called Humvees. They were the preferred vehicle by the military and could have over 15 different configurations, from troop to combat-ready transport. The HMMWVs were wider than they were tall, which gave them a low profile yet superior stability.

Michael looked out the window and shook his head in reproach. This operation was supposed to be secret, and his presence incognito. Someone from the States asked for this. Michael disliked it when his superiors provided unsolicited support. Part of his success in his career was being a ghost behind enemy lines until he needed to appear. While he had the use of a satellite link with his ground team, he checked in to ensure they were operational before exiting the Galaxy. The U.S. Embassy was over an hour away. During the drive, he could no longer communicate with Triple-S until he arrived.

"How was your flight, sir?" A junior analyst dressed in an oversized green puffy jacket from the embassy asked as he saluted.

"Long … why are these here?" Michael pointed to the Humvees.

"Admiral Jackson said——"

"Don't care. Not taking these to the embassy. Find me the plainest vehicle here."

"But—"

"Now, kid! Time is of the essence. Do you want us on the morning news? We're not riding in these targets."

"On it!" The analyst looked at both Humvee drivers in full military uniform with a nervous wave-off gesture. He made a phone call back to the base command.

Michael looked around and inhaled. The air was crisp and cold in his lungs. The sensation calmed some of the stress he felt about the delay. He decided it was time to enjoy the gifted White House cigar. It was the one benefit he appreciated from the lavish event. The Nicaraguan ambassador had given him a Padrón 1964 Anniversary Series Torpedo. Nicaragua was the best cigar maker outside of Cuba. This one won an award a few years ago. It was impossible to find in the States, especially with the embargo. It lit with a match, despite the freezing temperature outside. Michael detected notes of hazelnut upon inhalation, which segued into a complex flavor of smoked cocoa bean. The buzz came in seconds, smoking his first stogie in a month.

The pilot, about 20 feet away, saw Michael smoking

and with a cigarette in-between his fingers motioned to Michael if he could have a light. Michael tossed the small matchbox at him.

"Nice arm," he says. "Did your dad teach you that?"

Michael says, "No, unfortunately."

"Crown Victoria work for you, sir?" The analyst asked after getting off his call.

"Yes, as long as it's quick. We must get on the road."

While waiting for the car, Michael used the time to send an encrypted text to Captain Donnelly. He gave him an update on his ground team and his disdain for the Admiral's transport arrangement. Being a decorated commander had its benefits. With no repercussions, he voiced his opinions. He would never disrespect a senior officer, but he also didn't want a mistake made twice, especially with jeopardizing the safety of his team or himself.

The sedan pulled up, and Michael extinguished his cigar, saving the rest for a later time. Typically, he would toss a used cigar, as they didn't keep well unmaintained, but this one was too special to half-smoke. He entered the backseat of the car with the analyst. His puffy jacket took up half of the sitting area. He appreciated the office folks who helped them through challenging tactical situations in the past, but this guy was annoying.

"Aren't you going to be a little warm in that? It's a long ride," says Michael.

"You're right," says the analyst as the car drove off. "Wait, driver!"

The car halted, and with haste, he exited it, taking off his coat to place it in the trunk. This annoyed Michael again, even though it meant more space. A scrawny frame re-entered the vehicle, reaffirming Michael's nerdy perception of the man.

The roads were vacant, being several hours before sunrise. Avoiding the use of attention-grabbing Humvees was the right decision. Michael made some small talk with the driver, as he didn't trust anyone. He wanted to ensure the local wasn't working for the Russians. Most people would not notice the East Slavic language differences, but it was even more complicated when they spoke broken English. Michael could easily detect the vowel and consonant pronunciations between Ukrainian and Russian; however, when speaking English, native speakers had different stress patterns on words. The experienced commander knew to ask the right introductory questions, which required the responder to use certain words. Depending on how those words sounded, Michael could tell their native language.

After feeling satisfied, he put his head back to get a brief nap in. The car seats were much more comfortable than the cargo plane seats. As he did, the analyst began trying to get to know him.

Why was this kid trying so hard? thought Michael.

"How long you been a SEAL?" says the analyst.

"Started in the Navy over a decade ago, been a SEAL—"

Michael's facial expression froze.

"What?"

"Keep your head facing me."

"Why?" The analyst froze.

"We've got company on the left. Whatever you do, do not face them. They're trying to confirm our identities."

The driver looked in the rear-view mirror, then the side mirror. His grip on the steering wheel tightened. The truck's subtle attempt to match the sedan's speed made Michael suspicious. He also noticed the vehicle had dark window tinting. Luckily, the truck had big tires, making it twice the height it usually would be for the make and model. The high viewing angle inside the truck made it impossible to see through the sedan to Michael's side. The analyst, however, was an easy target. It was unlikely they had intel on the junior analyst, but his facial features might raise suspicion. The kid was as far from being Eastern European as a dog's face was from a cat's. An American traveling toward Kyiv during the morning would keep the truck's interest.

"Exit P19 west, driver," says Michael. "Don't signal your exit."

"That'll add 20 minutes to this ride," says the driver.

"Understood, do it!"

The driver waited until the exit ramp was almost unreachable before attempting an illegal move over the solid lines to make it. Sedentary gravel on the highway shoulder area kicked against the wheel well as the sedan made an aggressive move to enter the ramp. The maneuver worked. The truck barreled down the main highway with no illumination of brake lights.

"Nice driving," says Michael. "Keep your speed just above the limit until we get to the embassy."

"This is exciting, my first field mission," the analyst says.

Michael rolled his eyes while looking out the window. Was this the best they have in the U.S. Defense Attaché

Office (USDAO), or was he just lucky to get the greenest associate? He hoped his lack of response would kill the small talk. He desperately needed a quick one-hour nap on the way to the embassy. In order to satisfy both of their desires, he assigned his overzealous new helper a simple task.

"The time change is weighing on me. A nap would do me wonders before we arrive in Kyiv. Be on the lookout for suspicious vehicles that seem to either be following us or trying to stay at pace with us. I don't mind us taking a few alternate routes, but we can't waste any more travel time. I need to re-establish contact with my ground team."

"Got it, Commander. Do you want me to wake you if I see something?"

"Only if the driver can't shake the vehicle or the vehicle gets aggressive," replies Michael.

"On it. Would you like to borrow this?" He pulled a sleeping eye mask with a Batman logo out of his pocket.

"No ... thanks ... wake me when we get close."

An apartment building block ravaged by missiles from the war came into sight. The top and sides of one building looked like crumpled paper despite the brick and cement construction. Woken by the analyst, it was the first thing Michael saw. He remembered a report he had read about the toxic environment these air strikes created, as the old construction contained asbestos cement. Building rubble released airborne fibers, which, when inhaled, can cause life-threatening diseases. Despite the government's success intercepting Russian missiles, some shrapnel still reached buildings and people.

The embassy building was nothing special and would have blended into the other buildings if it weren't for the four Marines stationed outside. Since the start of the war, the facility had round-the-clock monitoring and protection. As they passed around the building and entered through the gated checkpoint, Michael observed a flaw in the security design. A 10-foot iron fence enclosed the building, with only a single entrance and exit. Although effective for access control and visitor monitoring, it could hinder evacuation during emergencies. If the enemy somehow took control of that entry point, they would trap everyone.

"We're up on the third floor, Commander; I'll take you there," says the analyst.

"Who's in charge?" asks Michael.

"Lieutenant Graton, sir, from the Royal Marines. He was on leave in Prague with his family and the closest officer to the embassy we could find on short notice. Captain Donnelly knew him and specifically requested that he take this mission."

As they entered the situation room, there was a heavy contrast between new technology and outdated decor. Decorated like an office building from the 70s, the room had modular furniture riddled with ugly, avocado-green geometric patterns. The brown, wood-paneled walls hid behind thin, large flat-screen monitors. The monitors showed high-definition camera views around the building and the greater Kyiv city area. Some monitors showed satellite views, while others had secure message readouts. Frantically working, Lieutenant Graton recognized new individuals entering the room. He turned around to salute and was visibly sweating despite the comfortable room temperature.

"At ease, Lieutenant ... everything okay?" says Michael.

"I'm afraid not, Commander. Let me get you up to speed."

CHAPTER
FIVE

U.S. EMBASSY, KYIV

Detailing the ground team's strategy, the lieutenant continued. He explained they split up to cover both the front and rear sides of the only inhabitable building on the airstrip. The control tower was too small to hold hostages, and the other structures had empty hangers besides some aircraft maintenance equipment. Snow was coming down hard and blowing sideways, making it easy to lose visuals after about 50 feet. Petty officers Turner and Chapman went around the back while Officer Stinson and Ensign Pham headed to the front. They agreed to check in every two minutes, but five minutes later, Ensign Pham lost contact with the other two.

"What was your next order?" asked Michael.

"I told them to proceed as planned through the front entrance, but they found the door secured," replied Lieutenant Graton.

"So?"

"So … Stinson wanted to go around back. It's because he figured the building construction knocked out their radio signal with the other two. He didn't want to risk making noise while blasting the lock on the front door."

"Dammit, Stinson!" says Michael. "You told him not to, right?"

Graton flushed with shame. "I tried, but he said Pham agreed and she was in command until you checked back in with them."

"She is, but I don't believe Ensign Pham would make that mistake. Did you actually talk to her?"

"She wasn't on the comm—Commander, there is something else. I'm sorry."

"Sorry for what? Did they rendezvous? What is their current status?"

"We lost contact with Stinson about eight minutes ago."

Michael turned sharply away from the lieutenant. He didn't want his frustration getting the best of him. He felt like striking the man. The helpless look on the lieutenant's mug needed to be wiped off. At his rank, it would be very unprofessional. He rushed toward the window, taking a deep breath. *That freaking truck on the highway had to delay us!* If not for their detour, their arrival could have been earlier. He would have been there in time to give his team the proper orders.

"What does our drone see?" Michael kept gazing at the rising sun from the window.

"We weren't provided one for this mission, but we're re-tasking Skynet 3B."

"I can help with that; I have 11 hours of training on her," says the analyst.

He tightened his muscular body until it felt like his shirt would rip apart, hoping it would prevent the boiling blood from reaching his temple. The satellite could see body heat signatures at ground level, but the snow could mask this technology. Motionless team members with injuries would be difficult to spot.

"Did you inform the admiral yet?" asks Michael.

"No-t yet." The lieutenant stammered, fearing he would anger the commander even more.

"Patch me in on a secure line now, please."

Michael considered what might have happened as the analyst and lieutenant scrambled to connect with Washington and locate the admiral. Despite his contradictory training, he knew Stinson was an act first, think later kind of officer. He had experience in a few combat situations with him. The nervous intensity when you're dealing with a life-or-death situation can change any learned behavior. He had tried to coach Stinson before. Stinson recognized his behavior, but a switch flipped when it wasn't training.

Jasmine was different. Her mental sharpness, ability to learn, and psychological screening scores to get into DEVGRU were off the charts. In some ways, Michael was jealous of her. *One woman having so many gifts, how?* Jasmine made quick strategic decisions that affected the tactical moves. He hoped she ordered Stinson on the proper hostage tactic to keep them all safe. It was strange that she missed her check-in, but perhaps she had good reason.

His mind wandered to a memory of her during a team celebratory dinner after a successful mission. No longer in uniform, Jasmine wore a classy cocktail dress. She looked so exotic that he almost forgot she was a soldier. Her high cheekbones provided an enhanced definition of her smooth, amber skin, supplemented by full lips that crinkled when she smiled. Her long, silky, black hair was styled with perfect curls that laid on her athletic but ample bosom. *Focus Michael! She works for you and needs your help.*

The analyst proffered the comm to Michael with a creepy smile.

"What's the status, Commander?" says Vice Admiral Jackson.

"Are you trying to make this mission a failure, sir?"

"Michael, what happened?"

"I get you're trying to protect me, but sending army vehicles for transport only puts me in more danger, and why the heck don't I have access to a drone?"

"Over the last few weeks, ground forces shot down several of our drones, and we're doing our best to get replacements out to the region."

"The situation is the team is unreachable. I'm taking Lieutenant Graton and going in," says Michael.

"We don't have clearance for that from the Defense Secretary. Let me get a team from one of our carriers in the Mediterranean there; they can be on the ground in less than four hours."

"The team could be dead in an hour, sir. Send the team, but I'm still going; this is Ghostwalker, out." Michael ended the communication.

"Holy crap, I thought I recognized you," says Graton as his eyes widened. "You're Ghostwalker?"

"Yeah, and I hope you packed a change of underwear; we're leaving," says Michael.

"Do we have authorization, sir? Never mind, forget it. I'll get the Black Hawk pilot started on flight prep."

CHAPTER
SIX

1 HOUR EARLIER, ORSHA AIRFIELD, BELARUS

After checking the hangars, the team realized the only viable location to hold the hostages was a medium-sized, gray-bricked office building structure near the airport control tower. The snow was whipping around the hangars, creating large 10-foot, snowy drifts that kept the team from adhering to the structures' walls, hoping to stay out of the open. Their white camouflaged uniforms worked well in the conditions, but they realized it would be daybreak soon, making their surprise incursion even more difficult. After surveilling the building from afar, there appeared to be two entrances. One was in front, opposite the runways, and one was in the back that faced a dense forest of thick, green spruce and oak trees, heavily covered in fluffy snow.

"We need to split up. You two take the back. Pham and I'll hit the front. Keep in contact every two," says Stinson.

"We using the shape charges if the doors won't budge?" asks Turner.

"Yes, take these four."

Stinson moved his shoulder-strapped MK18 rifle to the side while he searched through the side pocket of his backpack. He handed the charges over to Turner with a wink.

"We'll wait behind this hangar till you clear the back corner. Good luck, men."

The white uniforms disappeared as they moved to the building; the storm was not letting up. It felt like a lucky break for the covert mission.

Five minutes later, Pham and Stinson heard the radio beep signaling an incoming message, "We see the entrance, no visible cameras or personnel, looks to be solid metal, no windows, moving in to attempt a breach," Chapman provided the status.

Stinson's hand signaled Pham to move to the front entrance, about 200 yards from the hangar. They jogged with haste in a semi-crouched position, swiveling their heads around to check for signs of the opposition. They were about 10 feet from the door when the radio clicked several times. The pair looked at each other, confused. They settled into a squatted position close to the building wall. Pham attempted to contact the back door team several times with no success.

"Switch to the backup radio," says Stinson.

Already considering that move, Pham wondered why Stinson was giving all the orders. She was his superior. Stinson was the HALO jump expert in charge of that for the team, but his command technically ended once they were on the ground. It was important that the chain of command was crystal clear during missions. She again tried to contact the team using the backup frequencies.

"Got nothing; let's wait two more minutes and try again. Meanwhile, check that door." she orders.

Stinson nodded.

While waiting, Stinson inspected the front door with a two-foot concrete ramp walk-up to get to it, outlined with a basic cylindrical metal railing. Stinson tested the locked door and noticed it had a deadbolt as well. He dashed back to Pham's position on the wall.

"Still getting nothing but static on both frequencies; let's check in with command," says Pham.

Stinson took out his satellite phone and, after a 30-second conversation, put it back with haste. He motioned to go to the building's rear and departed from Pham.

Frustrated, Pham sprinted to catch up with him and pulled on his jacket arm to stop him.

"What are you doing? Did you talk to Commander Cooling?"

"He still wasn't there. We're going to find our boys."

"Not a good idea. They'll expect us if the men were compromised. This ruins our chance for surprise. Let's breach the front and assess the situation once inside."

"Sorry, Pham, Lieutenant Graton agreed with me; this is our next move."

Before she could command him otherwise, he was around the side of the building. Pham shook her head and re-raised her rifle to proceed around the building. The sun was rising, which warmed the cold air around her face. The warming feel calmed her but also meant the enemy would wake up, provided they didn't have troops on night shifts. When they reached the building's backside, the ground became soft. The pavement turned to forest ground.

They saw two figures in the distance, crouched near the building, motionless. Approaching with caution, they had their MK18s readied for action. The scene became very grim as they soon realized the two deformed bodies were Turner and Chapman. Bright blood stained their white uniforms, likely from the carotid arteries that were severed when they lost their heads. Their legs were two feet underground as they had fallen into a punji stick booby trap.

Not seen since the Vietnam War, these traps were holes in the ground, covered with a thin material on top, which camouflaged the trap. Inside was a group of sharpened bamboo sticks pointing upwards, many times laced with urine or feces. Not only did the sticks pierce deep into an unsuspecting soldier's feet and legs, but the substances on them would cause infections later. This was a more modern and insidious trap at the building's back entrance. It had large metal spikes pointing straight up, each with smaller thorn-like spikes pointing down. The SEALs would rip their legs apart, trying to free themselves from the spikes. They didn't even have a chance to, as someone swiftly removed their heads.

The scene was enough to make anyone lose their lunch, even for a trained special operations unit like the Silver Squadron. Neither Pham nor Stinson did, but their faces became intense with anger and survivor's guilt. Stinson reached for both slain officers' dog tags, so they could give them to the families. The tags were slippery as they were dripping with fresh, uncoagulated blood. Ensign Pham moved to the door in an offensive position. As she reached for the handle, the door exploded open, sending her flying backward almost into the pit of spikes.

"You must be lady luck!" A paramilitary lieutenant sneered as he aimed his RPK-74 automatic weapon at Pham's head. "Damn, I usually get someone to fall into the pit."

Two more cadets with gun sights aimed at Stinson accompanied the lieutenant. The SEALs couldn't resist. The cadets were laughing and mocking the SEALs in a Russian dialect. One of them raised his eyebrows in succession and smiled at Pham, realizing she was a woman.

The Russians stripped the American soldiers of their weapons and their radios. Their hands were zip-tied behind them. Despite her hands being immobile, Pham was confident in her ability to disable two men using Muay Thai kicks. She also planned to signal Stinson to handle the third man simultaneously. She chose instead to confirm the number of combatants and ensure the hostages' presence and well-being. The Russians guided them to a steel freight elevator that took them all to sub-level 3, the lowest floor. As the door opened, the smell of petroleum filled Pham's nostrils. A heavy-set older man wearing an ushanka and a white winter military uniform approached.

"Sorry, comrades, but we don't get much heat down here." He got within a foot of Pham and looked into her eyes. "Don't fret, my darling; I'll let you at least keep your panties on, unless you want your fellow here to wear them instead," General Petrovsky snickered, along with the other men. "Take her to the other hostages."

CHAPTER
SEVEN

While Lieutenant Graton and Commander Cooling loaded up the MH-60S Knighthawk, Michael pondered his next steps. He didn't have time to look up Graton's record or combat capabilities. He figured he would vet him on the way there, which was at least 80 minutes at top speed. Although Michael was prepared to go solo, having someone to rely on is always a good idea in challenging situations.

The armory at the embassy was satisfactory for the equipment they needed. The last thing Michael grabbed were several M84 flashbang grenades. Hoping the hostages were still alive, he wanted a non-lethal way to distract the enemy.

Before they left, they checked the real-time satellite images that finally came online. The weather made it difficult to confirm details, but the heat map showed a couple of faint signatures near a building off the runway. The commander hoped it was his team, masked by the cold weather, and not some forest animals. *Why weren't they checking in with Command?* As the Black Hawk ascended, Michael engaged with the lieutenant, accompanied by a Galaxy pilot staying in Kyiv overnight.

"How long have you been in the Royal Marines now?" asks Michael.

"About four years now. I attempted last year to get into SAS, but missed the cut," says Graton.

Great, thought Michael in disappointment. The SAS was the British equivalent of special forces like the Navy SEALs were for the United States. It didn't sit with Michael. He was going into combat with someone sub-standard for the mission.

"Yeah, it's a tough program, just like in the States. But, hey, even getting into the Royal Marines is a significant accomplishment. Have you seen any action during your tours?"

"A little; we were patrolling the Red Sea because of recent piracy activity there. There was a bulk carrier ship we boarded for a routine check. It turned out the pirates had already boarded and killed one passenger. I took two of them out before we regained control of the ship," says Graton.

"What's next for you?"

"Soon I hope to be a captain. My wife keeps having babies like we're a new football team. I could use a serious bump in pay."

"You know … half of that problem is you, right?"

They both chuckled.

~

The pilot tried to follow a path that was primarily expansive plains to avoid detection. Belarus did not have any significant mountain ranges, but it has a considerable number of forests, especially where they were going, in the north. Michael noticed a few people on the ground, gazing up in awe as a military helicopter passed over their farms.

The Belarus countryside had not seen war since the Second World War, but the folks were conscious of the current conflict between Ukraine and Russia. Michael imagined that many people probably felt anxiety about their country being so close to the dangerous fighting. He hoped the onlookers wouldn't alert the authorities.

Michael signaled to the pilot, extending his arm above his head with a fist, which meant it was time to start the landing. Graton and Michael jumped out and quickly put on their overloaded backpacks to start the hike to Orsha Airfield. The snowy weather had finally subsided, and the morning sun's rays were glistening off the frozen landscape before them. Avoiding roads, the trek would be exhausting in two feet of snow. They had brought snowshoes made of lightweight magnesium to make it easier, which they would abandon once they reached the runway.

"What's the plan?" The lieutenant huffed out cold air while his legs struggled through the powder.

"Well, we ain't going in the front; they'll probably be expecting a rescue," says the commander.

Do you know of another entry point? I thought there were only two."

"Correct, and we're not entering from the back, either."

"Okay, Commander, then what?"

"You didn't study the Airfield schematics, did you?"

"Was I supposed to?"

"Part of being ready for the special forces is antici-pating the enemy's next move and planning for the unex-pected. Your commanding officer can't always tell you your next order; remember that," says Michael.

Lieutenant Graton nodded.

"The building they're in houses the underground tankers for the airfield's jet fuel. There are several tanks. Now, while jet fuel can withstand frigid temperatures, much colder than freezing, the colder it gets, the higher its viscosity becomes. Thick fuel is difficult to pump and is not put into planes. It would affect performance. This airfield is too old to use insulated tanks, so they have a heating system to keep the tanks, lines, and pumps at a desirable temperature."

"I didn't know that," Graton says.

"The satellite images showed heat signatures only on two of the three tanks. I supposed it's because the air traffic is minimal at this site. This means the other tank is cold, and I'll bet my life it is empty."

"Wait … you want to enter the facility through the surface pump location on the empty tank?" stuttered Graton.

"Exactly, my friend! I might add that the fuel line is big enough to fit a person, uncomfortably, but it's about a 70-foot crawl, and we'll land right in the underground tanker."

Graton's face was slightly paler than earlier. Michael surmised he probably was claustrophobic. He had to lighten the load on Graton's emotions.

"Easy-peasy," says Michael. "I brought some oxygen in case we need it, and the tanks always have a doorway out.

The tanks require cleaning once a year, and that is how they access them for maintenance."

Graton appeared to be thinking hard for a moment. "Blimey, if I'm surprised by this plan, then the enemy will be as well. Look! I see the hangar just ahead."

The forest's edge opened to an expansive white field with eerie inactivity for such a large military base. The hangars and structures along the periphery of the airfield had roofs and walls adorned with layers of snow, accentuating their architectural lines. Michael stopped and pulled the folded map out of his cargo pants' pocket, where he had written notes. Graton asked to use his encrypted military phone to check in with his commanding Royal Marine officer. Michael questioned why he hadn't made the call earlier before they entered enemy territory. Graton mentioned he was distracted trying to fix the communication with the SEAL team. When Graton returned to Michael, they headed to the empty tank's fill cap location circled on his map. It wasn't visible because of the significant snowfall, but after some digging, they located it and cut off the padlock with a mini-high-powered blow torch. Upon opening it, the faint smell of jet fuel was a welcoming sign to Michael. The scent would have stung their nostrils much more had the tank been full.

"Follow my lead," asserted Michael.

He removed his backpack and dropped it into the dark metallic hole. Then he took Graton's pack and did the same. He switched on his bright LED forehead lamp and went into the hole, headfirst, with no sign of hesitation. Graton waited about five seconds before reluctantly following Michael.

The first thirty feet was like a steeply inclined carnival ride before leveling off. It was thrilling for Michael, as he loved the adrenaline rushes. He figured they had another 40-50 feet to crawl. He glanced back at Graton, whose headlamp lit up the path behind him. Graton was sweating profusely, despite the freezing temperatures in the underground tubing. It took another 10 minutes to crawl to the tank. The tubing changed direction to straight down, and Michael knew it ended at a pump on the fuel tank's floor. To breach the tank, he planned to cut a large hole in the horizontal pipe, allowing their bodies to descend.

Using a torch in a pipe with gas fumes could ignite a chain reaction that would cook them both alive, especially if the tank still had some residual jet fuel. The only option was a special gel Michael brought. The small tube resembled toothpaste.

The gel contained a heavy mixture of nitric acid, and other chemicals formulated to dissolve 98% of the world's metals. After handing an oxygen mask back to Graton, he outlined a large hole in the pipe in front of him with the corrosive gel. It quickly began dissolving the steel, and Michael used a suction device to hold the remaining metal in place so it wouldn't drop to the tank floor. Once he removed the metal cut-out, he coated the hole's edges with a solution that neutralized the acidic gel.

After a quick scan of the surface below, Michael smiled widely. The tank was empty, except for a shallow pool of fuel that the pump couldn't reach. Using a rope, he lowered the backpacks 10 feet down to the floor. He proceeded cautiously to not make any noise. He instructed Graton to move past the hole carefully and drop in feet first, while hanging on the edges of the dissolved pipe with his gloves. This would facilitate a softer landing. By extending their bodies, their feet would only be about 4 feet from the tank floor. Michael proceeded out and landed with a quiet splash.

BOOM!

Michael quickly turned around as the loud noise made by his partner reverberated through the empty tank. With a clang, the interior door to the fuel tank swung open, revealing three black muzzle tips. Michael quickly turned to face them.

"Welcome, Commander Cooling; I've been expecting you! Kak vy, Comrade Graton?"

CHAPTER
EIGHT

Graton smiled and air-kissed each side of the general's face. He looked back at Commander Cooling, laughing about the betrayal.

"I told you … I have a lot of mouths to feed!"

One cadet hit Michael hard on the back of his head with the butt of his rifle, knocking him unconscious. The cadets then exited the tank, escorting Michael's limp body on both sides. General Petrovsky followed and turned back to Graton.

"Don't forget the backpacks," Petrovsky pointed to them in the middle of the tank.

"Da," says Graton in Russian as he turned around.

As the general exited the tank, he took out his Zippo lighter, lit it, and then tossed it in while quickly locking the door to the tank. The jet fuel pool inside ignited, along with the residual fuel on Graton's uniform.

The faint sounds of screaming outside the fuel tanks made Jasmine cringe. A couple of explosion sounds happened later from the oxygen tanks in the backpacks. She was shivering from the cold temperatures as the perverted guards left her only in her underwear while being tied up next to the Ukrainian generals. It didn't matter; she was alive, but the situation seemed hopeless. She knew her decorated commander had experienced capture before, but with half of her team dead and Petty Officer Stinson's whereabouts unknown, they were facing unfavorable odds. As they dragged Michael's body away, she watched. Her posture relaxed, seeing him invigorated her hunger to escape.

The captured generals looked defeated, but she knew they were her only allies. She contemplated a strategy to get them to help. The biggest problem was they were being watched constantly. Even when they used the bathroom, the paramilitary cadets watched their every move. Her identity as a woman provided her with an advantage that most men overlooked. Jasmine was like Michael in that she always anticipated the worst scenario in a mission.

Before their incursion of the building, she slipped a two-inch blade wrapped in a thick rubber coating into her privates after urinating in the forest. The blade could easily cut through the plastic zip-ties around their hands and feet, but she needed a distraction even to attempt it. She engaged the generals to see how useful they could be to her planning.

"You speak English, yes? I'm sorry to hear about your families," she says.

"I do," says General Kuzma. "He barely understands," motioning to his fellow general. "Thank you. It looks like we will join our families soon."

"You two must still lead your armies and win this

senseless war. Will you help me? Wouldn't you rather die trying to escape than die feeling helpless?"

"Of course, I just need one minute with that monster GIP," says Kuzma.

"Follow my lead after we receive our meals."

It was late in the morning when they received their only plate of food, which typically comprised a tiny, plain, unseasoned baked potato and two measly pieces of under-cooked cabbage. The routine included the guards cutting free the prisoners' tied wrists that were tied behind their backs to a chain wrapped around a building column and retying their wrists in front of them while they ate. They gave them about 10 minutes to eat before being returned to the chain.

Jasmine got lucky. The guard she knew had an infatuation with her came to untie her. Since she arrived, he had been sneaking looks at her tan, curvy, slender body. As he retied her wrists together to the front of her body so she could eat, she squeezed her cleavage together.

"Spasibo, sir, could I please sit near the generals? I'm freezing," she shivered her body. The shaking of her chest got his attention.

"Da," the cadet says, flushing with embarrassment.

Leaving the food plates, both cadets walked back to their post. With their backs toward the prisoners, Jasmine pulled the blade from her vagina and opened it while concealing it under her plate just before the guards turned around. General Kuzma watched in awe at her swift actions as he took a bite of his potato.

All Jasmine needed now was a distraction. Her brain cycled through possibilities when she heard some popping sounds down the concrete corridor where the kitchen and other interior rooms were. The guards looked at each other inquisitively but stayed their post. About five minutes later, the sounds were louder and distinctly sounded like mini explosions. The guards appeared worried that they might get in more trouble for not checking on their general's safety than staying at their guard. They ran down the hallway to the source of the noise.

"General, can you tell the other general to act like he is choking to death when he hears the guards approaching?" With haste, Jasmine cut through the zip ties on her ankles, then cut through Kuzma's wrist and ankle ties. "Now, hurry, cut through my wrist ties."

"Got it!" says Kuzma as he translated her request into Russian to the other general.

Jasmine grabbed the tin-plated steel plate and ran toward the outside corner of the corridor entrance while ensuring the guards were not in eyesight. She gestured for Kuzma to imitate her on the opposite side of the entrance.

After a few more explosion sounds, they could hear yelling down the hallway in native Eastern Russian that sounded like someone was getting scolded. Jasmine figured the general was fine, and he was unhappy with the guards leaving their posts.

"The guards will come running when they hear the general choking. Just trip the one on your side and I'll take care of the rest," Jasmine kept her voice at whisper volume.

General Kuzma nodded but looked nervous.

Jasmine could hear the rhythmic sound of the guards' boots echoing down the hallway as they returned to the fuel tank area. Approximately 20-30 feet from the entrance, she urgently gestured towards the general still sitting tied up on the floor. His act was better than she had hoped for as he pretended to choke and gag, with strained breathing and his body squirming side to side.

The guards' boot rhythm quickened, signaling their realization of an issue and prompting them to run. As their heads led their bodies into the room, one of them went flying forward, and almost face planted. His rifle helped break his fall, but the butt poked hard into his stomach. The second guard immediately turned around just as Jasmine forcefully jabbed the steel dish edge into his trachea, crushing it, which permanently cut off all the airflow to his lungs. He dropped instantly. As the tripped guard got to his feet, Jasmine greeted his head with a roundhouse kick that sent him flying to the side, unconscious.

"You fight better than most men in my country," says General Kuzma.

"And mine," Jasmine crinkled the corner of her mouth up. "Free the general and grab that rifle and sidearm. I need to check on Sleepy lying over here."

Jasmine straddled the kicked, motionless guard and put his head between her palms. Abruptly turning his head further than normal, produced a deadly cracking sound. She took off his coat to have something to cover her bare skin and disarmed him.

Each now armed, they proceeded down the hallway to look for Stinson and Commander Cooling. The loud explosions continued. With their weapons in an offensive position, they walked along the hallway wall till they observed two more cadets trying to peer into a room through a small window. Another explosion occurred in the room, making one guard outside vomit on the floor. As he looked up, he spotted the generals and Jasmine. He began yelling something in Russian while raising his rifle.

Within a microsecond, Jasmine aimed the AK-74 at the second guard's head. He had just realized what his partner was warning him about. The bullet penetrated his right eye and through his skull. The first guard grabbed his deceased partner to use as a human shield. He fired rounds at the escaped prisoners. To avoid getting hit, the generals and Jasmine retreated backward to a defensive position at a turn in the hallway.

"General, can you lay down some cover fire so I can see what we're dealing with?" asks Jasmine.

General Kuzma double-checked his magazine clip to ensure it had bullets, inserted it back into the rifle, and began firing back down the hallway. Jasmine noticed the break-in return fire and looked around the corner briefly. To her dismay, another cadet had emerged and put a thick metal table in front of them so they could use it for cover. They re-engaged their targets. The thunderous roar of synchronized gunfire shattered the brief silence. The air filled with the sharp scent of gunpowder and the rhythmic clatter of spent casings hitting the ground. Further down the hallway, she saw a large man ducking while running away.

"Dammit! Looks like the general is escaping. General, can you please ask him to see if we can salvage any weapons from the backpacks in the fuel tank?" Jasmine motioned her head to the other general as she spoke to Kuzma.

A few minutes passed before the general returned, holding a device that looked like an olive Christmas tree ornament, but it wasn't. He handed it to Jasmine, who was happy to see it survived the fuel tank fire.

"This is a Sting-ball. It's a flash grenade that will release 100 rubber balls forcefully in all directions during its loud bang and bright flash. I'm going to attempt a table incursion. Toss the grenade ahead of me precisely three seconds after pulling the pin."

"What?" says General Kuzma. "Won't it injure you?"

"Probably, but what choice do we have? I'd rather have a bunch of welts on my body than be dead. I know this brand; they should go off five seconds after pulling the pin."

"Should?" The general raised his eyebrows high.

Jasmine used her small blade to tear a hole in the inside of her jacket. She pulled out bunches of insulation and stuffed it generously into her ears. To provide cover fire, she passed her rifle to the other general. She quickly checked the Makarov pistol's magazine count before cocking the hammer. She placed the grenade in Kuzma's hand.

She counted down while staring at the generals, "Three, two, one ... now!"

As one general fired in a direction away from where Jasmine was running, Kuzma pulled the pin, waited, and then tossed it toward the table. As it hit the table, the general's rifle ran out of ammo sooner than expected. The cadets poked their heads over the table. Realizing it was a grenade, they ducked again.

She barely made it over the table at her count of five as the deafening sound, luminous light, and balls peppered the hallway. She rotated mid-air to land on her back and fired two headshots. The cadets behind the table dropped; one of them flailed as the bullet hit him in the back of his neck. Jasmine stood up and put him out of his misery. Her gaze focused down the hallway at the generals.

"Hooyah!" she loudly voiced her SEAL battle cry. Jasmine's excitement shifted to disgust as she peered into the room beside her. It was like a scene from a horror movie.

CHAPTER
NINE

Someone had strapped Michael into a metal chair, leaving him only in his underwear and motionless. The small room smelled of sulfur, which had a pungent odor like rotten eggs. Colorful paper shrapnel littered the entire floor around him. GIP had attached firecrackers, big and small, all-over Michael's body and ignited them. His appearance made Jasmine tear up and dry gag. The limbs bore severe burn marks, some as black as coal from the skin side explosions. His right arm and legs looked like someone had put them through a tree trimmer's woodchipper. Jasmine checked his pulse, and miraculously, there was still one. She surmised it was because of the method they used to torture him. As he started bleeding from each injury, the general had wrapped the wounds tightly with silver duct tape so he wouldn't die quickly from bleeding out. His right eye had a bone fragment sticking out of it. It might have come from his shredded arm.

"Find our uniforms and gear! See if you can find our satellite phone," her voice shrilled, talking to General

Kuzma. "And check the rest of the rooms to ensure there isn't another cadet waiting for us. I need to stabilize him."

"Affirmative," says Kuzma.

Jasmine had some medical training for survival, but this was beyond her skills. If she could stabilize him before airlifting him to a proper medical facility, he had a chance. The first objective was controlling his bleeding and make sure he wasn't having breathing problems. To slow down any loss of blood from his torso, she tore up some nearby stained towels and created tourniquets for his arm and two legs. Although his breathing was slightly strained, she listened closely and discovered that it was near normal. Hopefully this meant there wasn't any blood in his lungs. She grabbed another chair to help keep his legs elevated. Her movements had to be extremely slow. As she lifted his legs, they looked like they would fall apart with any sudden movement from the hanging flesh and deformed bones.

Once finished, she needed to see how the Ukrainian generals were doing with finding communication equipment. Barefoot, she ran out into the frigid hallway with her pistol raised. Her heart rate slowed as she saw Captain Chase Donnelly and six other SEALs jogging toward her down the hallway. Behind them were General Kuzma and his colleague. She stopped and stood erect, giving him a salute.

"It's awful, captain. Please tell me you brought a chopper."

"We did, and we apologize for not getting here sooner. We found Stinson; drugged out of his mind. He's a little beaten up, but otherwise in good shape. Are the prisoners alive?" says Chase.

"Yes. Can I have your SATCOM?"

"Doesn't work down here. We need to get to the surface. Where is Lieutenant Graton?"

"On his way to *Hell*, I hope! Fucking bastard was a spy," says Jasmine.

"Jesus, I know his wife; now I wonder if she knew. Where is he?"

"You mean what's left of him? Check the left fuel tanker down that way." Jasmine pointed with her finger. "As soon as General Petrovsky got what he wanted, he ended Graton."

"We have been following Petrovsky for years. There was no sign Graton was involved. Son of a bitch!"

"Captain Donnelly, with all due respect, we don't have time for chit-chat. The commander is stable but needs immediate help."

"Right … Grant, check on the fuel tank. We need evidence of death for the family and military records. Petty Officer Dalton, get Ensign Pham what she needs to transport the commander out of here quickly. I'll check in with Command."

Jasmine watched as the captain approached the room where Michael was. His hand went over his mouth as he entered with his head sulking. Seconds later, he passed by her as he sprinted down the hallway to get to the surface.

Two Black Hawks prepared for takeoff after being summoned from their secretive positions. One Black Hawk now had the remains of Petty Officers Turner, Chapman, and Lieutenant Graton, along with four of the rescue SEALs, under Captain Donnelly's command. Stinson was finally coming to from his daze, but still moved in a disabled fashion, requiring assistance. The Ukrainian generals helped load Michael, now on a stretcher, into the second helicopter.

"Why so many people on that UH-60?" asks Ensign Pham.

"They're taking the generals back to Kyiv. We're going somewhere else," says Captain Donnelly.

"Where?"

"Tell you soon. We killed two of them, and I saw several other bodies. What happened to General Petrovsky?"

"After starting our incursion on the guards, I saw him running for the exit. Strange seeing the Tigr vehicle is still here."

"The forest must have concealed his getaway vehicle. There were no signs of movement when we arrived. We need to torch this place. Did you say the other two fuel tanks were full?" asks Chase.

"Think so; easy to check; the fill caps are right there." Jasmine pointed to an area on the runway.

"Take this," the captain handed a grenade to Jasmine. Her eyes lit up. "These have an 8-second timer. We each will drop one into the fill tubes, then run like hell for the chopper. Got it?"

"Do we have to waste a grenade? With probably a million gallons of jet fuel in each tank, one will do the trick."

"Funny … remember your training. Always have a backup plan."

"I just hope your plan doesn't send our chopper to the moon!" Jasmine shook her head.

Both went to their respective drop areas, broke open the locked caps, and checked the intensity of the smell. Jasmine gave the captain the thumbs up and watched as his fingers counted down from three. The igniters dropped, and Jasmine began running as fast as she could. As she counted down to eight, she briefly pondered the chance of a faulty grenade and promptly recognized the captain's plan as more commendable. The ground rumbled under their feet just as they leaped into the chopper.

"Go! Go! Go!" Chase yelled at the pilot.

The fiery energy at the epicenter of the underground facility tore through the earth with an unrestrained fury. As the explosive force surged upwards, it bubbled the concrete around the building while the structure succumbed to a violent force that completely disintegrated it. Bricks, metal, and billowing smoke flew in multiple directions. As the smoke cleared, many fires outlined the space where the building used to stand. The pilot circled back one more time. A debris-filled crater the size of a professional baseball stadium was all that remained. The carnage also took out a line of trees behind the once-standing building. Jasmine never liked to see her work disturb nature, but she rationalized it was unavoidable given the circumstances.

"Which hospital are we going to, Cap?"

"We're not going to a hospital. The vice admiral has strict orders."

"What?" says Jasmine with raised eyebrows. "Even our base medics don't have the equipment to help Michael." The two other SEALs riding with them seemed as shocked as Jasmine.

"Our final destination is not a base. We're heading to Necker Island."

"The island owned by Richard Branson?"

"Yes, we lease part of the land from him," says Chase.

"We? You mean the Navy?"

"No, Strategic Intelligence, Section 10 or SIX, for short."

"Okay, I'm completely lost now."

"I know as much as you, but they will properly care for him there."

"Then why don't we know about it?" says Jasmine.

"My understanding is it's funded privately by an eccentric multi-billionaire. I swear, that's all I know. Here … I'm sure you're starving. Take this MRE."

"Please tell me you have hand-sanitizer," Jasmine said, wiping dirt and blood off her hands with a clean t-shirt from the chopper's interior storage.

Chase rolled his eyes. "Yes, it's taking up precious space in my fatigues, just for you."

Jasmine smiled for the first time in days while cleaning her hands. Opening the vacuum-packed military ration, she dug a plastic fork into the preserved beef ravioli. She didn't realize how hungry she was till the cold pasta activated her taste buds. She glanced back at the stretcher in the rear of the Black Hawk with an unspoken affection. Conflicting emotions of distress and hope followed.

CHAPTER
TEN

HIGHLAND, CALIFORNIA

Martha was tending to her garden and couldn't wait to see her bleeding hearts bloom in a month or two. Spring was her favorite time of year, primarily because of her love of flowers. Last year, her heart-shaped plants complimented her cherry blossom tree's vibrant pink colors. This year, she hoped the new seeds she planted a couple of years ago would finally bloom, adding some white and violet shades to the serene setting at the end of her back patio. She was obsessed with keeping her tree healthy as it protected the plant with its shade during the hot summer months in Highland, California, part of San Bernardino County. Unlike many coastal towns in the Golden State, the inland village had distinct seasons, which allowed her to plant perennial plants that experienced periods of dormancy during the winter months.

While digging near the brick edging, Michael's well-being crossed her thoughts. She heard from him last before his trip to the White House to accept his award. Extended periods of being out of touch with Michael were common for her. She knew his missions were a priority and contact with the outside world could endanger him. She reluctantly forced herself not to reach out unless she knew he was on leave. Sometimes, she would call Vice Admiral Dante Jackson to get an update, knowing that appearances, speeches, and clerical work took up most of his time in his position. Just then, her phone rang, and the caller ID was "VA Jackson." This was a first, him calling her and a strange coincidence as he was just in her thoughts.

"Admiral, this is a switch. Were you expecting me to call soon?"

"Hi Martha, no … how are you?" Admiral Jackson says with hesitation.

Martha caught her breath. "Something is wrong. Just tell me."

"The mission didn't go as planned, but Michael is alive—"

"Why is your voice so solemn, then?"

"Sorry, Ma'am, he is gravely wounded. We're taking him to a special facility in the Caribbean."

"Caribbean? He needs the best doctors, like the Mayo Clinic or Johns Hopkins!"

"We have everything we need where we are taking him. He will be in excellent care. We want you to come there. Just in case things get worse."

"Of course. Have you informed his father?" asks Martha.

"We haven't spoken or heard from Michael Sr. since he

retired years ago from the Marines. We don't know where he is. Have you talked to him?"

"No, but strangely, he is sending me his pension checks, which I never asked for. What about SI2? Doesn't he need to visit for maintenance occasionally?"

"I'm afraid to say the SI2 facility closed over 10 years ago."

Martha was concerned about both Michaels. Despite Michael's father leaving her right after their son was born to focus on his career, she still cared for him. Michael was the only man she connected with so effortlessly. She hated his selfishness primarily because of its impact on her son being raised without a father rather than for her own gain.

"Martha, you still there?" asks the admiral.

"Yes … sorry … all of this brings up suppressed memories. Can you send me the address so I can start booking my flight?"

"No need; a car is coming by in two hours to take you to March Air Reserve Base in Riverside."

"An Air Force plane, why?"

"Ma'am, I can explain everything when you get here. Please don't share your destination with anyone. For Michael's safety, please follow my instructions," says Admiral Jackson.

A moment of awkward silence occurred on the line. Martha agreed and thanked the admiral before ending the call.

An unsettling anxiety passed over Martha as she put away her gardening tools. She didn't understand why the admiral was so cryptic in his message. She knew that her son Michael's command on the SEAL team required secrecy, sometimes as high up as the Secretary of Defense, but this was his health. Michael had already earned high decorations as a Navy officer, despite his young age. He deserved the best attention after all his sacrifices for his country.

While packing for her trip, something told Martha to pack her SIG 380. Michael was always worried about her living alone and had bought the gun for her several years back. The 380 had much less recoil than a 9mm. This made gun handling easier for her smaller hands. Michael would take her to the range to practice and learn during every one of his visits.

Martha distinctly remembered him telling her that there was a trade-off for an easier-to-handle gun. Guns with smaller bullets have less stopping power to incapacitate an intruder. Michael had bought her hollow-point ammo that expands on impact. This results in more internal tissue damage and less chance of exiting the body. *Don't stop at just one!* She remembers Michael saying, which meant to fire off at least three or four rounds if the intruder kept coming. This would help compensate for the smaller bullet's lower performance.

As she zipped her suitcase, she said a few prayers for Michael. The lack of detail from the admiral on his condition was concerning. Captured a few times in the past, Michael had told his mother about some past missions. To her disdain, he liked to give her the gory details over dinner, which typically made her lose her appetite immediately. Being transported in military vehicles, she didn't know when she could eat again. While waiting for her ride, she headed to the kitchen to warm up some leftover home-made lasagna.

CHAPTER
ELEVEN

NECKER ISLAND, BRITISH VIRGIN ISLANDS

As the island came into sight, it was much smaller than Jasmine expected, maybe about a mile wide from her rough estimate. With a stunning palette of turquoise and cerulean hues, the surrounding water was absolutely breathtaking. The vibrant reefs couldn't hide below the transparent surface, and schools of fish darted about. The sand sparkled from the sunlight hitting the beaches, outlined with various tropical trees and plants. There appeared to be two key signs of civilization on the island. Details of a charming resort became visible as the helicopter flew over the first area. There were pickleball courts, a large swimming pool, and several communal areas. Some buildings had thatch roofing to solidify the tropical island feel.

"Wow! Is that where we're going?" Jasmine's eyes widened.

"You wish," says Captain Donnelly. "That is a high-end resort for the rich and famous. Guests have exclusive access to the resort and full-service staff, including a Michelin-starred chef."

"How much does it cost?"

"More than we make in a year, I think,"

Jasmine's mouth watered from the thought of freshly prepared island food. From Europe, they took a military plane to the base in Guantanamo Bay, Cuba, then aboard another Black Hawk to the Caribbean island. She had her fill of cold vacuum-packed meals, but there was no time to get proper food. Commander Cooling was on life-support, and they agreed to keep him sedated in fear the stress of realizing what had happened to him would only make his recovery worse.

A white building emerged on the island's far side, away from the resort. The SH-60 aircraft landed on the roof's helipad. Several medical technicians in white overcoats were waiting there with a wheeled stretcher to accept Michael. Jasmine and Chase helped get Michael out of the helicopter and onto the stretcher. As soon as they did, the pilot signaled to Captain Donnelly and departed immediately. The island personnel didn't greet either of them, but hastened Michael to the service elevator. Jasmine grabbed Chase's arm to stop him.

"Okay, can we talk now, since we have some privacy?" she asks.

"Ensign, I told you everything I know. Let's get inside. Vice Admiral Jackson is waiting for us."

"He's here, too?" she says.

Chase pressed the "L" button as they boarded the elevator, but Jasmine noticed the "SB-3" button was already lit.

"We're not going with him?" She peered directly into the captain's eyes.

"Not yet. Please be patient."

The lobby door opened, and Jasmine immediately caught a soothing smell of coconut and vanilla. She and Chase exited to a large room with brilliant white walls and richly decorated with tropical plants, mahogany furniture, and turquoise-colored cushions. The front of the room boasted floor-to-ceiling windows, offering a breathtaking view of the northeast island coast and the Atlantic Ocean. A man in full Navy uniform stood with his back to them, gazing out the windows.

"Greetings, sir," Chase says as they closed the distance between them and the man, stood at attention, and began saluting.

Turning around and smiling widely, Admiral Jackson returned the salute. "At ease. Nice to see you, Ensign Pham; it's been a while. I can see by your expression you have a lot of questions."

"Yes, sir, I want to ensure my commanding officer gets the proper care."

"Then why did you guys bring him here?" Jackson's face tightened.

"What? Captain said—"

The admiral guffawed, threw his head back, and smiled with satisfaction. Jasmine sighed deeply and shook her head.

"Sir, please. It's been a long trip," says Jasmine.

"I know, I apologize, I just couldn't resist. Our host is waiting in the private dining room. Does Beef Wellington sound good?"

"Okay, I forgive you."

While heading to an early dinner, Jasmine noticed the scarcity of people in the large facility. Everyone she saw wore all white, except for a silver and turquoise metal badge on their chests. Some wore white lab coats; others wore white pants with white button-down short-sleeve collared shirts. Some smiled as they passed, but no one greeted their group.

"Sir, this place is odd. Maybe it's on a need-to-know basis, but what's with the cloak-and-dagger tactics? Seems like overkill," says Jasmine.

"That's right, Ensign. I assure you; it was of the utmost importance. To outsiders, this is a rehabilitation center catering to the rich. The top three levels provide that care. The three sub-levels are entirely different. They contain a sophisticated research center that less than a dozen people worldwide know about. You might make number 13 now." says Admiral Jackson as he opened a 10-foot glass door to a room with all the decor of a fancy steak restaurant.

"Great!" Jasmine rolled her eyes. "Is this where you tell me I may never leave now that I know the big secret?" asks Jasmine.

"Ensign, you've been watching too many movies on Netflix," says Chase.

"Well … Captain, she's not far off in a matter of speaking. It's been about ten years since we've let outsiders into the facility. Once you understand the situation, confidentiality is imperative."

The admiral led them to a set table with a spectacular view of the ocean. Two people sat there. One was unfamiliar.

"May I introduce you both to Mr. William Streeter?" says Chase.

A man with jet-black hair stood up from the white-clothed table and turned around to greet them. He exuded an air of refined elegance, as his appearance was meticulous. His well-groomed short mustache and beard perfectly framed his square jaw. He stood a few inches over six feet and wore a royal blue wool sport coat with a dark metallic shimmer. Underneath, he wore a white button-down shirt and white slacks. As he extended his hand to shake, a shiny, expensive gold watch with a unique black face revealed itself.

Martha, who arrived shortly before Jasmine's group, was sitting at the table. When their eyes met, she smiled at Jasmine.

"It is great to have you all here, despite the grim circumstances. Please have a seat. My chef has prepared a delicious three-course meal. I'm sure you're all starving after your journey," says William.

"We appreciate your hospitality, Mr. Streeter, but I would really like to stay with Michael. May I please see him?" asks Jasmine.

"That's precisely why we're here, dear. My tablet has a direct link to his room, where they're keeping him stable and evaluating the extent of his injuries."

"Please call me 'Ensign'," says Jasmine, not appreciating William's informal tone.

William smirked, "Noted. Let me connect with Dr. Bell."

William connected to an app on his tablet that brought up a video call with the doctor. Behind the doctor, Michael lay completely still on a hospital bed with several life support machines connected to him and a white sheet up to his neck.

"Greetings, everyone," says Dr. Bell. "We have done a preliminary evaluation of Michael's current condition. Three of his four limbs have suffered significant trauma because of the intensity and proximity of the fireworks blasts. Even if we could repair the tissue and bones, the risk of infection remains very high. We removed the bone fragments from his right eye, but it is not repairable. Both of his ears have tympanic membrane perforation. Sometimes, a ruptured eardrum can heal without treatment, but the process takes weeks. Michael's eardrums have too many membrane holes to heal properly, unfortunately. I'm sorry I don't have better news. William, would you like me to start the operation?"

"Thank you, Doctor. Let me catch them up on our dealings here. Start going through our pre-op checklist," says Mr. Streeter.

Nausea overwhelmed Jasmine. As she looked around, the captain and Martha had their hands covering their mouths in shock. She shuddered, thinking about Michael's future after the tragedy. Michael was brilliant but hated being behind a desk. He wanted to be active in the field whenever he had the chance. Even his hobbies, like sailing and working out, required physical exertion. Being confined to a wheelchair or having prosthetic limbs would not suit him.

"Gang," says William as he read the solemn vibe in the room, "I know this is not the news you wanted but let me tell you a story that I know will give you hope for Michael."

CHAPTER
TWELVE

"During the early 2000s, I was an angel investor in Tesla's founding. I knew it had great potential, so unlike some founders, I held my stake until well after it went public. You won't see my name on the list of billionaires because I invested in Elon Musk, not directly in the company, through a hard-money agreement. A portion of his publicly disclosed stake in Tesla is my ownership through this private partnership. Now, while he invested in space travel research, I wanted to see what I could do right here on earth, thus the founding of SIX or Strategic Intelligence, Section 10," says William.

"Just how much are you worth?" asks Captain Donnelly.

Jasmine asks, "After the first billion, does it even matter?"

William smiled widely and continued with his explanation.

"I met Dr. Bell over a decade ago. His education and

research experience extremely impressed me. He's not only an MD but also has a PhD in materials science."

"What is that?" asks Martha.

"It's a rather broad field but primarily involves the study, design, and improvement of materials' structure, properties, and performance. One invention you're probably familiar with is carbon fiber, which is used extensively now for its high strength, flexibility, and lightweight properties. I started SIX to help advance humans past the relatively weak endoskeleton that we're all born with. We even received several large grants from the U.S. government for our exoskeleton research."

"You mean you're creating military exoskeletons for our troops, like the aliens in science fiction movies have with a protective shell around them?" asks Jasmine.

"You're much smarter than you look," says William. "In a way, yes, but in parallel, we worked on something even more impressive."

Jasmine didn't take a liking to the quip but held her facial expression, pretending to still be interested and not affected by his sarcasm.

"After hiring more scientists, we figured out how to use the exoskeleton technology in an endoskeleton application."

"You've lost me now," says Captain Donnelly.

"Sorry … I'm trying to tell you all that we can help Michael. We can repair him. We have the technology. Michael will be the world's first AIonic man." William's eyes widened.

Everyone's eyes lit up. They glanced at one another, searching for signs of understanding in their expressions.

Jasmine noticed Martha looked confused but also wanted to ask a question.

"Martha, do you have a question?" asks Jasmine.

"Yes, thank you," says Martha. "Is AIonic like bionic?"

Jasmine didn't expect such a technical question from the older woman. She had heard of bionics being used many decades ago, but she also knew that the government scrapped them because of safety concerns. She knew nothing more detailed than that.

"Martha, I assure you these are not, and Michael will not have to endure the issues his father went through," says William.

"What!" Jasmine's forehead creased. "Michael's father had bionics?"

"Yes," says William, "Michael's father had bionics after a war injury. As a matter of fact, Dr. Simon Bell is the son of Michael Sr's prosthetist."

Jasmine got up suddenly from the table and started scratching her head. A million questions were racing through her mind. The general began whispering some things to William.

"What are AIonics? Don't you think we should ask Michael what he wants? Have you done this type of surgery before?" Jasmine's questions came at a rapid pace.

"Calm down, Jasmine. I'll make sure you all have time to ask your questions. AIonics is a new technology that leverages artificial intelligence to enhance the performance and maintenance of artificial limbs and other sensory components. I can get into the foundation model we developed for the neural networking, but I might lose you all—ahhh … the food has arrived."

Two waitstaff started putting down plates of food on the table. The first plate had a colorful spinach salad, complete with crumbled feta cheese, slices of red onion, halved olives, and toasted pine nuts. A steaming plate followed, containing a bed of Dauphinoise potatoes with a large piece of beef wrapped in a golden-brown puff pastry. Cut in half, the Wellington revealed its desirable pinkish doneness hue.

The buttery garlic scent of the meat infiltrated Jasmine's nostrils, and she couldn't wait to consume it. Despite her strong urge to sit, she realized it was the perfect moment to address Martha while the hungry men were distracted.

"That looks amazing, but first, Martha, can we talk for a few minutes?"

Martha had just taken her first bite of the crispy salad. She wiped the corner of her mouth with a napkin and walked about 10 feet to where Jasmine had moved.

"I'm sorry; I know you're hungry, but I feel as if William has already decided on this. Are you okay with this? You must have some legal guardianship of your son if something happens to him in the field," says Jasmine.

"You really care for him, don't you?" says Martha.

Jasmine nodded.

"I do feel a little in the backseat on this one, but to be clear, Michael set nothing up to give me legal responsibility for the decisions on his care. I feel like a fool now for not forcing him to. Even if he had, what choice do we have? It's a risky operation, but it's better than Michael being confined to a wheelchair with one arm."

Jasmine's voice elevated. "They're using Michael as a science experiment!"

"Before you got here, Mr. Streeter said they had

successfully done a similar operation to a chimpanzee. He didn't go into any technical details yet, but he mentioned they had to put the chimpanzee down a month after the operation."

Jasmine snaps her head back. "That is not making me feel any better, Martha! What was all that bionic talk? Michael's father had bionics in him?"

"Yes, it was several months after I met him. They deployed him to assist during the Gulf War. While trying to save one of his 'brothers', he stepped on a buried land mine. I was pregnant with his son at the time of the accident. Anyway, after his operation, our relationship went sideways because he devoted all his time to his enhanced body. They probably forced him to work around the clock. Either way, we only saw him around the holidays. I haven't heard from Michael Sr. in over five years now."

"You did an amazing job with Michael on your own. Come on, your food's going to get cold," says Jasmine guiding Martha's arm.

As they sat down, William poured some red wine freshly opened into everyone's glasses. The admiral's body was bouncing from a funny remark made by the captain.

"Everything okay?" asks William as the two ladies took their seats.

"Perfect," says Jasmine, "we haven't seen each other in quite some time. Just catching up on some things. We didn't want to bore you all with our banter."

"Well, Amen to that," William shook his head while grinning. "I've never figured out why women have such long talks. It seems like a waste of time."

And you never will! Thought Jasmine, trying to get her feelings past his obnoxious narcissism.

"Would you two like some Bordeaux? I believe this one was just under $10,000," William asks while inspecting the label on the bottle.

Both ladies nodded as they dug into their plates of food. Jasmine had never tasted such a perfectly cooked Beef Wellington. The pastry crunched while the tenderloin melted in her mouth with a hint of garlic, mushrooms, and other subtle herbs. A sip of the expensive wine surpassed her expectations of complementing the meal. She briefly wondered if her fascination was purely because of her empty stomach, which could make any meal taste good. Her thought diminished when others at the table started complimenting William on his chef's expertise. She held back any compliments, given his ego was already being massively stroked.

Jasmine shifted her attention back to Michael's care while waiting for the expected dessert.

"So, what happened to the monkey?" asks Jasmine.

The odd question took William aback a bit, but then he quickly realized where she was going.

"Oh, so that's what you two were talking about," he says, shaking his finger at Martha as if to relay she had done something terrible.

"We attempted replacing two chimpanzee limbs with AIonics, and the operation was a great success. One method we used to take advantage of the superior AI engine is to connect the technology to the brain's prefrontal cortex. This part of the brain performs the decision-making, problem-solving, reasoning, etc. Our research has shown that the subject could better control the artificial limbs by allowing the engine to help make those micro-second decisions.

"For instance, imagine if the chimpanzee wanted to jump from one tree to another. He wouldn't know the distance, nor had he attempted it before. Leveraging the visual and audio inputs, the AI would give the chimp the exact amount of leg force he needed to make it from one tree to the next. We know this because we turned off the AI in several experiments, and the chimp sometimes fell short or jumped way past the target. It was amazing!"

"Sounds like mind-control to me," Martha says.

"Why did you kill the chimpanzee?" asks Jasmine.

"Ladies, we have learned a lot since then. Unfortunately, the AI worked too well, and the chimpanzee began exhibiting behaviors as if it were human. It even figured out how to get out of its secure habitat thrice. We couldn't have a powerful, smart chimpanzee walking around in the real world, so we made an ethical decision."

"Martha and I don't want to see Michael be your personal cyborg, Mr. Streeter, no offense."

"None taken, Jasmine; The ambiguity of this experimental operation can be frightening. I assure you; Michael's thoughts will be his own. We have figured out a way to inform him when a thought is from the AI, and he can make his own decision from there. Let's finish this delicious wine, have dessert, and retire for the evening. We promise nothing will happen to Michael until we talk again. Tomorrow morning, I'll take you all to visit him in the lab."

CHAPTER
THIRTEEN

SEVASTOPOL, UKRAINE (RUSSIA OCCUPIED)

General Petrovsky had a barrack designed specifically for him at the military base in Sevastopol. The base location was strategically close to the Black Sea and the Ukraine. His team's performance history had impressed the Ministry of Defense, and they rewarded him with some luxuries most generals would never get. As he sat in his indoor jacuzzi smoking one of his Cuban cigars, a scantily clad server handed him a cocktail glass half-full of Beluga vodka.

"Will there be anything else, GIP?" she asks.

"Where is Natalia?"

"She is prepping the bedroom for your massage."

"You will join her, right?"

"Of course, sir," she says with a masked smile.

"Please call Katya in. I have an assignment for her."

"Right away, sir."

Katya was a deceptively innocent-looking Russian

woman in her mid-twenties. Violence was all she knew in life, watching the Russian mafia butcher her parents at the tender age of eight. Her parents had owned a gastronomic restaurant in Moscow, which meant it specialized in high-quality cuisine and culinary expertise. Weekly, the mafia would demand their share of profits, often violently targeting her father, occasionally for no reason other than their own foul temperament. In times of economic down-turn, mobsters sought additional funds to compensate for diminished earnings from their other controlled ventures. Despite being a popular dining spot in the city, her parents would be upset as they barely have enough to keep the restaurant running.

After her parents' death, the mafia took her in and trained her on every interrogation tactic under the sun. Instead of learning what most kids learned during adolescence, Katya learned martial arts, espionage, and foreign languages. She hated working for the organization that killed her parents, so when General Petrovsky asked the mafia boss to have her join his paramilitary, it was one of the happiest moments of her life. This made her devoted to the GIP's needs and one of his most loyal followers.

A winter wind swept over the base grounds as she walked toward the general's living quarters. Despite the temperature being in the low single digits Celsius, Katya was not wearing a coat. She had trained herself to with-stand uncomfortable conditions and always appear more formidable than anyone around her. She wore an all-black outfit made of Luxtreme, a moisture-wicking, stretchable fabric designed for high-performance or, in her case, preci-sion combat strikes from her limbs. The material hugged her athletic body so that every curve was visible. She always wanted to look professional to her boss. Her hand grabbed the tightly braided strand of jet-black hair that extended below her buttocks and flung it over her shoulder to the front. She grabbed the end of the braid and observed the black, three-inch, spiked titanium ball attached. It looked like something from a historical Viking weapons book and the reason for her code name. She noticed a dark red stain on one spike. Licking her fingers, she rubbed it clean before opening the door to the general's headquarters.

"Good morning, Mace!" The general greeted her with her code name upon seeing her.

Her initial inclination was to look away, noticing that the tub was not bubbling, and the overweight, hairy general was completely nude, sitting in the water. As this would show weakness, she focused her gaze on his eyes.

"Sir, how can I help you today?"

"Is your passport still current?" asked GIP. "I need you to take a brief trip."

"Yes, sir. Where?"

"This is my personal mission, so please keep it discrete. The Kremlin does not sanction this, but in some ways, it will aid our future strength. The President couldn't plan his way out of the paper bag. I must do the forward-thinking for him. Understand?"

"Yes, sir."

"I need you to take a trip to D.C. and find out everything you can about the current status of Commander Michael Cooling. I maimed him before the damn U.S. Navy got in my way, so he's either dead or recovering somewhere. He's a decorated veteran, so they probably took him to the best hospitals. I would start at Walter Reed Medical Center. Here is a platinum American Express under your alias; use it for every expense."

Katya bent closer to the general to grab the card, careful not to break her comfortable facial gaze.

"Just me, sir?"

"Yes, this must be discreet. Once you know what happened to him, buy a burner and call me on the secure line. I'll provide further instructions."

As he finished speaking, two gorgeous females entered the room completely naked and glistening from the oil all over their bodies.

"We're ready for you, sir," one said.

Katya immediately felt sorry for them. She considered herself lucky that the general made no sexual requests or suggestions. He treated her like one of the boys, and she appreciated that. As she left the building, she heard the general's phone ring. By the unique ringtone, she remembered it was someone close to him.

"Baby, how are you?" asked General Petrovsky.

"I heard you failed!"

"What do you mean, Dear?"

"Don't 'Dear' me, I visited the cadet taken to the Belarus hospital. I got him to tell me what happened just before he succumbed to his gunshots."

"And you believed him?" says the general.

"He said the Navy foiled the plan, and you abandoned it. Do you not care about avenging my fiancé killed by that bastard? Did you know I just received the invoice from the hall where we were supposed to have the reception? They told me we canceled too late."

"Honey, please calm down. I already have my best person on it to make sure the commander didn't survive. I just need a little more time. Please give me the hall's contact info; don't pay that invoice. I'll have someone pay them a visit."

"I'll text it to you. Please keep me updated; I'm going crazy with all this grief. Some of my friends and I are heading to Cuba to escape this cold. I need to work on my tan and maybe find someone to fuck."

"Way too much information … take one of my men with you for protection, please," says Ivan.

"Okay, how about Sergei? I wouldn't mind having him be my oil boy." Irina let out a squeaky laugh.

"Fine. I need to go." Ivan quickly ended the call.

CHAPTER
FOURTEEN

Jasmine slept better than she had in weeks, but the sun's rays peeking through the dense pine trees and the chirping of a variety of bird species woke her up. The stressful mission and uncertainty with Michael had weighed on her, but the expensive wine aided her in getting to sleep the night before at a reasonable hour. Having stayed in lavish hotels previously, she couldn't ignore the luxurious room, yet this place surpassed all expectations.

A constant, subtle vanilla smell filled the room, its source unknown to her. The fixtures, flooring, furniture and counters exuded 5-star decor, but the most impressive feature was the wall opposite of the king-size plush bed. The enormous LCD screen had so many pixels, it appeared to be a solid wall. Voice-activated, the screen spanned floor to ceiling. The night before, she experimented with the "plain wall" view, resembling a typical hotel drywall with some imperfections. Instead, she chose the "midnight ocean" view, giving her room a beachfront appearance. She remembers staring at the white-cresting waves as the tide came in over the white sand and the cycle never repeated. Usually, videos like that repeat their pattern over and over, but she never saw it in the 20 minutes before she fell asleep.

She had asked the wall to wake her at 0700 hours with a forest view. A digital screen on the entry-door displayed the day's agenda. The agenda showed Mr. Streeter's organization skills, but the only parts Jasmine cared about were the visit to the treatment room after breakfast. She messaged Chase to confirm their simultaneous presence in the dining room. The one thing she wanted to avoid was a conversation with the arrogant host.

"How did you like Mr. Wally?" asks William to Martha as they walked to the elevator after breakfast.

"Mr. Wally?"

"The digital wall in your room. I named it that. Did you know Mr. Wally has a generative AI brain? He can sense your mood based on your heartbeat, body heat, and audio cues. He can also remember your wall preferences and suggest them."

Seriously? That's creepy. I got undressed in front of that wall!

"Isn't that an invasion of privacy?" Jasmine asks.

"Not that I'm aware of. Don't worry, it can't see you and if you read the instruction card left on the desk, you can ask it to stop listening for any period of time."

"Thanks, but that doesn't seem much better. Where is the Vice Admiral?"

"He had to head back to Washington for an urgent matter," says Captain Donnelly.

As the elevator opened to the third sub-level, a five-foot

tall man, probably in his early forties, with a thick black mustache, pleasantly greeted them. He was wearing a white-lab coat that had its pockets full of many small instruments, including a pen protector in his chest pocket. Seeing the group, he appeared excited, as though he hadn't interacted with visitors for months.

"Nice to meet you, Dr. Bell," says Martha. "Where is my boy?"

The five entered a room that combined elements of a hospital surgery room and an automobile factory. There was computer equipment and monitors all over, getting feeds from multiple places. Most of the screens had either graphs, charts, or undecipherable codes scrolling. Michael was in the middle with four high-powered lights above him. His right-eye had a bandage over it and only the top of his chest was visible beneath the white covers. Medical staff had attached several wires to his head and body while he appeared to be sedated. No bulges under the bottom half of the cover suggested his legs were no longer there. Martha quickly ran over and grabbed his hand under the cover.

"You said you would do nothing till we talked again." Jasmine's eyebrows scrunched.

"We—"

"Let me answer, Mr. Streeter. This is my fault," says Dr. Bell. "Our monitoring last night raised an alarm. Both of his legs had a minor infection. Then, his body started showing signs of septic shock, which is an inflammatory response to infections that cause serious side effects, like organ failure. Antibiotics showed no response, thus removing the source was necessary. I'm sorry, but it was our only alternative."

Martha cried quietly; gripping Michael's hand tighter. Jasmine walked over and put her arm around Martha to comfort her while whispering in her ear.

"Martha, why don't we hear the doctor out before we decide? If it seems too risky, we'll just ask for regular prosthetics."

"O-o-o-kay," says Martha, wiping some tears away.

"Okay, Dr. Bell and Mr. Streeter. What can you all do for Michael?" asks Jasmine.

William smiled compassionately and motioned everyone to the adjoining room.

The room smelled like rubbing alcohol and on the tables appeared to be amputated human limbs. As they moved closer, the leg and accompanying arm looked like healthy, living flesh, including real-looking hairs, and a few birthmarks. Black material protruded from the limb edges, with fine wires replacing the cavity where bones would be.

"This is a sample of what we will fit Michael with," said Dr. Bell. "Here, hold it ... touch it."

Martha reluctantly reached out her hands, and the doctor placed the leg in her hands. The weight pressed into her hands, but she could still hold on.

"Oh, my goodness, it feels so real, but heavy."

"Believe it or not, it's only about 10% heavier than a real leg, but the skeletal muscle layer, covered in flexible borophene, is almost 200 times stronger than steel, yet an excellent superconductor."

Sensing everyone's' confusion, William piped in, "The good doctor is saying that while the leg looks and feels human, it is materially and functionally superhuman. The same for the replacement arm."

"I've never heard of borophene. Is that like graphene?" asks Jasmine.

"I'm impressed," said William. "Correct, but where graphene is an allotrope of carbon, borophene is from boron. When added to carbon fiber-type materials, it results in superior strength, yet still being very lightweight. We were going to use graphene, but for millions more, we could manufacture borophene. I wanted the strongest."

"That sounds so lavish … and why does he need super-human limbs?" asks Martha.

"We were hoping he could go back to doing what he loves. It will only protect him from harm."

"What is the skin made of? It feels so soft," asked Jasmine, stroking the forearm on the table.

"Ahh, that is one of my favorite features," exclaimed Dr. Bell. "Over a decade ago, we found that a bark spider, native to Madagascar, produced a spider silk that was an astonishing 10 times strong than Kevlar. You know … the material in bullet-proof vests. As you can imagine, sourcing spiders for silk is a difficult and a dangerous business. My research team took it one step further and started studying silkworm. Years of research proved that by manually manipulating the silk, we could create a silk that is 65% stronger than spider silk. Of course, other materials have been added to it for the texture, color, etc."

"Oh wow, he'll be bulletproof!" Captain Donnelly's eyes widened.

"And then some …" says William, grinning.

"Unless he gets shot in the chest!" Jasmine says.

"There's something we wanted to talk to you both about," William glanced at Martha and Jasmine. "You've felt the material. We thought it's best to add it to his entire body, especially since he has nearly third-degree burns in several places."

Martha and Jasmine exchanged glances, attempting to assess their respective opinions.

"Just not his two heads. Deal?" says Jasmine.

William and Dr. Bell let out a good laugh in unison while nodding.

"How long will all of this take?" asks Martha.

"We estimate he will be in surgery for at least 18 hours. Besides the physical, there are a lot of electronic connections, tuning, and, most importantly, the brain interface."

"We didn't talk about his eye or damaged ears," says Jasmine.

"They'll be replaced, looking just like his own, but with better performance," William says.

"Why do all this for him? The technology and research must have cost millions."

"Decades ago, bionics cost several million dollars. AIonics is pushing one billion after looking at last month's balance sheet, but it will be worth every dime. We still have the exoskeleton contracts from the government. This is just a sub-project of that, mostly funded by my personal funds. I like to think of it as a giant, technical leap forward in prosthetics."

"I hate to break it to you, Mr. Streeter, but very few will be able to afford these limbs," says Jasmine.

"I always say innovation before commoditization."

Martha and Jasmine walked back to Michael. Martha kissed his cheek and whispered softly. The women and Chase took one last look around at the symphony of technology, hoping that money and research would save Michael's mobility before they started walking toward the elevator.

William followed but was then pulled aside by Dr. Bell.

"You didn't tell them about Michael's healthy arm."

"I think they've had enough shock for one morning, don't you? I would like the surgery to begin as soon as possible."

CHAPTER
FIFTEEN

TALLINN, ESTONIA

Estonia became independent from Russia in 1991. Located in Northern Europe it shared its eastern border with Russia. It's one of the three Baltic states along with Latvia and Lithuania, and General Petrovsky vacationed there often. Typically, his trip would include a visit to its capital, and then a fishing trip to the Pärnu river. The river boasted world-class salmon. He loved the taste of broiled salmon, especially after a fresh catch. He usually fished alone since most of his acquaintances knew better than to go with him. A story circulated about a senior lieutenant of his. He apparently drowned on a fishing trip with Petrovsky. Many believed the general killed him for something as ludicrous as catching more salmon than the general caught.

His trip this time would have to be cut short, given his overloaded schedule. He was meeting with a highly paid government informer. Afterward, he would go back to

Polohy's front line to inform the officers of their next actions in the fight against Ukraine. The Minister of Defence had clearly communicated the war and Red Union offensive were the general's only priorities. As he waited for his contact while taking a sip of his hot, herbal tea outside of a coffeehouse in Old Town, his phone rang.

"Katya, what have you found? My impatient daughter calls me daily even while she is on vacation. I'm waiting for someone. I have little time."

"D.C. is a dead end. I've reached out to all my contacts here, and no one has heard anything. I also found it strange that there was no record of a burial service for anyone involved in Belarus, not even the two SEALs killed outside the building. They didn't have personal addresses, as I heard they lived on a military base. The only lead I have on Michael is his mother's address in California. There is no record of his father or any other immediate family."

"That's a start. How did you manage to get that?"

"I decided to test my charm. I went to a bar near the Capital and met a federal analyst. My attire made him eager to join me in my hotel room. I gave him some story about how I knew Commander Cooling in high school and wanted to send him a congratulations card for winning the Medal of Honor. He said he couldn't give me his home address, but if I wanted to send it to his mother, he would provide that."

"Fantastic, Mace, and the loose end?"

"Terminated."

"Just a second," GIP raised his index finger to the man approaching and motioned for him to join. "Please sit down —thanks for the update. Talk to you soon."

Ivan ended the call and put away his phone. He offered a handshake. Despite the cooler evening, the man's hand was warm and sweaty.

"Thanks for meeting with me," says the general.

"I don't have long ... I only get a half-hour lunch break."

He continually glanced behind, along the alley, and past the general's shoulder.

"You're drawing attention to yourself, comrade. Just relax and nothing will happen," insisted GIP.

"Do you have it?"

"You don't trust me? As you can see, I came alone. Normally, I have at least three officers with me in public places."

"I know, sir, but I'm taking a gigantic risk here." Beads of sweat rolled down the man's temple.

GIP opened the leather messenger bag that was draped over his shoulder. He lifted a gold bar partially out of the bag, just enough to let the setting sun behind his visitor gleam brightly off it.

"Okay, okay, put it back!" The man motioned downward with his hand.

"Is the rumor true of a Ukrainian gift?"

"Yes, in exchange for our generosity in providing military aid, the President has agreed to ship nine slightly damaged Leopard tanks to Estonia. My understanding is the repairs are nominal. However, they must be taken out of service to do them. They've also agreed to send over the spare parts. You'll just need to find mechanics to repair them," said the informer.

"1s or 2s?"

"My understanding is just Leopard 2s."

The general says, "Excellent! The 1s are becoming a maintenance nightmare now. Your country has no other battle tanks in service now, correct?"

"No, that's why this deal is so huge for us. We can use them to protect our eastern border."

"When is the delivery?"

"I'm sorry, I don't know that, but I can tell you the train line they are using. You just need to keep tabs on those scheduled deliveries from Kyiv via Riga. They're going by general freight, not military, because of costs."

"Any more information? You know if you tell anyone of this conversation, my men will execute your entire family."

"Yes, understood," The man wiped his brow with the back of his hand.

"Then let's celebrate! Here … take this. This bar weighs like over 10 kilograms. My shoulder is killing me. Let me get us a shot inside."

"I still need to go back to work. I shouldn't—"

"Nonsense! This is how Russians seal every deal. 44 milliliters of vodka will not kill you."

The general went inside and ordered shots while monitoring the informer. As he waited, he became eager to update his superiors about the information he had learned.

The two raised their shot glasses up and flung their heads back as the chilled fluid warmed their throats. They shook hands, and the man departed down the cobblestone alley. The general sat back down, appreciating the dusk-colored orange sky. Out of the corner of his eye, about 25 meters away, the man collapsed, convulsing violently. Before too many people took notice, he walked over, lifted the messenger bag, and headed to his hotel casually.

CHAPTER
SIXTEEN

Dr. Bell was happy with how the surgery was progressing and the expertise of his team. They brought in surgeons from some of the best institutions in the United States, like Johns Hopkins and Cleveland Clinic. He wanted some doctors from Germany, but the risk was too high. This project was top-secret. The medical team had sedated Michael with several types of anesthesia, including general and epidural. An epidural would ease pain after Michael's surgery, even while awake. His vital signs were stable despite completing one of the riskiest parts of the operation.

While his internal organs and torso remain in-tact, his frame would be reinforced to withstand the energy and pressure from the AIonic limbs. This required a type of advanced shock absorbing system that was fused to his pelvis bone for his legs and to his scapula and clavicle for his arms. The system was intelligent enough to convert the massive additional energy into reserve energy for the limbs. This prevented the stress from transferring to his bones, which easily could cause them to shatter. The limbs were very lightweight. There was no reason to modify Michael's spine. The doctor instead installed a few microscopic monitors along several of the vertebrae. These gadgets would take measurements for later evaluations.

As he prepped the new legs for insertion into the torso, he glanced over at the silver tray table that now held Michael's severed left arm in nearly perfect condition. *The ladies are going to kill me*; he thought. They didn't know the choice to install two artificial arms was one of experience, not desire. He hoped that, when it was over, Michael Sr. would visit to provide insight on the weakness of only having one bionic arm.

The digital wall intercom by the surgery room's door buzzed. Mr. Streeter's face appeared on the small LCD screen while he waited for someone to answer.

"Little busy down here, William," says Dr. Bell after walking over to answer.

"I know … I know … sorry, I'm just too excited to sit up here and wait around drinking 100-year-old scotch."

"You know, it could take weeks for Michael to be back on his feet."

"Even with the Convalescytes?" asks William.

"Yes, the genetically modified stem cells will only work as fast as his body will allow. We have to be patient."

"Okay, can you at least call me when you work on the eye? That tiny component alone cost me over 20 million to manufacture. I would like to inspect it."

"Sure, thing, William. I suspect it will be at least another four hours before we start that."

Simon walked away from the intercom, shaking his head. His fellow surgeons briefly looked up and gave him a sympathetic look, which was clear even through their surgical masks.

Dr. Cynthia Moore was examining the artificial limbs carefully. She was a bit puzzled as she looked closer and ran her fingers across the synthetic skin.

"Something I can answer?" Dr. Bell asks.

"What? … Oh yes, sorry, I'm fascinated by this skin and cannot for the life of me understand why the skin has pores … like actual skin," she says.

"Remember, you're under strict NDA. Anything I tell you now is highly proprietary, as the technology doesn't exist anywhere on the planet. At least as far as we know."

"Of course, Doctor."

"The byproduct of the energy created by his limbs is simply water," says Dr. Bell.

"Wait … we're using hydrogen fuel cells?"

"Yes! Sort of … we actually don't need that many cells or big cells because his body will function like an actual body. His consumption will fuel his limbs."

"On my way here, I read the notes from the bionic operations years ago. They used radioisotope thermoelectric generators, like the ones they used in space probes. Why are we not using that technology?"

"Couple reasons. First, it's difficult to properly insulate to keep the radiation from leaking into the body. A body's cavity is too crowded to implement the proper barriers. The best ones, like lead, are way too heavy. Second, bionic history has shown us that despite their best efforts, they detected radiation in measurements taken near the artificial limbs. Matter of fact, Michael's father was leaking radiation, but somehow his body adjusted to it. It was the main reason he didn't maintain a relationship with his son or the mother. He feared long exposure would sicken them."

"Jesus! How devastating for him," says Dr. Moore.

"The government department that made him stopped supporting his older technology many years ago. Not even sure if he's still alive."

She gasped. "How do you plan to incorporate these hydrogen molecules into these new AIonics? Is Michael going to carry around a hydrogen tank, like an old man?"

"Don't be silly. We don't need hydrogen molecules. Michael's body will create the hydrogen," Dr. Well was confident he had given his peer enough clues.

"Are you telling me hydrolysis will happen inside his body by drinking water?"

"Precisely! The limbs will use hydrolysis to break down the water molecules into positively charged hydrogen ions that will move through cathodes to generate electrical current for his movements. Those protons and electrons will then have a reduction reaction using the oxygen he breathes to release the byproduct, water. This water will seep out of the pores in his artificial limbs and appear as sweat, just like natural limbs."

"That is genius!!" Dr. Moore's voice ricocheted off the glass-enclosed room. Some of the other doctors turned around, distracted by her loud outburst.

"Well, thank you! I actually helped develop the miniature system. Of course, he will have some ways to store hydrogen in case he ends up stuck in the Mojave Desert." Dr. Bell's mouth clicked.

"Doctor, I feel so fortunate to be part of this unprecedented procedure. Let's get going on his legs."

"Give me five minutes. Want to check on how the others are doing with his ears."

As Dr. Bell walked the few paces over to Michael's head, he suddenly worried how he was going to keep all these doctors from accidentally telling others about their intriguing experiment here. This job was a wet dream for these doctors. Some doctors love to brag to their colleagues, especially given the inherent competition between highly educated individuals. There was an experimental drug he had heard about that helps prevent short-term memories from becoming long-term memories. The military was considering it for troops going into battle to help prevent PTSD. Some researchers were nicknaming it the new "*morning-after pill.*" Simon quickly turned around and took out his pocket notebook. He jotted a reminder to have William see if he could overnight it to the facility.

"How are we doing over here?"

"The tympanic membrane and cochlea are too big. We had to cut away some of the temporal bone to fit it in. By the way, I was told to test these ears, but I think the machine is broke," says one doctor.

"Why?" asks Dr. Bell.

"Because the ear tested hearing a simulated sound almost two miles away! That's seven times farther than dogs can hear, and they hear 4-5 times farther than humans."

Simon slapped his hand lightly on the doctor's shoulder and leaned over to whisper in his ear.

"The machine works just fine. Wait till we test his balance. Cats worldwide will be extremely envious."

CHAPTER
SEVENTEEN

Katya wasn't happy sitting in the economy section of the 757. She had used all her frequent flyer miles flying first-class from Moscow to Washington with a stopover in Turkey. It was worth it, though, given the 16-hour travel time. Her mind began plotting how she would convince the general to let her charge in a first-class ticket for the trip home. That meant she needed results he would appreciate. She forgot to buy water before boarding in her rush to make the gate. First class was already receiving beverage service when she passed their seats. This made her envious. The flight attendants' primary concern for economy class was only seating and carry-on bags. The only positive thought she had upon arriving at her row was her luck in getting a window seat with a last-minute one-way ticket.

She placed her oversized black backpack in the over-head and took her seat in the empty row. She hoped the plane wasn't full and the middle seat next to her would be vacant. *Isn't that every traveler's hope?* Her mind quickly realized that greedy airlines enjoyed packing as many people as possible into their undersized seats.

Katya immediately checked for new encrypted messages on her phone before putting it in airplane mode. Pulling the spy novel out of her bag, she began reading. The book was called *Smiley's People* by the late author, John le Carré. She enjoyed reading novels that portrayed characters who were like her. She even got an idea from a novel she read about a unique way to kill someone. Katya thought the book portrayed it as too humane. The unfortunate soul she killed using that method suffered much longer. She hoped that someday people would read about her style. To ensure this, she documented many of her missions in an online, encrypted journal. The security set on the journal made it automatically decrypt in the year 2100. She figured she would be long gone from this Earth by then.

While reading, she noticed people staring as they passed by. It wasn't uncommon given her non-traditional look. Her long black hair was braided into two strands this time. Her weapon of choice would've never made it past security. She had black lipstick on and three silver-pointed half-rings in her right eyebrow. One reason she traveled light, with just a backpack, was her attire. She primarily wore black skin-tight outfits, so a couple of extra outfits took up very little space. Her top, today, had a triangular sheer front that extended down to her bellybutton. It accentuated a semi-transparent view of her busty cleavage. She enjoyed watching husbands and boyfriends try to sneak a glance while with their significant others.

A middle-aged woman sat in her row, in the aisle seat.

Without greeting Katya, she started texting someone on her phone after filling her seat pocket with a bunch of sugary snacks. Soon after, a man, probably in his early seventies, paused at the row. The woman in the aisle seat immediately unbuckled and stood up. The man entered the row. Katya raised her head to find the man's eyes fixated on her chest, then swiftly shifted to her face. He smiled creepily at her. Katya turned her head to look out the window.

Katya's book was on an exciting chapter, but she couldn't help feeling annoyed by the old man sitting there doing *nothing. Who comes on a 6-hour flight with nothing to keep them busy?* No phone, no book, no magazine, no food, just staring over her lap out the window at a boring tarmac. She hoped he wasn't a talker—.

"Whatcha reading?" he asks.

F-U-C-K!!!

"A book," says Katya.

The man laughed heartily at her curt response.

"Of course it is! What is it about?"

"It's an old spy novel from the 70s. You've probably never heard of it."

"Try me, I've been around the block quite of few times as you've probably guessed."

"'Smiley's People.'"

"That sounds like a comedy to me."

Katya was already tired of the conversation. She offered to exchange her seat so the man could stare outside and not over her.

"Oh, no! I wanted the middle seat. It gives me a chance to get to know two *new* people."

OH - MY - GOD! thought Katya. Now he was frying her nerves—.

"I like your outfit! My late wife could never pull off black. She wore the most colorful clothes. Might be a little eccentric for some people, but I loved her for that."

"That's wonderful, sir. I don't mean to be rude, but I'd just like to read my book, if you don't mind."

"Not at all, of course. By the way, I detect an accent. Are you from Europe?"

Why the hell did he say "of course" and then continue to ask me a question?

After Katya didn't respond right away, the man realized his error and motioned with his hand to zipper his mouth, and then tried to be funny by putting an imaginary key in his pocket. He extended his hand to the poor woman on the aisle seat and introduced himself. Katya decided it was better to sleep through the flight. She popped a black-market melatonin pill that almost instantly helped her drift away.

Katya felt a hand glaze over her left leg and immediately realized she wasn't dreaming as the preparation for landing announcement came over the cabin speakers. She jerked awake and caught the old man with his hands raised in the air, acting like he was surrendering.

"I'm so sorry, Miss! Your belt buckle was super loose, and we were about to land. I was just tightening it for you, since you were asleep."

The words that came to her mind would have surely

frightened the surrounding passengers. Instead, Katya gave him a look of disdain and lifted the window cover just as LAX airport came into view.

Skipping baggage claim, she made her way to the airport's FedEx office. She hoped the small package she sent the night before had arrived. The clerk found it after about 10 minutes and handed it with a smile to Katya. Next stop, the women's restroom. After entering a stall, she re-braided her hair into a single long strand and attached the contents of the package. The weight felt good on her hair, and she proceeded outside to grab a taxi.

As bad luck would have it, she saw her flight buddy again. He was standing at the curb waiting for the cross-walk light to change. The crosswalk took arriving passengers to the middle divider for ground transportation. Engaged in conversation, he was with a younger man in an army uniform. She approached him from behind inconspicuously to make sure he didn't see her.

She saw a large shuttle bus from the rental agency approach. With a calculated twist, she whipped her head and body, causing the spiked ball in her braid to strike the old man's head. Blood and small bone fragments gushed out of the impact area. His body tumbled into the lane from the blow. The army guy tried to grab him, but it happened too fast. The vehicle's brakes made a loud hissing sound before coming to a stop. The man's deformed body was dangling inside the rear wheel well. Loud screams rang out on the sidewalk as Katya took the opportunity to cross over the lane to a taxi with its roof light on.

"What's going on?" asks the driver as she hopped in.

Noticing the commotion, his head kept moving to get a better look.

"Time caught up with some old man."

"Where to?"

"I'm starving. Any good steak restaurants nearby?"

"You picked the right cab, lady, I know just the place."

CHAPTER
EIGHTEEN

Michael's eyelids felt heavy, and his vision was blurry, but strangely in only one eye. A glass wall on the left showcased a stunning view of the ocean. Seeing the sunlight dance on the waves was very therapeutic, especially as he tried to clear his foggy head. He began panicking as his memory brought back one of his last thoughts. He quickly lifted the white cover to check out his body, hoping not to see the trauma from the memory. To his surprise, his body looked normal, except for the tighty-whities underwear he was wearing. Despite his foggy mind, Michael knew those weren't from his wardrobe. He felt his right arm and while the hair looked real, the skin texture was slightly stiffer than he remembered. He also thought the amount of hair was less dense.

"You're awake!" Jasmine walked into the room with a wide smile.

Right behind her, Dr. Bell immediately went to a control panel on a machine linked to Michael.

"Jasmine … am I glad to see you. I was just remembering the nightmare in Belarus. Where am I?"

"A facility on Necker Island. This is your doctor, Dr. Simon Bell," she says.

"Great to finally meet you," Dr. Bell shook Michael's hand carefully.

"How did I get here? Where is Necker Island? … Who rescued us? Why don't I have any scarring? I'm so confused." Michael rotated his right arm to show them.

"Let's slow it down a bit, shall we?" says the doctor. "Do you feel any pain?"

"Nothing now, except a slight headache … that fucking asshole general! Did we get him?"

"I'm afraid not, sir. But I took out five of them before the calvary arrived," Jasmine raised her chin while pulling her shoulders back.

"You've always been my best frogman. How long have I been here?"

"Several days now," says Dr. Bell.

"Your mom was here, but she had to leave," says Jasmine.

"What! Why?"

"You were in terrible shape, sir … and we had to make some decisions about your care."

"Does the Russian general know I'm alive?"

"Only a handful of people know anything. We have even delayed the services for our fallen men to keep your status secret," says Jasmine.

"Why did my mother leave? We need to send someone to protect her. They might come after her to find me," Michael says.

"Why?" Jasmine's brow furrowed.

"Because the general has this vendetta against me for his daughter. During my rescue mission to save the Ukrainian President, I evidently killed her fiancé, who was also part of GIP's paramilitary."

"Who's GIP?"

"General Ivan Petrovsky. He likes to go by GIP for short, pompous prick!"

"That's why they tortured you? Jesus! … Her address is classified information. Doubt they can find her, but if it makes you feel better, I will call Admiral Jackson and ask him to send two MPs from the base."

"Yes, please, these people are ruthless. Why did my mother leave?"

"We didn't know how long it would take you to recover. Someone in her prayer group got Covid, so she had to host the next meeting."

"Yep, that sounds like my mom," Michael says, closing his eyes and shaking his head. "Speaking of recovery, how are my limbs fully healed in less than a week?"

Dr. Bell gently nudged Jasmine aside. "Let me take this one. We used molecular machines called Convalescytes. Think of them like immature cells advanced synthetically. They accelerate your recovery and can heal proportionally faster than human blood cells. You've probably heard of stem cell therapy to repair damaged tissues. This is the next evolution in healing therapy."

"I appreciate the explanation, Doctor. But why am I here? Shouldn't I be in a military hospital?" asks Michael.

With hesitation, Jasmine and the doctor briefly locked eyes before refocusing on Michael.

"Because—"

"How is my investment doing?" William entered the room with a big grin, wearing his workout gear and carrying a tablet.

Michael's brow wrinkled at Jasmine as his eyes looked William up and down.

"Who the hell are you? Where is Captain Donnelly?"

"Surprised you haven't heard of me yet. I'm the one who saved your life. William Streeter, nice to meet you." William extended his hand, then yanked it back, looking at the doctor. "Is he activated yet?"

Dr. Bell shook his head. William re-extended his hand without concern. Michael looked confused but shook it while sitting up in his bed.

"I'm really lost here! Would someone start explaining?" Michael's eyes beaded at the group.

"It's better if we show you, sir," says Jasmine.

Authenticating with his thumbprint, the doctor brought a nearby computer monitor to life. He pulled up an application that had an outline of a male human body. Grey shaded the head outline and torso. The limbs and ears had a shade of blue. The right eye was also blue but had a red outline. As the doctor touched each of the blue parts, they transitioned to red like a thermometer rising in temperature.

Michael felt a brief surge of energy, like the adrenaline someone gets when they're about to attempt something dangerous. He heard countless conversations simultaneously, as though in a sports stadium, then it became nearly silent. Out of his right eye, he spotted a small cobweb in the ceiling's corner at least 30 feet away. It appeared to fill his vision like he had just taken a picture up close. For some strange reason, he knew it was from the Lycosidae family, commonly called the wolf spider. He never studied spiders once in his life.

"What the hell is happening to me?"

"Extraordinary things!" says Mr. Streeter, his eyes animated with unrestrained enthusiasm. "You're officially the first AIonic man."

CHAPTER
NINETEEN

The doctor finished explaining the technical composition of his new limbs, as well as his enhanced hearing and vision. He elaborated on the interface between the AI engine and his various sensory and motor cortices in his brain, which helps him make better decisions or know things just based on sensory input. Michael stared at his legs for a good 30 seconds in silence. This was uncomfortable for the chatty benefactor.

"You'll be—"

"Excuse me a sec, Mr. Streeter," Michael raised his hand, palm out. "So … my body is nearly indestructible, but one well-aimed sniper headshot can take me out?"

"Good question," says Dr. Bell. "To give you the extraordinary hearing, we could have given you Dumbo ears or just amplify the sound—"

"Well, thanks for not making me a Disney character—"

"Let me finish, Michael. The amplification waves are so strong, the decibels could literally shatter your skull, so we applied a protective borophene and artificial spider silk layer there, too. It serves two purposes: to protect your skull and absorb the otherwise damaging waves."

"And you tested this? When?"

"Mostly theoretical, with AI simulations using a quantum computer," says the doctor.

Shaking his head slowly, "Nice to know I'm lab rat numero uno!"

"Michael, we had little choice with the condition you were in." Jasmine's voice softened as she spoke.

"I can't deny it. I want to return to the field. But I would have been happier just testing out your exoskeleton uniform. Why couldn't you just give me normal limbs that work?" asks Michael.

"Because you're different, Michael," says Mr. Streeter. "Any frogman can wear a combat exoskeleton. None of them has the instinct, intelligence, or military experience that you have. The investment in this tech is significant. It's completely undetectable by security scanners and is self-sufficient. An exoskeleton might help during war, but the actual wars are fought with espionage. Besides, it's in your blood to do this!"

Regret filled William's eyes as he immediately wished he could retract his last comment.

"Blood! What the hell are you talking about? Are you gonna tell me that my mother has AIonics too, now?" Michael's face contorted, releasing pent-up emotion as much as it could with the subdermal crystalline boron beneath.

"No, no, but …" Dr. Bell looked up at Jasmine and William, "your father was enhanced."

Michael processed the information, glancing at Jasmine for confirmation of the doctor's accuracy.

"I just found out, too," she whispered.

Michael shook his head and looked down. *All these years, all these years!* The damn government kept his father from his family because he was a weapon. *The impact on a fatherless boy was trivial compared to the safety of secret technology.* His anger grew inside.

"Can I have a glass of water?" His sharp words cut through the silence in the room.

Jasmine, sensing the mounting frustration, quickly poured water into a steel cup and put it in Michael's left hand.

The metal folded together like crumpled paper, flinging the volume of water straight up into the air.

"What the fuck, Doc!" Jasmine started a blaming stare.

"We had to!"

"His left arm was perfectly fine. Why did you replace it?"

Michael, unaware of his condition before the surgery, pierced his dagger eyes toward Mr. Streeter, knowing he was pulling the strings here.

"Everyone, calm down," says Dr. Bell. "Did you ever hear the saying, don't repeat the same mistake twice? Many of the patients who first got bionics decades ago only received them in their injured limbs. This limited their capabilities drastically. Soldiers had to fight using only their enhanced limb or switch stances if a threat came from the opposite side. Also, they could have had double the lifting power if both arms were bionic. The slight weight differential between the enhanced and regular limbs also affected their balance. Something that's necessary when you're jumping to the roofs of buildings."

"Wait! I can jump higher?" asks Michael, as intrigue replaced his anger.

"You can do lots of things. We won't know for sure until we get you out of that bed," says William.

"Since I can't even hold a cup right now, can I turn these enhanced limbs off or at least disable beast-mode?"

The doctor and Mr. Streeter chuckled.

"Once activated, there is no going back. You will get used to controlling them with practice. There is, however, one way to temporarily disable them, but only you can do it. Setting your body to low-power mode conserves hydrogen fuel and reduces your power. I estimate you could function for over two weeks without water in that mode. You won't want to do it very often though, the discomfort you experienced when I brought you online will happen again, plus you'll only have 10% of the strength you normally have."

"Please don't starve me to test this," says Michael. "I'm craving proper food. Can someone bring me something to eat?"

"Of course," Mr. Streeter folded his arms on his chest, "my Michelin chef can make anything. What are you craving?"

"Bo Luc Lac"

"Hmm, I don't know what that is. Excuse me for a few minutes while I get the chef started on this."

"Are you sure you should eat a heavy Vietnamese steak dish?" says Jasmine.

"His digestion should be completely normal, and we have extracted any chemicals needed for surgery. If his appetite is strong, no worries here," Dr. Bell's hands gestured affirmation.

Michael got out of his bed and walked to the panoramic window. His body felt good, but his mind was painfully racing. In the distance, as he peered past the turquoise water clinging to the sandy shore, he saw a green and white striped sailboat bouncing over the white waves that was crashing into its bow. For a moment, he pictured himself there, the warm ocean breeze on his skin and not a care in the world. He was thankful the SIX team had so much faith in him. They were putting all this technology, effort, and money into his well-being. He knew it came at a cost. That cost would be servitude.

He felt like a teenager with his first car. He wanted to explore his enhanced body's capabilities but sensed the doctor's need for post-operative tests. It was unlikely he would get out of the facility soon. He thought about calling his mother to investigate her role in the paternal cover-up but preferred not to discuss it over the phone. Still, she deserved an update on his surgery and despite Jasmine assuring him that MPs would watch her residence; he had a sinking feeling she was still in danger.

The sailboat appeared anchored now. It looked tiny, floating in a vast expanse of water, almost a mile from land. He tested his AIonic eye to get a closer look. A blonde woman was suntanning on the golden teak wood deck.

"Why is your face getting red?" Jasmine joined Michael at the window and followed his gaze.

Embarrassed, Michael says, "I didn't know the French bikini wax was still a thing."

Jasmine playfully smacked his arm, a burst of laughter escaping her lips as she shook her head in amused disbelief.

CHAPTER
TWENTY

RIGA, LATVIA

The view from St. Peter's observation gallery 200 feet above the capital was breathtaking. As Ivan looked north-west to admire the unique construction of the Vanšu Bridge, the crisp air invigorated his senses. If this church were in America, he was certain protective barriers would exist to block the wind and prevent suicides. He frequently pondered the country's excessive protection of its weak individuals. He knew the legal systems were mostly to blame for allowing families to sue establishments for their own family member's stupidity. For attractions, especially those with medieval history, he admired the greater freedom Europe offered. He briefly enjoyed the thought of tossing someone over the concrete parapet and figured he would have the chance if the secret meeting he was having soon went any other way but perfect.

His cadet had temporarily replaced the church's elevator attendant to keep their meeting private. Making something like an unscheduled security check seem official was as easy as sending a military-uniformed man to do the job, and the general reveled in it. The scheduled attendant was now on an early lunch break. Two burly men arrived shortly thereafter. The cadet escorted them to the elevator for the covert rendezvous. Once they reached the gallery floor, the elevator door opened. The general inspected the visitors, then signaled the cadet, who retreated downstairs.

Two men strolled toward the general from the elevator. They looked to be born and raised in the gritty streets of Riga and stood at an imposing 6 feet 3 inches with broad shoulders, shaved heads, and matching snake tattoos on their necks. The only method to differentiate the twin brothers was by inspecting their faded facial scars. Even their black leather jackets matched.

"General Petrovsky? I'm Kristap Vilks, and this is my brother, Kaspars."

"Call me, GIP. I only asked for one person. Was that not clear?"

"It was, but Kaspars and I work better together. We watch each other's back. We'll do it for the same price as one man. You'll get more for your money. If something happens to one of us, the other is your backup plan. As you can see, we're twins, so very difficult to tell us apart."

"I suppose that is agreeable. Next time be clearer in your communication. We can't afford any slip-ups on this one," says GIP. "Did you secure a position at the Central Railway Station?"

"Yes, it was easy. Most people are looking for jobs at the new fancy Rail Baltica Central Hub. That one's almost operational, so they had lots of openings. We took a nighttime janitor position and have keys for everything," says Kristap.

"I already got this out of the station manager's locker," says Kaspars, as he showed off a shiny black and silver Breitling chronometer watch.

His brother became flush with embarrassment. Before anyone could say anything else, GIP, who was at least three inches shorter than Kaspars, took him by surprise and flung his body over the barrier surrounding the observatory while keeping a hold of his ankles. GIP's eyes were nearly black.

"How is the view, you fucking nitwit! Do you think that watch will survive the fall?" asks the general.

"General, please," Kristap got up close to the general. "Please forgive my brother's foolishness. Theft is in his nature."

"I don't give two shits what is in his nature. You're there to observe and do as I say, *NOTHING ELSE*! If you can't follow orders, then go back to the Berġi sewer you two came from."

GIP motioned to Kristap, who assisted with lifting his brother back up. His brother stood up, visibly shaken, but quickly collected himself.

"You don't think I know what neighborhood you two came from? If anything goes wrong with this operation, every trace of your bloodline, wherever they live in the world, will perish. You got me?" GIP's face was flush.

The brothers confirmed and nodded in unison. The general straightened his jacket that had become disheveled by the skirmish.

"Sometime ... we believe in the next two weeks, a

freight train shipment of tanks from the Ukraine will pass through Riga on its way to Estonia," says GIP.

"Why would the President do that? They're amid a war with you guys?" asks Kristap.

"Once again," the general's eyes pierced Kristap's, "you're not here to ask questions, only to follow orders. The less you know, the better."

The general huffed and pulled out a Nicaraguan cigar and cut the end off before lighting it. He took a few puffs, then exhaled, blowing the smoke into Kristap's face.

"I need you to check the arrival schedule nightly for a shipment from Kyiv. As soon as you see one appear on the schedule, call me from this burner phone. *DO NOT* use this phone for anything else. Not even to call each other. Got it?"

Both brothers nodded.

"Is that all, General?" asks Kristap.

"That's part one, part two happens when the train arrives at the Riga station. Typically, trains won't stop, but this one will. That's because it will have to, thanks to my operatives. Your job is to incapacitate any security presence while my men climb discreetly aboard the train and eventually into the tanks."

"Got it, but our parole prohibits us from possessing any guns. They come to our flat every week for inspection," says Kaspars.

"Don't worry about that. My men will bring you what you need that day," says GIP.

The general left the cigar in his mouth while digging into the inside pocket of his jacket. He glanced inside the envelope, then handed it to the smarter brother.

"Half now, half when my men are aboard the train. Now that our business is concluded, where can I get the best grey peas and bacon?"

"Try the pub on Peldu iela. It also has good black balsam," says Kristap.

"Go now ...," the general motioned with his hands toward the elevator, "my man downstairs will take you anywhere you like."

The general opted to finish his cigar before he headed back down. He was enjoying the complex spiciness with a subtle hint of sweetness flavors. He thought he detected cocoa, but the part he loved the most was the distinct leathery undertones in the smoke.

He realized he hadn't heard from his daughter in a while. Hopefully, she was too busy partying in Cuba to care about her vendetta. Mace only reported in when she had something useful to report. He trusted her skills completely and realized he never gave her enough credit for her services. After conversing with those two imbeciles, he appreciated her professionalism even more. The general felt elated as he envisioned the Red Union plans coming together. No one, even the sneaky Americans, would suspect Russia to invade one of the Baltic States while at war with Ukraine. Russia's Ministry of Defence could also deny any involvement if a rogue paramilitary group orchestrated it. These tanks would have been the first tanks that Estonia owned, hoping to boost their vulnerable sub-par military. The general would ensure this never came to fruition but use them instead to help overthrow the Baltic government under force. Repairing them on the way to seize the President was the trickiest part.

Another couple of tanks would capture the Prime Minister.

CHAPTER
TWENTY-ONE

The two and half-hour drive to Highland from the airport gave Katya time to go over her plan and contingency plans for her unscheduled visit. She stayed near the airport after grabbing dinner. Through a sophisticated man-in-the-middle attack on a satellite ground station in Riverside County, she intercepted the satellite photos of Martha's residence from her laptop. She sought to understand the exits and land layout, as well as if there were any nosy neighbors.

Her plan was to attract bees with honey before going down the torture route. She planned to once again imitate a high-school friend who had an interest in finding the commander. Throughout her teenage years, she never revealed her infatuation for him because of a lack of courage. After reading about his award in the government news, she thought it was fate. Perhaps explaining that she also worked as an analyst and couldn't help but look up his last known address. It was the best she could do and the worst-case scenario. If it didn't work, she would resort to what she knew best: intimidation.

The contingency plans involved tactics if they had provided the woman protection. She suspected that if the commander was alive, he would have ordered it. The military didn't trust local police, so March Air Reserve Base would likely provide protection. Aware of their combat training, she expected they would send army reserves from that base. Most Army personnel had undergone training in close-quarter combat through the Modern Army Combative Program or MACP. Katya preferred hand-to-hand combat over guns. She relished the opportunity to witness the fear in her victims' eyes by getting up close and personal. Searching for stray bullet casings or, even worse, extracting bullets embedded in victims to ensure no evidence was left behind was something she despised. She carried a Makarov pistol strapped to her leg, but only used it as a last resort.

Martha lived in a cabin-type home that was at the end of town and nearly built into part of the San Bernardino Mountain range, which lied northeast of Highland. The town was perfect for lake enthusiasts, with three of them within a 10-mile radius. The GPS alerted her that the home was within a mile. She found a nearby hill that had a perfectly elevated view of the dirt road that led to the woman's home off the main street. There were only two homes on that unnamed road, which meant privacy for its residents, but also easy anonymity for an intruder. As she scanned the area, she spotted a view of Martha's colorful garden, which illustrated a dedication to recreational horticulture that Katya had never seen before. Sturdy, natural wood-toned logs were used to construct the home, stacked one upon another. The back of the house featured a stone chimney set between four large windows that spanned the height of the home. The windows faced the mountainside, which surely made for a spectacular view while relaxing in the rustic rooms inside. A porch made of wood encircled the home. In the back, Adirondack chairs surrounded a chiminea, creating a cozy atmosphere for occupants on chilly evenings. Katya briefly envied her target's perfect retirement home, longing to escape urban life.

Katya observed a medium-built man, probably in his twenties, wearing a LA Dodgers baseball cap, sitting on a folding chair, under a tree that was at least 1000 feet from the home. While working on a laptop, he often glanced towards Martha's home. *BINGO!* she thought. She directed the binoculars down the dirt road away from the house and stopped at another odd view. The entrance to the main street had a plain-looking sedan parked near it, positioned off to the side to ensure the pathway remained clear. A muscular, dark-skinned man was leaning against the trunk, smoking a cigarette in a white ribbed tank top with his back to Katya's view. Just then, he turned in her direction and she almost dropped the binoculars.

Back in Russia, any serious thoughts of a relationship appalled Katya for a couple of reasons. At some point, the companion would inquire about her occupation and if uncovered, she'd have to eliminate them. Then there was the reason if she had somehow fallen in love, it would be a weakness that her enemies could exploit if discovered. This might also result in her partner being tortured or killed. Her goal was to hold a powerful position in a male-dominated field, including those who worked for the Kremlin. She avoided playful interaction with paramilitary personnel, enhancing her lethal image. She, like all women, craved intimacy and satisfied her desires during her travels. *Why was this bodyguard her dream man?*

The man had a chiseled, closely shaven face, adding to his formidable and sinister appearance. His chest bulged like he was intentionally flexing, only to be supported by a wide frame with shoulders the size of softballs. The midday heat caused perspiration that glistened in the sun as he moved. *Maybe I don't have to kill him*, she thought. She guessed the guys were on shifts and would depart when replacements came. She didn't want to approach the house anyway till nighttime, so she waited it out.

The passing hours were unkind. She couldn't stop grabbing sneak peeks of the man while she went over some additional jobs that the general sent her on her encrypted computer. At about dinner time, she noticed the man closest to the house leave on his motorcycle as another sedan pulled up next to her hunk. The new team exchanged some words with the muscle man before he drove away. Katya quickly packed up her things and headed toward the dirt road.

Despite knowing the quickest route, Katya decided against going to the target's location. At a four-way stop, she spotted the bodyguard in his sedan just coming off his shift. As he started moving from the stop, she slammed her foot down on the accelerator. Her rental took a left turn, smashing her bumper right into his left front quarter-panel. His car swerved right several feet. The bodyguard jumped out of his vehicle and headed toward hers.

"Lady, are you okay?"

Katya manufactured some actual tears, which immediately wreaked havoc on her black eyeliner below her eyes. She had a black low-cut V-neck on and pulled it lower at the stomach to make her cleavage pop.

"Uh ... I think so. I didn't expect that airbag to hit me so hard in the face," says Katya.

"Do you have any water? We need to get the bag dust off your skin. It can cause irritation." His tone was slow and soft, his body movements gentle.

His calm demeanor surprised her, especially when she was clearly in the wrong. That went a long way in her book. She pulled her flask from her backpack and handed it to him.

"Here, take my hand. Let's get you out of there."

"Thank you, sir." Katya forced a sniffle.

A second later, he pulled off his tank top, exposing his upper body. Creating a ball out of the shirt, he poured the water over it. He motioned toward her face to use it to wipe away the dust and make-up. Despite his extreme gentleness, it wasn't what Katya had on her mind. He smelled so good. His muscular chest and abs were so tantalizingly close she wanted to jump him right there. It was difficult for her not to stare. He finished wiping off her arms and again, using body language, asked permission to wipe her neck and chest. She pulled her shoulders back to help.

"I'm so sorry. I don't know where my mind was."

"Don't worry, it's a company car." The man took out his cell phone. "Calling the police so we can get you out of here quickly," he says.

"Oh ... oh my god, please, sir, no. If I get one more

point on my driving record, my insurance will surely drop me. Is there another way we can take care of this?"

As he reassessed the damage to his car, he looked back at Katya. He appeared to hide his glance at her breasts, but she caught him. He locked eyes with her.

"Okay, did you want to pay me out of pocket?"

Katya frowned.

"I'm a little short in that department. It's dinnertime. I saw a decent-looking bar and grill on Boulder Avenue. Can I treat you to a bite? I'll check my bank balance to see what I have for you."

"Oh, you mean 'TJ's Bar & Grill'? Yeah, they have the best burgers in town. I'll meet you there, but first, let me take care of your steering wheel."

Katya watched as he pulled out a military knife from his boot and sliced around the edges of the airbag. His dark back muscles were contracting and extending in a visually appealing dance of strength and grace. She looked away and bit her thumbnail in agony.

He presented the clean steering wheel with one hand, holding the airbag in the other. "Here you go. Now, it won't get in your way. Just don't go hitting anybody anytime soon."

Katya laughed to make him feel like the funniest person in the world.

"Oh, give me your phone."

"What for?" he says.

Katya added a contact name and number, then showed him.

Semone Marek XXOO, Mobile ...

"Thanks, I'm Carter."

CHAPTER
TWENTY-TWO

The walls in the dingy room at Hampton Inn could not keep out the loud cable program next door. Katya didn't care, as it helped mask the cheap headboard's rhythmic banging against the wallpaper. She felt a euphoria in her loins and was light-headed until Carter loosened his grip.

"No, don't stop! Grip harder!" She spoke in a commanding voice, as the sweat dripped down her back.

"Sorry, I don't want to hurt you."

His enormous hands covered her entire neck as she came, but she couldn't scream. The asphyxiation coupled with her climax sent pleasure to every part of her body. She fell next to Carter onto the hard, gritty bed sheet.

"I've never done that to a woman. Sorry, if I messed up."

"Oh no, Sweetie! You were just fine. Have you ever had it done to you?"

"With this neck?" He pointed to his linebacker-sized neck.

Katya laughed. "Maybe you just need two sets of female hands."

Carter had let her finish first, so he straddled Katya again, but his heavy, muscular frame was too much for her. They switched positions, and his hands guided her hips up and down while his eyes watched her enhanced C-cup breasts dangle sensually over his body.

Katya lifted his head gently off the pillow and began wrapping her silky, long hair braid around his neck. This surprised him a little, but the sexual moment prevented him from overthinking it. She raised her eyebrows and began pulling the hair tighter. He nodded in agreement. He lifted the spiked ball at the end, now lying on his upper chest, with a confused look at her choice of fashion. Katya shrugged her shoulders and tilted her head toward the right. Carter shook his head and smiled.

As he moved her hips faster, anticipating the end, she quickly slid off him and to the side of the bed frame. His body, headfirst, moved toward hers. With both feet now firmly gripping the shaggy carpet below, she pulled on her braid with all her arm and body strength in a sudden jerking motion. The haste unraveled the black noose around his neck and ended with the spiked ball slicing through the circumference of his skin dramatically. Crimson blood was squirting in every direction. He squirmed on the small bed, using his hands to hold back the bleeding, but it exited his body too rapidly. His dark brown eyes had a look of despair and betrayal. His body finally stopped moving. His buttocks were up in the air, propped up by his still rigid phallus.

Now that's a first, thought Katya.

It was about ten o'clock at night when Katya was strolling down the dirt road toward Martha's house. The bodyguard in the car at the entrance died in his sleep.

That's what you get for napping on the job!

The second guard, further down the path, noticed her in the full moonlight and approached her with his hands raised, palms faced out.

"Can I help you? This is private property."

"Is this your property?" asks Katya.

"No, I'm—"

The side of her thick-rubber boot sole connected forcefully with the man's front jaw, accompanied by a cloud of dirt and pebbles. His head yanked left, sending his body to the ground. Knocked out, Katya snapped his neck to make it permanent.

The wooden stairs creaked under her as she went to the front door and pressed the video doorbell. A crackled voice came through the minute doorbell speaker.

"Who are you? It's after 10 p.m.,"

"I'm so, so sorry, Ma'am, but I had car trouble on my way here. I just want a few minutes of your time," says Katya.

Silence persisted uncomfortably for a minute.

"Step back a few feet and please rotate your body." The doorbell commanded.

Katya did so and was glad she had re-tucked her long braid inside her lightweight jacket. A porch light turned on moments later as the door opened. Martha appeared holding her SIG handgun at her side, but still pointed at Katya.

"You should be more careful. You could get killed coming out here this late. I'm not talking about people, hungry mountain lions like to hunt at night," says Martha.

"Jeez, I didn't know. I wanted to get here by afternoon, but my car broke down. I'm an old friend of Michael's."

"Oh, sorry," Martha realized she was still pointing her gun at the visitor. "Can you come back in the morning?"

"I barely could take off work for this trip and need to get my car into the shop tomorrow morning. I just need a few minutes of your time."

Martha hesitated, looked the visitor up and down, and reluctantly motioned her to come in.

"It's cold out there, let's talk inside. Would you like something to drink?"

"Thank you, Martha. My name is Semone."

As they walked toward the kitchen, the house had an open concept. The great room, as her spying surmised, had a picturesque view of the hills. Moonlight illuminated the sitting room through the tall windows. A fireplace, with glowing ashes, provided the only other light. Adjacent to the great room, a sizable kitchen showcased a grand marble island adorned with accent lights. The lights glowed an ocean blue from the color of the small shade.

"This area is awesome, feels so open and inviting," says Katya.

"Well, thank you. Now, how do you know Michael again?"

Martha grabbed the kettle to fill it with water. Katya noticed her set the gun down on the corner of the island.

"I'm a little embarrassed. I had a crush on your son in high school. You don't have to make me tea. I'll just take a glass of water."

Katya had specialized training on losing her eastern European dialect when speaking in the States, but she realized she accidentally slipped up. She made water sound like "vater". Russians sometimes have difficulty pronouncing certain English words. Words starting with a "w" are some of them. She also noticed Martha pause.

Martha tried to grab the gun, but Katya was quicker and slapped her. She fell backward toward the cabinets in the kitchen corner. Her face scowled at Katya as she grabbed her left elbow, grimacing.

"You know," Katya grabbed the gun and waved it back and forth in her hand. "I was kind of hoping we could be friends, seeing I love your house. If you tell me what I need to know, I believe we can be."

CHAPTER
TWENTY-THREE

NECKER ISLAND

The island facility's gym surpassed Michael's expectations. It had state-of-the-art equipment that appeared to have been recently purchased. The pulley machines were high tech. Rather than using pins in pre-made holes, an electronic panel lets you adjust the weight instantly. The north wall in the gym had floor-to-ceiling windows. Rays of sunshine, undisturbed by a cloudless sky, created a mesmerizing spectacle on the tranquil beach below. The turquoise water was so clear, it looked almost drinkable. Despite the inviting view, he had work obligations. The doctor closed the gym for a private event to avoid disturbance from the rehabilitation guests. Excited to test his new body's capabilities, Michael couldn't help but worry about his mother. She didn't answer his phone call from the night before. He rationalized that he probably called too late. Jasmine had offered to visit her, even though they had hired military security, and Michael was grateful for that.

"Where should we start?" asks Michael.

"How 'bout the bench press?"

Dr. Bell put two 45-pound weights on each side of the shiny chrome bar.

"Seriously, Doc? I could do this weight before I had super limbs."

"Patience, Michael. Can we start slow, while you get used to activating your AIonic muscles?"

Michael laid under the bar and grabbed it shoulder-width apart. His hands felt minor pressure as he pushed up on the bar, but no chest tension. His shoulder and arms were doing all the work. He asked the doctor to load the bar with weights continuously for experimentation.

"That's it," says the doctor.

"What do mean, that's it?"

"I can't fit any more weights on this bar."

As he slid off the bench, his eyebrows raised. A slight bend was present in the middle of the bar, along with eight large cast iron weights on each side. He quickly calculated the load in his head.

"That's almost 800 pounds!"

Michael looked amazed as he walked around the bench. *If my high school football team could only see me now.*

"Doc, if I'm only using my arms, how am I going to keep my chest muscle from deteriorating?"

"Those chiseled-looking granite slabs you're carrying under your chin are not pure muscle. We added extra layers of borophene and spider silk to give it a bigger appearance, plus it will protect you better. According to my calculations, you probably could sustain the impact of a small ballistic missile in the chest without damage. Well ... maybe not. Your body would probably fly backwards hundreds of feet."

Michael was halfway listening as he sat back down on the bench. He was eager to try an idea that was burning in his mind. He rubbed his open palms together to remove any moisture before laying under the bar. With one hand and several visual checks, he gripped the exact halfway point of the steel bar. He sensed the extra pressure on his palm, but the bar came off the rack hook with ease. He smiled as he performed five reps before racking it.

"Hooyah!" Michael jumped off the bench. "What next, Doc?"

"How about this curved treadmill over here? I changed its display so it can display three-digit speeds instead of two."

"You have some high expectations of me, Doc!"

"Just in case," his lips curving in contemplation. "This one is non-motorized, so it moves only under your power."

Michael approached the black machine with the curiosity of a cat. Despite his lack of experience, the intriguing appearance of the machine caught his attention. The treadmill's belt comprised equally distant horizontal rubber slats, which moved freely as he mounted it. As he walked, the friction pulled the belt behind him under his gym shoes. He surmised the curve helped more when running. The natural leg stroke as someone runs causes each footstep to start at an angle. A slightly upward incline of the belt allowed the shoes to maintain more surface tension through the movement.

"Wait!" The doctor made a halting motion with the palms of his hands. "I need to strap you in for safety."

The doctor fastened a thick leather belt around Michael's waist, which was tied to the front handlebar by a mini bungee-looking cord.

Taking the doctor's advice, he started slowly to get used to the platform. The doctor's custom display began counting his speed, in miles per hour, with red numeric digits. As Michael ran faster, he noticed something odd. His breathing tempo stayed the same, no matter how fast he went.

20 mph

33 mph

75 mph

As Michael took his eyes off the last reading, his eyebrows pinched together, observing Dr. Bell taking notes nonchalantly, like his super speed was no big deal.

"It doesn't faze you that I'm faster than a cheetah at this point?" raising his voice over the mechanical whirling of the machine beneath him.

The doctor lifted his hand while holding the pen and motioned a repeating invisible circular path, urging Michael to push harder.

A creaking, grinding sound pierced Michael's ears suddenly. He discerned its origin beneath the belt. He glanced down, careful not to lose his balance, and somehow had a thermal image of the roller beneath the belt. It was bright red. Just as he glanced back at the display, now showing *110 mph*, the belt snapped off with force. Michael gripped the horizontal handlebars as a clinking crashing sound erupted behind him. The flying belt shattered the mirror on a cement building column.

"Well, that was exciting!" Dr. Bell's smile stretched from ear to ear. "I guess I forgot to check this treadmill's margin of safety."

"Margin of what?"

"It's just boring engineering talk, but usually manufacturers will over-engineer something for safety. That way, the design can withstand stress much higher than normal use before it fails."

"Whatever you say, Doc. Was that display correct?"

"Oh yeah! Plus or minus two miles per hour margin of error."

"There you go again with that *margin* talk."

Michael wiped his brow with the back of his hand and then cocked his head after touching his moist legs.

"I have to hand it to you—you weren't wrong about the hydrolysis byproduct. I didn't expect the rest of my body to do nothing, but probably should have listened to your instructions more closely. So … if my limbs do all the work, I guess I could run a marathon daily. Yet I'd still have a lazy old man's heart. So much for getting my cardio in."

"Not exactly." The doctor's eyes gleamed with pride and crinkled in the corners. "We programmed the AI interface to signal to your brain when you're active. Your brain's hypothalamus and pituitary glands will then respond to the stress cues by releasing endorphins. The simulated signals also increase your heart rate."

"I'm not sure how I feel about that. Next thing I know,

you're going to tell me you programmed my brain to tell me all vegetables taste like candy."

"Nonsense. Things like your digestive, reproductive, and excretory systems are still the same."

"Shit, Doc—" Michael shook his head.

"Yes, that's what I meant by excretory."

"No! Shit, Doc, can we get back to the fun stuff? All this technical talk is killing my superpower buzz."

"Absolutely. We've got a few more things I'd like to test. Tomorrow, we get to go outside and run my obstacle course."

Michael ached to get out into the sunshine. This was the longest he had ever stayed inside while on a tropical island.

CHAPTER
TWENTY-FOUR

MIAMI INTERNATIONAL AIRPORT

Jasmine felt vulnerable inside airport terminals. It was the only time she wasn't carrying weapons on her body. At home, her Glock was always nearby, safely stored in a biometric safe. When she traveled, it stayed under the pillow next to her head. She didn't feel threatened or in danger, but her weapons were an attachment she couldn't shake. Like the attachment a social media influencer has with their mobile phone.

Kunais, which translates to throwing needles in Japanese, was her other deadly accessory. Some women never leave home without their designer purse. For Jasmine, it was her throwing knives. She kept her six-inch flat steel blades in her boots above her ankle or at the top of her silk stockings if she wore skirts or dresses. She preferred knives to bullets, as they're quieter and result in cleaner immobilizations, especially in close combat. It didn't hurt that the battle gods, if there were any, had gifted her with exceptional speed and accuracy. There is a rule that law enforcement has long relied on, called the *21-Foot Rule.* It states an assailant wielding a knife can cover 21 feet in the time to draw and fire a gun. Jasmine believed in that rule so much that she tattooed a tiny *21* on the inside of her throwing wrist.

Walking to the seated area around the gate while waiting for her flight to LAX, she couldn't help but judge people she saw. Knowing it was wrong to do so, some people just invite criticism. An overweight kid was sitting in a gate row. His face made him look about the age of a middle schooler, but his size made him seem older. It was 8:09 a.m. and he was munching on an oversized meat-lover's pizza, thanks to the airport restaurants that serve their specialties no matter the day or time. Next to him, on the stained carpet, was one large empty bottle of Pepsi and then a second one, that was half-empty. He was so entranced by his Game Boy, while his parents chatted with their travel friends, that no one noticed his toddler brother wandering into the main walkway loaded with hustling people.

"Ma'am, is that your kid?" asks Jasmine.

The woman smiled at Jasmine and followed her gesture. As she did, she hurried to grab her son just before a motorized baggage cart passed in her son's path.

Two concealed knife throws, and Jasmine could have discreetly eliminated the parents, leaving no trace. Perhaps it was a good thing she couldn't bring her knives to the terminal. The temptation of knocking off parents who don't give a crap about their kids' welfare would've been hard to resist. Thankfully, her Christian mind always prevailed in times like these. She pulled out some alcohol wipes and cleaned the cheap vinyl seat. She glanced out the windows while standing there, waiting for it to dry.

"Bitchin scar," says the middle-aged man sitting across from her.

Thinking the well-trimmed, red-haired man was talking to her, Jasmine used her index finger to point at her chest. The man with a very light complexion, auburn eyes, and a warm smile nodded. He was of medium build and dressed in a charcoal suit with subtle baby blue striping. His silk tie complimented the suit stripes, and his leather dress shoes looked like they were just shined. The phrase intrigued Jasmine, unusual to hear slang from a well-dressed man of his age.

"You mean this?" pointing to the skin abnormality on the front of her neck.

"Yep, was that from a tracheostomy?"

"No … I could tell you … but then you'd wind up like the guy that did this."

The man's eyes opened wide, and his forehead lines deepened, "Yikes!"

Jasmine sat and quickly changed the subject, "Heading to LA for business?"

"No, personal. Unfortunately, my dad passed away a few days ago. I need to claim the body and arrange for services."

"Oh, sorry to impose and for your loss. If you don't want to talk about it, I understand," says Jasmine.

"No, it might actually help. It was so sudden. I mean, we drifted apart when I moved across the country, but I was hoping to fix that one day. Now, I'll never have the chance.

It's even harder, because right after I moved, my mom passed from cancer. He was alone, but luckily he was a guy who can make friends easily."

"Was it an accident?" asks Jasmine.

"That's what they're saying, but I have this weird feeling it wasn't."

"Why?" Jasmine's eyebrows furrowed, and she leaned closer to him to listen.

"He was coming back from visiting some friends in D.C. and on his way to the taxi, he fell in front of a shuttle bus."

"Oh, my god!" Jasmine genuinely felt bad, but overreacted, covering her mouth with her fingers as if she rarely heard of people dying. She had to keep her innocent appearance, despite her actual experiences on the subject.

"The scene was pretty bad, I heard. What I don't understand is they interviewed a witness that was talking to him before it happened, and he swears my dad was pushed somehow. There was no evidence or suspects to corroborate the witness's story, so they ruled it an accident. His body had all sorts of cuts, bruises, and mutilations."

"That is—"

Passengers in Group B, you may now board the plane ...

Jasmine looked down at her ticket, but already knew the answer, "That's me. By the way, I'm Jules."

As she pulled the suitcase handle to extend it for rolling, she reached out her hand to the man.

"Again, I'm so sorry for your loss. I hope you find peace soon."

The man froze with tense shoulders, but then realizing the conversation was over, arched his eyebrows upward.

"Nice to meet you, even if it was for a few seconds. I'm James. Thank you for listening."

Jasmine walked to the jet bridge line-up as passengers patiently waited for the flight attendant to scan each of their tickets. It was an odd conversation to have when you first meet someone. It reminded her of Michael's mom, who was like a second mother to her. She was glad to have volunteered to check on her while her son recovered. *Come to think of it, I asked the base to update me every 24 hours on their surveillance.* It had been 26 hours by now. While handing her ticket to the attendant, she fumbled through her side backpack pocket for her mobile. The line kept ringing on the other end———.

"Hello."

"Mrs. Cooling, is that you?" asks Jasmine.

A few seconds of silence followed. "Ohhh … yes, hi, Dear. I'm sorry, my mind is in another place. Haven't had my coffee yet."

Jasmine detected a slight shrill in Martha's voice.

"That's right, sorry to call you so early. Just wanted to check on you. Listen, go get your coffee. I have a busy day. I'll call you back after work, about eight hours from now."

"Okay, thank you."

The call ended with neither saying goodbye.

The tiny hairs on the back of Jasmine's neck stood up. It could have been morning brain fog, but Martha didn't seem herself. Since she wouldn't be able to use her phone on the plane soon, she thought about checking in with the MPs watching Martha. If someone had reached Martha, then the guards were already dead. Even if a new shift started, spooking them might only escalate Martha's situation or get more military personnel killed. It's not like Jasmine didn't trust MPs, but they were no SEALs. If the Russians wanted Martha dead, then she would be dead already. Jasmine recited a quick prayer for Martha's safety before heading down the aisle to her seat.

CHAPTER
TWENTY-FIVE

SEVASTOPOL, UKRAINE

The ringtone made the general squirm in the leather booth. The host at Restobar Smach always had the same table for Ivan. He typically arrived without a reservation. The host would swiftly relocate anyone sitting at that table, regardless of their meal progress. The staff had to deal with long faces until they softened upon seeing who was taking their booth.

Why does she always call at the worst times?

GIP was a foodie and didn't like anyone disturbing his indulgence, even his own daughter. His face sorrowed as the garlic and bay leave aroma of the plate of Beshbarmak tantalized him. The attentive waiter noticed the call coming in and motioned to keep his plate warm while he took it.

"Irina, dear, I trust the Mojitos are treating you well."

"Father, you know they make the best ones down here; I don't know if it's the Cuban rum or the freshly picked mint. I called because I need a favor."

"Here, I thought you called because you missed me."

"Don't be so dramatic, Pops. Of course, I miss you. But really, is this a good time?"

The general surveyed the restaurant, observing customers who smiled after each bite. He envied them.

"Good as any. What's going on?"

"Well … I was shopping on my phone while sitting on Sergei's face wearing my bikini, only I forgot to put the bottoms on," Irina giggled. "Do you know what happened?"

Trying to sigh away from the phone, the general cringed at the visual that included his paramilitary cadet. Knowing he now had to execute one of his men was not upsetting, but the mental image she portrayed was very disturbing.

"Irina, what did I tell you about sharing everything with me?"

"But you said always to be honest with you—"

"Yes, I said that when you were a teenager. I don't need to know about your sexual escapades now that you're in your late twenties."

"Sorry, it just comes so naturally with you. Anyway, my credit card is maxed out."

"What!" The general's face flushed in disbelief.

"Can you make the limit higher or something?"

"No, I can't. You spent a million and a half rubles in less than a week?"

"Absolutely not. There was already a balance on it from my shopping last week in Moscow."

"I should make you stay there and find a local job to pay for the rest of the trip," the general gritted his teeth.

"It's only a few more days. I promise, I'll be frugal. I

won't shop anymore or rent any more yachts. I'll just sunbathe on the beach till we leave."

"I'll pay down some of the card later tonight. Listen … I just sat down to dinner. Can I call you tomorrow?"

"What about our father-daughter project? The cute guys in Cuba don't fu—"

"IRINA! For fuck's sake! Michael's mother will give up information any minute now as she is a prisoner in her own home," says GIP.

"Great, thanks, gotta go, have lunch plans. Love ya!"

While shaking his head, the general looked over his shoulder to find his waiter. His arm extended, and he curled his index finger in a beckoning gesture. The waiter sprang forward and headed into the kitchen to retrieve the general's entrée.

Still steaming when the plate arrived, the GIP's mouth watered. The waiter topped off his glass with a honey-pepper flavored vodka, called Nemiroff.

Ignoring the waiter, he stabbed the tender beef with his fork while twirling the broth-laden egg noodles around it. The meat melted on his tongue while his mind distanced itself from the delusional and erratic thoughts of spreading Russia's stronghold through the rest of Europe.

Back at his headquarters, the general decided to re-watch one of his favorite military movies, *Stalingrad.* A film about the successful Soviet defense of their city during World War II. He especially enjoyed the firing squad scene where the German captain told his corporal that if he missed the young Russian boy in the prisoners' line-up, he would join them. The general found amusement in the boy's fearful eyes before he was shot at point-blank range. Even the general thought it was odd that he sided with the Germans when they were killing his own countrymen. He rationalized enjoying the captain's focus, devoid of empathy, in pursuit of war objectives.

His mobile phone rang with a number that the general recognized as he owned the phone that was calling. Quickly setting his vodka bottle down, he eagerly answered.

"General? This is Kristap."

"No shit, son, don't you remember? I gave you that phone."

"Of course, uh … we have something you might want to hear."

"Anytime now, I'm kind of in the middle of something."

Although Ivan was interested in the update, he never liked others to feel as if their thoughts were more important than his time.

"There is a large shipment coming by freight through Latvia in five days. Its origin is Kiev, but more importantly, it mentions that the load will be slightly wider than the flatcars."

"So … How do you know this is my tanks?" says GIP.

"Because I checked. Leopard 2s are about 10% wider than the standard train cars. They requested a sweep of the train line to ensure nothing, such as tree branches or signals, was too close to the tracks. Lastly, the category on the bill of lading says 'military'."

"Damn, Kristap, you have proven to be more useful

than I expected. Are you keeping your dumb twin brother out of trouble?"

"Yes," Kristap says. He wasn't about to tell the general how his brother had almost caused them to lose their job by showing up one evening smelling of Balsam, a traditional herbal liqueur.

"Alright, shoot me a text on this phone with the expected time of arrival. Don't forget to provide the address where you're staying. I'm sending my best operative to meet you there to make sure everything goes as planned. Additionally, nearly a dozen cadets and two mechanics will need rooms. Book rooms for the evening before, close to the station. Text me all the arrangements."

The general ended the call as the Latvian continued to talk.

GIP didn't waste any time to call his contact at the Kremlin. His extracurricular activities caused him to neglect updating them for a while, so he had to catch up.

"General Petrovsky, we were beginning to think you defected."

"I wanted to visit some of the front lines before I provided you an update on the war and OP91." A quiver accompanied the general's voice.

The man waited patiently on the call's other end.

"We knocked out some sea drones that were targeting one of our warships. The men are in good spirits, and I've secured a freight shipment date," says GIP.

"That's great. What about the explosion at Belarus airfield?"

The general's brow perspired while his forehead crunched.

"Not sure I follow you, sir."

"Isn't it your job to know everything that's happening in Eastern Europe? Maybe we need to limit your expense accounts, as you seem to spend more time wasting money than getting intel."

Dammit, Irina!

GIP fabricated an excuse.

"A small fire at the barracks caused us to replace expensive equipment. I apologize."

"Our allies there are looking to us for answers. Luckily, that airfield was mostly just used for refueling, but that asset caused the damage."

"You know I heard their safety check records are pathetic there, maybe—"

"Don't give a damn what you heard, GIP! We don't need any more attention or blame on us, especially before Estonia. Send me a report tonight and your plan for the shipment."

The call ended abruptly.

The general looked at the clock. It was nearly 11 p.m. Consuming half a bottle of vodka at the restaurant and another half at home put him in an unfavorable position. Given the signs of irritation by his superior, the report would need to be extremely detailed. Worst yet, he had to create fake receipts to make up for his daughter's irresponsibility.

CHAPTER
TWENTY-SIX

William proceeded down the metal elevator to the secure underground room where Michael had his operation. Arriving at sub-level 3, he stopped short of the tempered glass entrance door, noticing a discussion between his most attractive employee and Michael, who was lying on the treatment bed with just a towel over his hips. Bundles of fiber optic wires connected to all his limbs and the back of his neck.

Sofia was the head nurse at the Necker facility. She also was the only nurse with knowledge of the SIX program. Born of Colombian descent, she was a citizen of the United States. For maximum security, Streeter only allowed US Citizens to work at SIX. She was in her early thirties and about five and a half feet tall. Her silky-smooth, caramel skin and wavy brown hair only complimented her bright, jade-green eyes that always had long lashes attached. Even when William had a work conversation with her, her provocative eyes aroused him. If not that, it was the way her figure filled out her uniform. When she bent over or sat down, her white nurse's skirt was just short enough to reveal the top of her satin leg stockings. The small amount of skin showing drove William crazy.

While removing the wires connected to Michael, the two conversed, and Sofia smiled excessively. Her button-down shirt had one too many buttons undone. That, coupled with a lace push-up bra, a staple from her room's dresser, gave her breasts more cleavage than normal. William stayed in the shadows but activated the intercom to hear the conversation inside.

"It's amazing how fast you've recovered, Michael," she says.

As she reached over his chest to remove a wire from his right shoulder, Michael tried not to show how much he enjoyed the view.

"Thank you. It's because of you all. Everyone has been so accommodating."

"Are you still getting the headaches?"

"Only after the Doc hooks my brain up to that contraption behind me. I suspect I'll have one after this evaluation," says Michael.

"Sorry about that, Commander. I can bring you something for that. I just need to finish removing these wires, then you can be on your way. It's amazing how these connect to your AIonics without having to be physically connected inside."

"Yeah, Doc said that the fiber optic light penetrates right through my skin with instructional signals. He had to make some programming adjustments to the microchips inside. To your point, glad I don't look like a human phone switchboard. You know, the ones you see in old movies?"

Sofia laughed and then paused while looking up and down his muscular body.

"Do you mind?" she says with an open palm in the air. "I heard the skin feels just like actual skin. Can I glide my hand over it?"

"Sure, … I guess."

Sofia started gliding her perfectly manicured hand over his shoulder, following the form of his artificially developed pectoral and stopping at his ribbed abdomen.

"And down there?" She glanced toward the towel covering his pelvis.

Michael swallowed. "Thankfully, they left that alone. I mean, if ain't broke, don't fix it, right?"

Sofia grinned widely. Her hand gently continued under the towel to his pubic area and wrapped around his growing penis.

"Wow!" she says, "I can't even tell the difference between your actual skin and the artificial skin."

His face turned beet red. "Yeah … um …," Michael let out a sigh, "Doc did good."

William decided it was time to break up the party.

"I trust my favorite SEAL is doing okay?"

Michael's eyebrows shot up, and his mouth gaped. "Yes, Mr. Streeter, feeling great!"

"Come on Michael, just call me William."

Sofia kept working and didn't even acknowledge William entering the room. This irked William, as she never gave him more than he asked for. He started a conversation solely to gaze into her eyes.

"Sofia, any updates for me?"

Sofia slowly turned around, having just set the final

wires on the rack behind Michael's bed. "Doctor Bell said for you to join him in the atrium upstairs. He has some technical updates for you."

"Thank you. How is your brother doing? I heard he was having trouble in medical school?"

"Oh," acting as if she didn't expect the question, "He's fine now. He found a study group that he really likes and they're helping him understand the material better."

Sofia swiftly went to the door, glancing back solely at Michael. William couldn't stop staring at her perfectly round ass that fully filled out her skirt but was in perfect proportion to her slender body.

"Michael, I left a few strong aspirins on the table next to you. If that doesn't help, buzz me from your room, and I can bring you something more effective."

As the door closed, William watched until Sofia was out of sight.

"Damn, Michael, looks like you picked up a new admirer."

"Nah, she is just doing her job. I will say, though, she's easy on the eyes."

"Take the rest of the day off. You've been training hard. I need to talk to Doctor Bell. I have a potential mission for you."

"Seriously, you mean I get to get off this island?" says Michael.

"Only if the Doc thinks you're ready. That's what I'm meeting him about."

"Can you tell me about it? I'm going stir-crazy here. To be 100% honest, maybe I'm not ready. The reason I needed this treatment today was to tune my AI."

William frowned. "What happened?"

"I ... or the AI ... um ... I don't know. Hard to tell if it's me or the AI CPU, but I missed a target yesterday."

"What target?"

Michael shook his head. "Doc wanted me to jump from the beach to the helicopter pad atop the facility."

"Yeah, so what? That should be easy for you."

"I overshot it quite a bit."

"What's a bit?"

"I'm unsure of the total, but I flew over and landed in a palm tree on the unincorporated part of the island."

"Wait ... beyond the property line? That's at least ... two hundred yards from the front of the building!"

"Yeah, if you say so. I got back inside easily. Your barbed-wire electric 20-foot fence was no match for me."

Lost in thought, William stepped away, hand over mouth, the other tucked under arm. He paced around the room. His mind was racing at the possibilities.

"Michael, that is unbelievable! We didn't expect that kind of distance."

"Sure, but if I can't control it, what else can go wrong with these super limbs?"

"Don't worry, Commander," William made direct eye contact and upturned his lips, "You'll get the hang of them. I have a ton of faith in Doctor Bell and YOU."

CHAPTER
TWENTY-SEVEN

HIGHLAND, CALIFORNIA

Tiny gravel stones on the narrow dirt path crunched under Jasmine's Navy boots as she cautiously approached Martha's home. The late winter evening produced a cool breeze that glided over the sweat droplets on her face and neck. The air carried with it a faint smell of sagebrush, native to the area. There were lots of evergreen trees and bushes along the path, keeping the home hidden from view. She already passed the car at the entrance. She resisted the urge to punch the sleeping guard and wake him up. With a devious thought, she considered twirling a throwing knife to test its force against the driver's side window. A searing pain in the shoulder that he would never forget was less important than blowing her clandestine activity.

The guard closer to the home was behind a tree on a lawn chair, entranced by his phone's ability to produce short bursts of dopamine with every scroll. Next to his chair, leaning on the tree trunk, was an M4 Carbine rifle.

Great location choice, Moron!

The M4 was standard issue for personnel in the U.S. Army, but it only had an effective range of up to 600 yards. The guard stationed himself several hundred more yards from the home. If an intruder approached, the guard's chance of hitting his target at that range would be slim to none. Cloaked in darkness, she pondered walking right past him on the road to gauge his response.

Focus Jasmine.

The home sat in front of a scenic backdrop of small mountains that glowed faintly with the half-moon's light. The home appeared dark except for the porch light. From the side with only second-floor windows, Jasmine approached. The air was cooling down to what felt like high-40s Fahrenheit. She noticed some smoke drifting upward from the brick chimney at the back of the house. Her senses picked up the smell of birch, a wood that ignites easily, has high heat output, and gives off a pleasant aroma. The sign of life inside calmed Jasmine's nerves.

As the home came into view, her confidence in the cedar deck not creaking elevated. It appeared new and well-built. The light danced on the cedar wood at the top of the deck as the fireplace inside reflected off the ceiling through the large glass windows. Standing a foot from the glass door, she hugged the outside wall.

As she brought her head around for a peek inside, the glass exploded outward, nearly sending fragments into her face. A whoosh of air accompanied the glass, along with a dangling female body. The figure had such a velocity that it easily flew the length of the 20-foot deck and dropped into the hidden yard below.

After being startled, Jasmine recomposed herself and pivoted inside with her Glock raised. A man resembling Michael was standing next to Martha.

"Freeze!"

His arms went up instantly, and Jasmine saw Martha confined to a chair with barbed wire. Bloodstains outlined the wire on her clothing. Her mouth had what looked like a peeled lemon with a rope through it, apparently being used as a sour gagging device. Her eyes looked defeated but widened briefly once she recognized her new guest.

"I'm only here to help," the man says.

Jasmine quickly assessed that the man was not armed and was cooperative.

"Don't you move!"

She hurried outside to the deck's edge where the body had gone. The ground, black as night, had movement about 100 yards away. Her flashlight beam caught a limping, slender figure in dark clothing. The figure turned toward Jasmine just long enough to produce an evil feminine grin, then disappeared into dense foliage.

Jasmine turned back to the house as she watched the man carefully remove the gag from Martha after handing her a glass of water.

"Who the hell are you? Martha, do you want me to subdue him?"

The man didn't respond, as if he couldn't hear Jasmine. His focus was completely on getting Martha free. He used his fingers to hold the skin back while he removed the barb from Martha. Martha grimaced in pain but was surprisingly braver than Jasmine expected. The surrounding wire wasn't tight, but it didn't need to be. If she even moved a millimeter, the barb would stab her skin deeper.

Jasmine knew where her medicine cabinet was down-stairs and darted for it to retrieve disinfectant and bandages. As she arrived at the bathroom, her 911 call connected. She cited a home invasion with an injured owner and provided the address while rummaging through the cabinet.

She started helping the man by working on Martha's ankles, which were also bound with the spiky wire. Working together took nearly as long as the ambulance's arrival. The goal was to release her from the chair without causing more damage.

When the paramedics arrived, they connected an oxygen mask to Martha and an I.V. They re-bandaged some of her wounds before putting her on the gurney. The police had also arrived and wanted some answers, but Jasmine somehow convinced them to wait on the front porch.

With a furrowed brow and deep sigh, Jasmine's eyes pierced the familiar yet aged face. "Start talking!"

"It might be hard to believe, but Martha is an old friend of mine. I wanted to help her," says the man.

"And how did you know she needed help?"

"I like to check in on her now and then," he says. "I usually just watch her from afar."

"What? Are you a Peeping Tom?"

"No, no … you got it all wrong."

"Please explain because I'm about five seconds from laying you out—and how did that woman fly 50 feet? Where is the cannon you shot her with?"

"Can we start over?" he says.

Jasmine's shoulders relaxed. "Yes, please."

"My name is Michael Trenner. I dated Martha a few decades ago."

His steel-blue eyes glanced warmly at her with a need for acceptance she had seen before. His square jawline perfectly complemented his masculine neck, but it was the crinkle at only one corner of his smile that sealed it for Jasmine.

"You're Michael's father!"

"In the flesh."

Jasmine's eyes softened. "Martha says she hasn't heard from you in years. Michael can't recall the last time he saw you."

"It was for their protection, trust me."

"So, you have bionics? That's how you tossed the intruder."

"I do, but I'm not that strong anymore. I might have the power of three men. The decay has taken its toll."

Jasmine turned her head slightly, squinting. "Decay?"

"I'm leaking radiation. The experimental type of Plutonium they put in me is well past its half-life."

"I just had a bad flashback of a chemistry final in high school. Can't you get the government to fix you?"

Michael walked to the pantry and grabbed a broom. He stepped outside to sweep up the broken glass.

"Remember Google Glass?" he says.

"Vaguely. Weren't they like wearable smart devices or something?"

"Right, it was like a head-mounted smartphone which could discretely capture photos and videos, voice recognition, etc. A friend of mine was an early adopter and bought like a thousand units. He was hoping to make a reselling business out of the supply. At fifteen hundred a pop, it was no small investment. Fast forward two years and he was homeless, as Google abandoned the technology because of privacy, social acceptance, and lack of developer support concerns. My point is, companies don't care, especially government companies, what happens to consumers of their products. When they abandoned bionics in the 90s, they abandoned everyone they supposedly helped as well. As a matter of fact, there are less than a dozen of us left. We meet up a couple times a year in the Bahamas. Kind of like a support group for the bionic rejects."

Jasmine says, "Jesus, that's terrible. I didn't realize they used them on that many people. What happened to the others?"

"Mostly radiation sickness, but also a few suicides. When you're a walking radioactive waste, you tend to be a loner. Some people can't handle a life void of human contact."

Jasmine's face soured with hesitation. "You might not like what I'm about to tell you then."

Michael Sr. stopped cleaning and looked directly at her.

"Your son has them now."

"Has what?"

"Bionics … well, I guess they're actually called AIonics now."

"Different lipstick, same pig," Michael dropped his head, shaking it.

"The good news is nuclear technology does not power them. I don't quite understand it all, but they're hydrogen-power based."

"Terrific, he'll be the next Hindenburg disaster."

Jasmine scoffed, "Don't be so negative. They invested a lot of money and research into this. Don't let your experience ruin his life, too. He could use a supportive father at this point. You should go see him."

"I fear it's too late for us."

"It's never too late to rebuild a relationship. Give me your number, I'll send you the details. We use this encrypted app as the project is super secure. I'm probably going to get in trouble for telling you all this."

Michael hesitated, then pulled out his phone. "Nice meeting you, Jasmine. Let me finish cleaning up here and repairing the sliding door. I'll put Martha's hidden key back when I'm done. Go back to Michael. Maybe I'll see you again one day."

"I hope so," she says.

CHAPTER
TWENTY-EIGHT

JALISCO STATE, MEXICO

Michael drove his rusted Ford Ranger past fields of blue agave, catching sight of the Tequila Volcano in the distance. Although it was now a dormant volcano, its size was formidable, scaling 10,000 feet at its highest peak. Considered a stratovolcano, if it was active, its eruptions would be catastrophic. These types of volcanoes have a conduit system inside that channels magma deep within the Earth's surface. Michael remembered his mother explaining how a stratovolcano, named Mount St. Helens, in Washington, exploded in the early 80s and sent ash over 11 states. During Tequila's active period, its lava flow contributed to enriching the soil so the agave culture could thrive in Jalisco. The region in Mexico produces 95% of the world's tequila.

Michael was loving his AI interface. His artificial eye would take in an object and almost instantly provide his mind with a multitude of interesting or critical facts about it. He had to force himself to think of something else to stop the input. He felt like a walking search engine and in some ways felt solace in that, given it was his first mission alone. The only external electronic device on him was a cheap flip burner phone with the ability to make encrypted calls, but not much else.

The dirt road kicked up a trail of brown dust as he drove toward the distillery. They would see him coming from miles away. A full-grown agave plant could never exceed 8 feet. Being the tallest object for acres around made a sneak attack impossible. His mission was simple, but extremely dangerous. The DEA back home had gotten a tip that liquid fentanyl was being trafficked through Mexico using tequila bottles as a cover. To the untrained eye, the bottle was indistinguishable from the alcoholic version. Somehow, the cartel was sending boxes of fentanyl bottles mixed in with legitimate boxes of tequila to the US by leveraging the same distribution channels. The commander's mission was to bring home proof and possibly identify a way to disrupt the network. It was a tricky and highly political scenario given there were over 150 distilleries in the region, and they suspected only five percent were part of the criminal trade.

As he pulled up to the metallic gate, a man dressed in National Guard uniform approached the driver side window carrying an AR-15 rifle with a modified scope. A layer of sweat covered his skin as the day had peaked above 90 degrees and the small station with dust-laden open windows clearly had no air conditioning.

"Hola," says Michael, "Hable inglés?"

"Sí, what is your business here?"

"I have an appointment. I'm the reporter from the States, Trent Thompson."

Michael handed the guard his passport that was meticulously crafted in his likeness.

"Stay here," says the guard, walking back to his station.

Michael felt defensively naked. It was his first mission without weapons, or at least how he used to be armed. As a SEAL, he would have the latest technology on him and his favorite weapon, a silver SIG Sauer P226. He used .357 SIG cartridges which were known for their high velocity and flat trajectory. His body was now a weapon, but an untested weapon in the dangerous field of battle. He contemplated his next move if the guard came back with his rifle raised. The gate opened before the guard returned. His arm poked out of the station window to wave Michael on toward the building.

Michael's cover was a story he was doing for his fake employer, The New York Times. The Mexican government requested the editor to write this piece following negative press about tourists caught in cartel violence. It was the DEA's golden ticket to attack the heart of the drug issue. The goal was to showcase sustainable practices of Mexican distilleries, which produce tequila with minimal environmental impact compared to global whiskey and vodka distilleries. Other Times reporters had already interviewed several other establishments in Jalisco, but the SIX organization made sure Michael had El Arenal on his agenda before visiting his current assignment. El Arenal was a municipality with several tequila producing sites, all legit with no evidence of trafficking. SIX figured if the current site knew he wasn't just visiting them, they would be less suspicious of an outsider.

The road changed dramatically from the gate entrance to the building. Dirt paths transformed into a wide granite road lined with canary palm trees that were each meticulously wrapped with accent lights. This driveway exuded luxury compared to the three distilleries he had visited yesterday. After about 200 yards, a yellow building with a terracotta Spanish-tile roof came into sight. It had distinctive semi-circle arches with white concrete columns shielding a shaded patio.

Several couples were sitting around wrought-iron tables with tasting glasses. Further from the building were larger structures where, undoubtedly, the real magic happened. Three men, armed at their waists, awaited the commander by the building steps. A fountain composed of copper resembled a man wearing a sombrero that stood at the center of the circular driveway. Michael drove right past them, showing no indication of seeing them, and parked at the furthest spot from the building.

As Michael exited his car, he could hear the men's conversation a hundred feet away. Their voices forced a subdued and slow tone, uncharacteristic of Spanish.

"Did you check with your girlfriend in El Arenal?" says the man in the white-stitched cowboy hat to his short, skinny colleague.

"Yes, sir, she gave him a tour of their operations. She said she never left his side, except during his meeting with the director of operations."

The cowboy glanced toward Michael as he approached. His tall, muscular frame bulged out of the fitted, short-sleeve, white-collared linen shirt. He snickered.

"I bet she hated every minute of that workday, motherfucker."

Skinny noticed his colleague's smug face and glanced over at Michael, creasing his forehead.

"Well, did she think he was a real reporter from the Times?" Cowboy asks.

Skinny just kept watching Michael intently, without a response.

"Hey, dumbass, I asked you a question!"

"Sorry, boss, yes, she said he even told her about a couple of trendy restaurants to visit in downtown Manhattan."

"You mean when she visits her new hunk while you're away on tequila business?" The cowboy's diabolical laugh turned the heads of visiting patrons.

Michael stopped a few feet from them and extended his hand to Skinny.

"You must be, Miguel. Nice to meet you."

Miguel looked back at his boss, then at Michael with wide-open eyes. "Uh, I don't think we've ever met."

Michael says, "No, of course not, but I recognized you from your girlfriend's desk pictures. She couldn't stop talking about you and the important job you have here at the facility."

Miguel's body relaxed. A crooked smile appeared while he shook the visitor's hand.

The cowboy put his hand on Michael's shoulder. "I'm Carlos, the operations manager, here. What do you think so far?"

Briefly glancing around, Michael redirected his attention to the fountain.

95% copper, 49 inches tall, tribute to the owner, Luis Sanchez, erected 2010

"So has Luis's family owned this since it started in 1861?"

"Amigo, you know more than I thought," says Carlos. "No, his family is the second owner. The first family nearly drove this establishment to the ground."

Just then, Michael received more site history, and it wasn't pleasant.

You mean the second family put the first family into the ground? He thought.

"Well, that's why I'm here. I'm interested in the various improvements that have occurred in the tequila industry. Where shall we start?"

"That's a stupid question, amigo. We have some of the best tequila in the state, but never take tours on an empty stomach," Carlos says, grinning.

The other men guided Michael upstairs to the tasting room.

CHAPTER
TWENTY-NINE

SOMEWHERE NEAR LAX AIRPORT

Walking into the 5-star hotel with torn Lycra pants revealing part of her butt-cheek was not desirable, but Katya didn't care. Her left arm was badly injured, and her face had scrapes with dried blood and mud. Failing to meet her objective for the first time, she deserved a treat to lift her spirits. She knew her boss might frown upon the price tag of the hotel when the expense report hits his desk next month, but it was the least of her worries. She approached the young Asian girl, behind the front desk, who had a proper look as opposed to her pending guest.

The clerk's eyes widened when she looked up from her computer.

"C-a-n I help you, miss?"

"One room, please, on the highest floor possible," said Katya.

"Do you have a reservation?"

"No—how do you get your hair so silky and straight?"

The girl's red lips puckered before a gentle smile creased her milky white cheeks.

She says, "Oh … well, thank you, I use a keratin treatment."

The hotel manager interrupted the conversation, swiftly moving next to the girl.

"Everything okay, here?" he says.

"Everything but the interruption," replied Katya.

The manager's face started blushing.

"We're good, sir, just pulling up her reservation now. She's had a rough day at the beach. Let's get her comfortable." As she typed, her eyes met Katya's with a wink.

As she walked to the elevator, a family of four, with two young children, moved to hug the wall upon passing her. The air had a captivating marine smell with hints of bergamot and jasmine. After pressing the button labeled 33, she leaned against the polished mahogany wall that glowed from the crystal small chandelier that hung from the elevator's ceiling. The first order of business was stabilizing her arm, then a warm shower and room service.

It took about five minutes just to remove her skin-tight top from her torso. She bit down on her metal hair ornament to keep from screaming at the top of her lungs.

The smaller forearm bone, her ulna, was now protruding from her skin. Her tight shirt had kept it in place and minimized the bleeding, but now it had the freedom to move. Katya remembered being thrown like a rag doll at Martha's house. Her velocity propelled her dozens of yards until she halted at a tree's base. She had used her left arm to protect her head from the impact.

She was thankful it wasn't her shooting arm and that the bigger radius bone responsible for most of the load when using your arm wasn't broken. Still, she wouldn't be juggling anytime soon and needed to find a doctor on the dark web who won't report treatments. For now, she used her small medical kit, that she always kept in her bag, to help stabilize the wound.

After painfully stitching the skin one-handed with no local anesthesia, she reset the bone and almost swallowed the mace ball attached to her hair. She had clenched it with her teeth to deal with the excruciating surge of heat from her arm. The tight medical tape wrapped around the forearm helped, but she hoped room service could bring her a few chopsticks to act like stabilization rods around her arm.

As her sweaty, blood-stained naked body was about to get into the oversized shower with dual heads, her burner phone rang. Katya's eyes narrowed into tight slits, and her brow furrowed at the sound of the caller.

"Hi-ya, Mace. How's it going?" screeched the voice.

Sighing, "Who the hell is this?"

"It's Irina," in a bubbly tone.

"Why are you calling me on your father's phone? Did you even activate the encryption?"

"What inscription?"

"You stupid dimwit!" A man started yelling in Russian on Irina's end of the call.

"You can't talk to me like that. Have you killed that soldier yet?" Irina says.

"Fuck you, Irina. I wouldn't care if you were the President's daughter. If you ever call me again, I'll take my

Makarov and pop both of your oversized boobs with a bullet, then save the last one for your anus!"

Katya heard muffled rustling and Russian expletives through the speaker. Irina's crying in the background became quieter as the seconds passed.

"Call Secure" words blipped on the small liquid crystal display.

"I sincerely apologize for that, Katya," said Ivan. "Why couldn't I have had a daughter like you?"

"My report will change your perspective."

"Why? What happened?"

Katya says, "They had an Auggy."

"An augmented soldier?"

"Yeah."

"Crap, I haven't even thought about one of those in almost a decade. I thought they all died from complications."

"We could only be so lucky. This late middle-aged one didn't look like a soldier but sent me packing in a terrible way. My arm is messed up."

"Damn! I'll send you the doctor we have on our payroll in California. Text me where you're staying. Only an *Auggy* could ruin your perfect mission record. Did you gather enough intel to find the commander?"

"Send me the doctor's location. I'll go to him." She didn't want the general to be cognizant of her luxurious accommodations just yet, especially after a bad report. "I got a lead. There was a woman that I saw and discovered she was on the military back channels as being the first female in the Navy to become a SEAL. Guess who her commanding officer is. Sometimes, being unique puts a spotlight on a person that's undesirable. I was able to hack into one of military's travel databases using SQL injection. I've tracked some of her movements to see where she is going next. The States have such a formidable military and superior technology but haven't minded the little things, like securing the database of their travel management vendor. It's laughable."

"Good work, Mace, and don't worry about Irina's sense of urgency. Things are coming together for Estonia, so I might need you there instead. Get some rest and heal up," says Ivan.

As Katya stepped out of the shower, she wrapped a soft, waffle-textured hotel robe around her wet body. A delicious smell emanated from the adjoining room. Upon her request, they had delivered her room service cart inside the room. It had a white designer linen over it and on the surface was a set of gold-plated utensils wrapped in a rose-colored napkin. The dome-shaped silver cloche covering her food was reflecting the singular flickering tea light candle. Near that was a crystal ice bucket holding a bottle of Taittinger, her favorite champagne, and two slender crystal flutes. As she lifted the cloche, the perfectly cooked tenderloin wrapped in bacon excited her senses.

Crap, where are they? She thought.

Katya moved some things around and checked under the linen cart cover, but it revealed nothing.

"Good evening, Ms. Marek. Nice to talk to you again." The hotel clerk answered her call. Katya had used her alias, Semone Marek, to check-in.

"You were the one who checked me in, no?"

"Yes, Ms. Marek. Something wrong with your room service?"

"How did you know?"

"Our motto here is once you engage a customer, you stay with a customer. We want all their needs covered for their entire stay. Customers having to swap between departments is not a five-star experience. Plus, it's more personal that way, don't you think?"

This blew Katya away. *Never in Russia*, she thought.

The front desk clerk continued, "I see you asked for chopsticks. Did they forget them?"

"Yes—"

"On my way … oh … and we'll comp your champagne for the inconvenience."

While pouring champagne, Katya heard a light knock at the door. She took a sip while walking over. The front desk girl was standing there in her white buttoned down short-sleeve shirt and navy knee-high skirt. Katya figured she couldn't be over 20 years old. Her hands cupped a folded napkin that was laying across them. The two metal chopsticks were laying on the napkin.

"Thank you for bringing them so quickly, it wasn't urgent," as Katya gently lifted the chopsticks off the napkin.

"It's our pleasure, Ms. Marek. Is everything else to your satisfaction?"

"Haven't tried it yet, but this champagne is exactly what I needed."

The girl leaned in closer and with a flutter of her long eyelashes, her cheeks flushed as she gazed intently into Katya's eyes.

"Will there be anything else, miss?" she asks

Katya smiled widely, and her heart skipped.

"You know they actually gave me two of these," gently rocking the crystal flute in her hand. "It'd be a shame not to share." She moved to the table to pour a second glass.

The clerk entered the room as the door automatically closed behind her. As Katya motioned to hand over the bubbly, the girl was intimately close, tugging at the robe's belt, until it opened.

CHAPTER
THIRTY

Tequila kept pouring in front of Michael, and he wondered how his body would react. It was his first time drinking alcohol after being enhanced. Would it mess with his AI interface and give him false information? He also needed to remember to keep drinking water. His AIonics leveraged hydrolysis to function. He briefly wondered if the percentage of water that's contained in most food and beverages also contributed. *Why didn't I ask the good doctor that when I had him?*

"Amigo, we saved the best for last," says Carlos.

An attractive server with an off-the-shoulder baby blue top with ruffles at the bust line approached the table with a silver tray carrying a unique-looking bottle and five shot glasses. As she set everything on the table, she never took her big brown eyes off Michael. He couldn't help but notice the beads of sweat dripping between her cleavage. The room lacked air conditioning, perhaps due to their frugal reluctance to operate it. Odd, considering they sold bottles of tequila there that were over a thousand dollars a pop.

Suddenly, it was as if she was topless. He saw right past the clothing material and knew the exact size and color of her nipples. He shook his head, immediately looking down at the table.

"Everything okay?" asked Miguel.

Michael nodded. "Yeah—been a while since I had so many shots."

I need to be careful with that feature, but holy shit!

"This one is an extra-aged añejo," says Carlos. "Three years in a French oak barrel."

Miguel couldn't stop looking at the server and Michael, for a moment, felt sorry for his sweet girlfriend that he met yesterday. After the server poured each glass, including one for herself, they all toasted with a "Sah-lud!"

"I don't mean to rush things, Carlos, but I gotta get going soon. Could we do the tour?"

"Absolutely, amigo," Carlos wrapped his arm around Michael's shoulders, briefly shaking him. "Damn, amigo, you're built like a brick shithouse!"

"Oh, you know the States … there's a gym at every corner. Guess it's become an obsession for me."

As they walked toward the milling room where the agave syrup extraction occurs prior to the fermentation process, Michael saw a sign for the bottling room. That had to be the entry point for the fentanyl being delivered. The buildings on the property were quite large, and it took over five minutes to reach their first stop. Carlos introduced Michael to the floor manager, who began explaining some of their sustainable practices. While nodding gently, Michael began contemplating a strategy to get some alone time.

"Gents, will you excuse me? Sorry, I think I had one too many shots of your tasty tequila," says Michael.

Carlos chuckled while pointing. "Absolutely, amigo … the baño is back down the hallway, on the right."

After Michael exited the room, he overheard Carlos whispering to the floor manager. "These pussies from America don't know shit about tequila."

The trip to the bottling room would normally take 10 minutes to walk. Michael did it in 45 seconds with his super-speed. He had to stop once when he spotted a worker. Luckily, it was after quitting time and the room appeared empty. The door was locked. Michael grabbed the stainless-steel door lever and turned clockwise slowly. The lock resisted with a metallic scraping sound before finally giving way from the force from his hand.

The inside reeked of alcohol, like an old dive bar with a gritty floor that's impossible to fully clean. The room was roughly the size of half a soccer field. There were two assembly lines for filling bottles, a packaging area, and a shipping station with a scale and light amount of computer equipment. A ribbed metal roll-up door with a dock suitable for an eighteen-wheeler occupied the corner. Clear glass outlined the dock to prevent the outside elements from contaminating the product.

With his x-ray vision, he could see behind large pallets with stacked boxes spread throughout the floor. In the middle of the room, there was a wire mesh cage with boxes of tequila stacked at least fifteen feet high. His vision zoomed in and made out some temporary label attached to the shrink-wrapped pallets. Each label had a one-inch calavera image stamped on it. In Spanish culture, this meant skull. No other shrink-wrapped pallets near the shipping area had that image.

Bingo!

As he made his way to the cage, he saw a padlock as big as his palm locking the entrance. He locked a grip around it, pulled it down, and it snapped it off within seconds. Michael chuckled inside because the energy he felt he needed to pull it down was like what he felt when he used to pick oranges of his mother's tree in the backyard. Even before others, Michael heard the alarm he activated.

Shit! I should have scanned the inside of the padlock.

The roll-up door creaked, and Michael could hear approaching footsteps from inside the building. He tried to block it out and focus. Grabbing a small vial from his pants, he poured a small amount of the liquid from one of the tequila bottles into it. With his phone, he snapped pictures of the multiple addresses, but then realized it wasn't necessary. One look with his eye committed them to memory, including the four-digit code after the zip code on the pallets destined for the U.S. The sounds were getting louder, and he knew he had seconds left. The pallets in the back required pushing aside the stacked ones. As Michael applied pressure to the side of one stack, he realized distillery staff were now inside the room. The sound of charging handles snapped back on their AR-15s.

CHAPTER
THIRTY-ONE

ORANGE COUNTY, CA

A vehicle matching the rideshare app's description approached the curb at a rundown strip mall in Little Saigon. Jasmine waved him down holding her bag of bánh cam, a Vietnamese dessert which is basically fried sesame balls filled with a sweet bean paste. The last thing she wanted to do was visit her parents empty-handed. She walked around and checked the car's rear to find the license plate. It irritated her that a company that employed so many contractors had very few vehicle validations. Their track record for passenger safety was subpar, and women definitely don't want to get into a car impersonating an Uber. Personally, it didn't matter to her, since her hands deadlier than most men in the States, but she always worried about the rest of the untrained female population, plus she was late. Dealing with a power-hungry person was the last thing she needed. She always reminded her younger sisters to match the license plate to the app's ride information.

She loved visiting her parents to see how her sisters were but lamented at the impeding dinner conversation. It undoubtedly would be her mom asking her about her progress in finding a suitable husband. She appreciated Captain Donnelly giving her a few days' leave, but the trip from Coronado's naval base to her parents was long. She would have visited after checking on Martha, but she had to go back to the base to lead a scheduled recruits' training. She didn't own a car, since she was always traveling for the SEALs, which meant public transportation and a ton of disinfectant wipes. The train ride up north alone was almost two hours. As the driver pulled up to her parents' home, Jasmine glanced at her tactical watch. She briefly contemplated if showing up empty-handed was better than being twenty minutes late.

"Sissy!" Her sisters greet Jasmine in unison as they open the front door.

Jasmine hugged them both tightly, much longer than a normal hug. Constantly risking her life at work, a family's embrace becomes a treasured solace.

"How are you, Hoanh?" Jasmine's mother appeared out of the kitchen, wearing an apron and holding a wooden spoon.

"Great, Mom! It's good to be home. Where's Dad?"

"Where he usually is. Drinking Crown Royal and watching Vietnamese cooking channels. I don't see the point of it. I do all the cooking."

Jasmine's lips curved upward. "But I bet he never runs out of dinner suggestions."

"You got that right, honey. Dinner is almost ready. Why don't you wash up from your trip?"

"Oh … these are for you and Dad from Bakery Hồ #3 in Little Saigon."

Jasmine's mother tilted her head and mouthed gratitude. As Jasmine walked to the bathroom, she wondered why she expected any different treatment from her father. Despite not having been home in almost six months, he still refused to get up and greet her. She had to come to him. She hoped some of the old ways would die with his generation. Her phone rang as she closed the door.

"Martha, thanks for calling me back. Are you back home now?"

"Soon, dear, soon. They want to wait till the internal swelling goes down more and re-wrap my arm."

Jasmine says, "Your arm? Was it broken?"

"Almost! I tried to be like Michael and reach for my gun, but that woman smacked me to the ground pretty hard. It's my left arm. Thank goodness I'm right-handed. I was so messed up; I didn't even know what happened. Did you guys get her?"

"Afraid not, but Michael's father was the real hero. Have you seen him since?"

"No, but he's my guardian angel."

The corners of Jasmine's mouth turned downward. "What did she want from you, if you remember?"

"Something about Michael Junior. She injected me with some drugs to make me more compliant, so my memory is foggy."

They want to know if he's dead or alive and where to finish the job.

"Well, I'm glad you're on the road to recovery. I'm visiting my parents, so I have to go. Will call you in a few days."

"Wait! How is Michael doing?"

"Not sure, Ma'am, on a classified mission, I heard. Talk to you in a few days."

Immediately after ending the call, the tiny hairs at the base of her neck hairline stood up. The call wasn't encrypted. What if they had bugged the hospital or, worse, her own parents' home? Did they even know she was involved? She recalled the assailant's evil smile before she limped away from Martha's property. She had to warn Michael somehow.

Biting her bottom lip, she considered doing something she was not supposed to do. She was told specifically by her captain not to call Michael while he was on a mission, unless it was a national emergency. Orders were orders, but Michael and everyone around him were in danger. She knew now that the woman who harmed his mother was after him. Given how they treated him in Belarus, the Russians might lose their patience since their plans kept getting interrupted. They might also know that he's alive. During Navy SEAL training, they had given Jasmine sodium pentothal and sodium amytal. The drugs can make you say things you won't remember saying. Martha might've told the assailant something inadvertently. The encrypted call rang Michael's phone.

Jasmine could hear a bunch of commotion and loud noises as Michael answered. "Sir, it's Jasmine."

"I know that," says Michael, "sorry, a little pre-occupied here."

"What is going on?"

"I, unfortunately, have a small Mexican army after me right now."

"What? Why did you answer the phone?"

"Well, for one, I'll always answer your calls, and two, I'm trying to decide my next move," says Michael.

"Are you being shot at?"

"Let's just say the only thing between me and them is a water tank."

"Just jump off the property! I heard your legs are like a human grasshopper."

Jasmine heard a hearty laugh on the other end of the call.

"That would work, but the security cameras above me would record that. I don't think SIX wants me to expose the AIonic agent to the world yet."

The loud bangs and metallic ricocheting stopped. She heard something in Spanish that sounded like an ultimatum.

Jasmine says, "Real quick update. Your mom is okay, but the same people who tortured you attacked her. They're still coming after you and might know you're alive."

"I was hoping you were going to tell me you missed me, not give me another thing to worry about. Thanks for the update. Gotta go, will call you later tonight, if I'm still alive."

"Michael!" The call went dead.

Jasmine looked in the bathroom mirror and said a quick prayer. She washed her hands, and it took longer than normal, especially when she had feelings of stress. Looking around, there were no guest towels.

Geez Mom! You know I hate touching other people's used towels to wipe my hands.

As she entered the dining room, everyone was already sitting and waiting. Her dad had a scowl on his face.

"Sorry! Had to make a work call," says Jasmine.

"Speaking of work," says her mom as she made her husband's plate. "How's that handsome-looking boss of yours? You know, the one who was on TV for the award. He'd make a great husband."

"Mom, please!" Jasmine's eyes rolled while her sisters giggled.

CHAPTER
THIRTY-TWO

Michael stood behind a steel, pill-shaped water tank nearly the size of a school bus. Four, short metal legs two inches tall supported it on a concrete platform. He wondered how it was not leaking water after all the bullets that hit it. It must have been extra thick metal to help keep the water insulated and prevent evaporation. The army knew he was hiding behind it. Dashing here became his only choice, having ripped through the metal wall at the back of the fentanyl pallet cage. They were calling out orders for his surrender in Spanish, and his augmented hearing could tell by the sound their footsteps made on the gravel that they were close to the tank. He hoped a distraction would allow him the ability to run away quicker than their eyes could catch.

He crouched close to the tank, pressing his palms against its surface. With both hands pushing upward, he leveraged his amazing squatting strength. The tank's leg braces creaked until the thick bolts gave way to the enormous stress, allowing the structure to separate. As it came free, Michael exerted a final powerful push like he was tossing a giant shotput. The steel cylinder was about four feet off the ground before it fell and started rolling in a terrifying manner toward the men behind it. Michael wanted to see what happened, but this was his chance to use his powers unnoticed. He bolted backward along the side of the building to avoid the cameras and disappeared within seconds.

The sounds of crushing bones and skulls replaced the swear words in Spanish. Two simple-minded guards tried sending more bullets into the tank to slow it down before being hit by the multi-ton object. A few men escaped, only to witness their comrades' blood painting the gravel.

Michael reached his vehicle and in his nervous haste, accidentally ripped the driver's side door off before getting in. His car raced toward the gate where two men with rifles blocked the exit. They had been alerted, and it was now open season on the foreigner. Before he even reached the gate, the car's engine started smoking, and the guards shot out all the windows. He kept his foot on the accelerator while ducking under the dash as best as he could while keeping one hand on the steering wheel.

When the bullets started coming from a different direction, he knew he was past the gate. He could hear the car's cylinders begin to struggle as the radiator was no longer functional. He adjusted his head up to get a line of sight. As he did, something struck his head and back multiple times, and it felt like hard-poking fingers. The engine failed, forcing the car's roll to stop in a patch of agave.

As he exited the car, he noticed several .223 caliber fired bullets lying on the driver's seat. His AIonic eye glanced back toward the distillery, calculating a distance of less than two miles. He wasn't safe yet; however, it was another first for him. Freedom came with little to no exhaustion.

In the trunk, he discovered a gallon of water that hadn't lost all its contents from the rifle attack. After consuming what remained, he began sprinting, hoping it was enough water to maintain the energy needed for his new body.

Michael realized shortly after that he needed a solution for his eyes. If he had remembered his sunglasses, they might have helped, but only the wrap-around kind. He was traveling so fast that the air was burning his human eye, forcing it to tear up. Thankfully, it didn't affect his AIonic eye. Now squinting with one eye, he looked back and almost tripped. He noticed a plume of dust in the air miles behind him. The army must have gone mobile.

He estimated one of the towns nearby was about five miles away, southwest. He headed that way instead of the other town a mile away. Temptation compelled him to look back again, observing the distance between him and the angry Mexicans. His foot caught a dead agave bush, and his body went flailing forward at over triple-digit speeds. He broke his fall with his forearms, but it ripped his artificial skin off from the road burn. He dusted off while observing the ugly transition where his arms went from pale skin near the triceps to black composite fiber.

Uh-Oh, Doc's not gonna be happy.

He reached the town outskirts in under three minutes and scanned for something to cover up his unsightly arms. It was dark by now, but somehow, he could see through it. An azoteas came into view with laundry hanging on lines.

To remain unseen, he chose a longer route to the structure. It was all women's clothes.

Terrific.

A long-sleeve pink blouse was the best he could find. He grabbed it and tore off the arms at the shoulder seams. He measured the length of his forearm to it then tore the narrower portion of the sleeves off to dispose. The remaining material barely fit over his muscular forearms, and it made him look like his next stop was a gay bar. He grabbed a worn-out baseball cap with the words "El Tri" written on the front. His AI told him it represented the Mexican national soccer team. Michael knew the army had to surmise he was on foot by now, and he hoped they assumed he would try to find transportation in the closer town of Tequila. They most likely split up to search in both towns, so his visit needed to be brief.

CHAPTER
THIRTY-THREE

RUBLYOVKA, RUSSIA

The man walked gingerly toward the estate that had a large water fountain at the entrance. It wasn't active because of the freezing temperatures, but the concrete sculpture looked familiar. The mansion stood quite large, positioned in front of a forested backyard. There were 12-foot-high iron gates surrounding the property line and evergreen shrubbery behind it to conceal the inside. A gold-plated two-foot-high plaque in the center of the gate, which had the word "GIP" in Russian, separated in half as the motorized double-door opened.

"I saw you admiring the statue at the fountain. Do you know who that is?" says General Petrovsky.

"No, sorry, sir, I do not."

"Shame on you! That's Vladimir Lenin. The original founder of the Russian Communist Party and the leader of the Red Army. A lot has changed in 100 years, don't you think?"

"Yes, and not always for the better," says the man.

"Well … that's up to you and me now. Isn't it? Welcome to my home, General Kuzma."

"Is that one of those new Tesla trucks?"

"Why, yes, I was number fourteen on the waiting list. Here, let me show you something. I always get a kick out of this after watching it on YouTube."

The general opened the Cybertruck's trunk with his remote. He grabbed two thick carrots that were in a plastic food container inside, oddly. He held the two carrots on the edge of the trunk opening. Half of each stick was lying past the edge.

"Watch this!"

As he held the carrots, he clicked his remote, and the trunk's tailgate started closing. When the metal reached the carrots, it sliced them in half before completely closing.

"Damn, that seems dangerous," says General Kuzma.

GIP's eyes narrowed while his mouth lifted higher on one side. He re-opened the trunk and pulled out the halved carrots, handing them to Kuzma.

"Now … your turn."

Two large men suddenly appeared and forcefully grabbed the visitor, pressing him against the vehicle. The larger thug positioned Kuzma's right four fingers over the trunk's edge. His hand futilely attempted to retreat. The trunk started closing again, and GIP stared into Kuzma's wide eyes.

"Did you tell anyone about your visit today?" he asks.

Kuzma was struggling, confused, "What? No, please?"

"Are you sure?"

"Yes! Yes! Please, General!"

An inch before his fingers, the tailgate started moving in the opposite direction.

"Caution is crucial, especially when visited by a leader from the opposing side of the war," says GIP.

The guards let Kuzma go, and he jerked away from the silver truck.

"General, you know why I'm here. Can we finish our transaction?"

"Of course, my friend. Hope you're hungry. My chef has prepared a delicious meal."

As they walked through the marble-floored foyer, there were all sort of ancient weapons hanging on the walls. Kuzma couldn't determine if they were replicas or genuine, but they appeared intimidating. A winding staircase led to the upstairs and in the half-circle foyer area below it was a coffin-looking box with spikes on the inside. Kuzma could have sworn he saw bloodstains on some of the spikes.

"That's what they used to call an Iron Maiden. Pretty effective torture device in the day, but certainly not humane by today's standards," GIP says, smiling.

Two attractive females in black and white French maid uniforms greeted them with a tray full of clear shots. GIP grabbed two and handed one to Kuzma. He nodded, and they clinked glasses before consuming. One maid grabbed Kuzma's hand and led him. He smiled at GIP and relaxed his shoulders. The home felt more welcoming now.

GIP says, "We'll have lunch on the back terrace. That way, you can check out some of my most prized possessions."

The terrace had floor-to-ceiling windows that could open for ventilation on warmer days. The room was about

12 feet above ground and provided an amazing view of the white wilderness behind the general's home. Countless trees filled the landscape with a handful of clearings. Two Artic foxes ran quickly into the clearing, then were gone just as fast. The room setup included a table, two chairs, a decorative tablecloth, and a chilled bottle of vodka.

"This is spectacular," says General Kuzma.

"Oh, you haven't seen nothing yet. Sit over there, please. You'll get a better look."

The wooden floor creaked a little as Kuzma sat. As soon as GIP took a seat, a man emerged holding two steaming bowls and a tray of Black Bread. Kuzma recognized the soup as Borscht. It's a hearty soup made primarily from beets, along with other vegetables like cabbage and potatoes. Typically, a cook will serve it with bits of meat, like beef or pork. This one had beef, and the smell woke his appetite.

"So, I'm curious," says GIP, "why would you help me after my men executed your wife?"

With his mouth full of soup-soaked bread, Kuzma looked up, "Actually, you did me a favor." He winked at the maid standing in the corner.

"How so?"

"She didn't accept my lifestyle. Can I help it if I get a ton of attention being a high-ranking officer in the Ukraine? For example, at last year's Christmas party, two of my female admirers ganged up on me and called me out in front of her."

"Called you out?" says GIP.

"Would you believe they asked her if she lets me do it

up her ass, like I did with them? And it was in front of the President!"

"That's embarrassing, the nerve of them," GIP tapped his index finger on the table.

Just then, Kuzma got up abruptly and headed toward the window.

"Is that an effin' tiger?"

"One of only 200 left in the world," says GIP, "His name is Dimitry. White Siberian tigers are very rare. Their color comes from a genetic mutation, called leucism."

"That thing is majestic."

"Sit down, General, your food is getting cold."

The general kept watching till the tiger disappeared, then sat down again to finish his soup.

"Your payment is being loaded into your vehicle as we speak. I also wanted to thank you for the Estonian tip. The contacts from Latvia are working out better than I expected."

Kuzma downed another shot of vodka. "Glad to hear. I can't wait to go to Spain and retire. Maybe I'll have you over when I buy my chalet." The general paused for a moment. "Wait ... sorry to go back, but ... doesn't that tiger eat your other animals?"

"No, I feed it regularly, so they all can co-exist in my little preserve here."

Making a loud slurping noise with his soup, Kuzma says, "That must be expensive. What do you feed them?"

"Swine—come to think of it, I've neglected him with my travels. He hasn't eaten in a week. Would you like to watch him eat a fresh pig?"

Kuzma's eyes widened, "Absolutely!"

A buttoned remote lay on the table next to GIP. He pressed a button, and a bell went off while the floor slid under itself next to their table, revealing a large viewing window. Within seconds, the majestic beast started pacing back and forth underneath the terrace.

GIP looked at Kuzma, "Ready? Here goes."

Pressing another button on the remote opened a trap-door beneath Kuzma. His body plunged, and he barely caught himself with his arms. In shock, he glanced back at GIP with an open mouth.

GIP says, "I told you Dimitry likes pigs. You know I left my wife because she cheated—"

The tiger leapt up and attacked Kuzma's left leg ferociously. It only took two tries to get it separated at his upper thigh. Kuzma nearly fell through the hole as the weight of the beast pulled down on him. He yelled in excruciating pain as GIP dipped the dark rye bread into his soup. As GIP watched the tiger devour the leg, he knew it wouldn't be enough. He signaled to the guards in the corner, who promptly pulled Kuzma out of the hole in the floor. The edges of the trap door started draining the massive amount of blood collecting on the floor.

"Get him to Dr. Zhuk to get that patched up. We don't want him bleeding out and dying. Dimitry enjoys his meat better when it's fresh."

CHAPTER
THIRTY-FOUR

AMATITÁN, MEXICO

It was a silent evening in the town, which made it easy to listen for intruders. Michael tried to stay inconspicuous, but a few boys playing soccer on the cobblestone road stared at his feminine arm bands. He approached a quaint little Roman Catholic church having evening service with the entry doors wide open. The instrumental and peaceful sounds of *Ave Maria* comforted Michael's ears after the violence tarnished them at the distillery. He briefly thought about how Jasmine would have enjoyed visiting such an intimate establishment. He admired how devoted she was. Despite her hectic schedule, she always made time for worship and prayer. Michael's prayers are cited when troubles required a higher power's divine intervention.

His AIonic eyes were in overdrive, trying to find a suitable vehicle to steal. He could have requested air support from Guadalajara, just 30 miles away. However, why disrupt this peaceful town with an Apache's noise? He would ensure the registered owner received replacement money from SIX for the old car.

What the heck?

The AI informed him that every car he inspected was less than 25 years old. The town housed one of the world's largest tequila distilleries, but not everyone shared in its prosperity. He headed down a street that had rundown homes. The AI again reported newer cars, despite their old appearances. He approached a four-door sedan and shed some light on it from his phone. It was a brown Chevy Impala but was far from its prime. His AI was telling him it was from the year 2000, but he knew it wasn't. He tried an experiment. He covered his AIonic eye and stared at the vehicle. No vehicle data popped into his mind. Using Google Lens on his phone, he snapped a picture and got back the result. It was an Impala from 1971 to 1976.

Terrific, now my AI is misleading me. That's S-A-F-E!

Michael checked his immediate surroundings, then pushed his fingers forcefully into the gap between the front door and the rear door. The metal bent inward like it was a sponge. Able to grip the door now, he pulled on it until the locking mechanism snapped. The inside looked worse than the outside. Empty beer cans littered the floor that was covered in multi-color stains. The vinyl seats appeared to have lost a fight with a machete. Still, it served Michael's purpose, because it had a mechanical ignition. He only hoped it had enough gas to make it to the airport. His index finger and thumb gripped the chrome ignition, and he twisted it with enough force to align the tumblers without a key. The car miraculously started and appeared to have a quarter tank of gas, which was plenty.

Using his eye's night-vision feature, he drove out of the town with the headlights off. Once he reached Highway 15, he felt it was safe to ring Jasmine again.

"Good to hear from you again," says Jasmine.

"Yeah, let's just say it's been a long day, and I've already damaged the merchandise."

"Your AIonics? What happened?"

Michael sighed. "My forearms look like props from a horror film and this damn computer they put in my head is playing tricks on me."

"That's not good. Heading back to Necker Island?"

"I have no choice. Can you make the arrangements to route me from Guadalajara? I really don't feel like explaining everything to Streeter right now."

"No worries. You won't be able to go direct given the secrecy, but we'll have transportation waiting at Guantanamo Bay. How long till you reach the airport?" says Jasmine.

"No more than an hour."

"Let me talk to our airport operative there. Can't guarantee a flight out tonight. Let me work on this. I'll email you the details. Stay safe."

"Understood. Goodnight, Jasmine, and thank you."

With a population of five million, Guadalajara was easy to get lost in. Michael had a simple goal; find a place to rest his eyes before his 8 A.M. flight. He really wanted to check in on his mom, but he didn't have a way to communicate with her safely.

Streeter better pony up one of these fancy encrypted phones for her.

He entered a souvenir shop to minimize exposure. Shopping malls would be riddled with cameras and law enforcement. The true extent of the cartel's influence in protecting the fentanyl industry was unknown. His face was probably circling among Mexico right now thanks to the cameras at the distillery. He picked up a long sleeve white Henley shirt with a beach scene and the word "Guadala-jara" across the front so he could ditch the pink accessory on his attire.

The motel he chose had no star rating, but it was an unlikely place to search. It was a fair trade. A night of restful sleep in a dirty, bug-infested room is better than sleeping with one eye open in a touristy hotel. The motel was next to a small cantina that had live music. A cold beer on a warm evening sounded like the perfect ending to the hectic day. He secured the room, took a quick shower and pulled down his soccer hat closer to his eyebrows before leaving for the bar. He sat in the back corner of the estab-lishment near the rear exit.

"You seem lost." The server sat herself in the other seat at Michael's small table.

"Why do you say that?" says Michael.

"We don't get a lot of tourists in this part of the city. It's not the safest."

"Not touring, oh … you mean this," pointing to his shirt. "Had a wardrobe malfunction earlier. I'm here on business."

She smiled wide with a perfect set of pearly white teeth.

"What can I get you?" as she stroked his leg with hers beneath the table.

This got Michael's attention, and he couldn't help but notice one of her small nipples showing inside her blouse, that wasn't buttoned at the top. She had long, black wavy hair to cover her chest, but perhaps it wasn't there for a reason. She was a slender, attractive woman, probably a little older than Michael, definitely a native.

"Thanks, just a Modelo is fine."

As she got up, she gripped his forearm lightly with her long, manicured nails, "Be right back, sweetie."

He hoped she couldn't feel the missing skin under his forearm through the shirt he was wearing.

The beer took longer than expected. When his server finally brought it, a plate of small tacos accompanied the drink.

"My apologies for the wait, those are on the house," she says.

Michael nodded and turned his gaze back to the energetic band playing. He felt her long stare before she retreated to the kitchen.

They smelled so authentic, and Michael quickly remembered he missed dinner with all the commotion earlier. It only took Michael about five minutes to finish the food and beer. With his stomach satisfied, he sat back to listen to the music. A cool breeze came in from the propped open back door that complimented his relaxed state.

"Can I get you another?" says his server.

"It's late and I have an early morning appointment. I probably shouldn't."

"Oh, come-on! You'd be the first guy in a long time to come in here and leave after just one drink."

Michael smirked. "Well, since you put it that way, hate to disappoint."

This time she returned within minutes, setting the beer on top of a new cocktail napkin. Michael lifted it for a sip, which revealed some words written on the paper coaster. "Off in 15 minutos XXX"

So much for going to bed early.

CHAPTER
THIRTY-FIVE

RUBLYOVKA, RUSSIA

Irina was lying on the white fur rug in front of the fireplace. An enormous pile of fresh birchwood was crackling away inside, with the occasional golden embers floating upward. The enormous stuffed polar bear's head propped her head up at the rug's end. She was typing away on two different phones and humming some Russian pop song. Her legs were open, bent slightly at the knees. A couple of uniformed house guards were in the massive great room. The one closest to the fireplace was visibly uncomfortable.

"GOV-no, Irina! What have I told you about your attire in my home?"

"What, Father? It's not like I'm naked or anything."

"First, your loose shorts are way too short without underwear. Second, can't you see this isn't a private room?"

"You mean Stupid #1 and Stupid #2? They might as well be statues. They do nothing but stand there looking bored out of their minds."

"That's their job, darling. Oh … and at least they have a job," says General Petrovsky.

"Well, I should've been married by now. He would've made plenty of money for both of us."

"Sure, but you're not … and therefore … start rethinking your life."

"I can't, Father, till I have closure. Did you get that stupid SEAL yet?"

"We're close, but something has come up that threatens our national security. That is the priority right now."

"Fine! By the way, I haven't seen Sergei since we got back from Cuba. Is he part of this national security ordeal too?"

"No, I had to let him go."

"What? Why? He was so good to me in Havana."

"I've told you before, Irina. Don't get involved with my men. They don't have time for relationships. When one of them comes back dead, you don't want to end up heart-broken again, do you?"

"Okay." Irina started texting on her phone, then stopped. "Promise I'll start looking for a job tomorrow."

"Thanks, Honey," says the general.

As the general headed to his study, he whispered into the guard's ear in the hallway.

"Whatever is left of Sergei, dispose of him in the fire pit. The last thing I need is my daughter seeing Dimitry drag the damn guy's head around outside."

The guard nodded and walked off quickly.

The general's study had a classical appearance. Heavy dark red drapes hanging from a brass rod adorned the large bay window behind his mahogany polished desk. On one side was a bookshelf filled with hundreds of military novels. On the opposite side, a picture light, enclosed in a brass casing, illuminated a couple of oil paintings. One painting stood out to the woman in his guest chair.

"Is that Stalin?" She pointed to the oil painting closest to his desk.

"Yes, it is called *The Morning of our Motherland.* An artist named Shurpin painted that in 1949."

"That's not the original, is it?"

"I wish, but it is a reproduction from the original. Brilliant man, Stalin!" says GIP.

"Wasn't he responsible for millions of deaths, some by execution?"

"Sure, but it's a small price to pay for industrializing the Soviet Union—not to mention repelling those Nazis. How is your arm, by the way?"

"Doc says it will take at least 8 weeks to heal—don't worry, it won't slow me down," says Katya.

"I have a better idea and a big surprise for you," the general's mouth curved deviously upward. He motioned with his head to a manila folder lying at the edge of the desk.

Katya opened it and her eyebrows lifted as her eyes widened. She quickly paged through the diagrams while skimming over the associated text.

"How? I thought this project was dead decades ago," she says.

"We got lucky, and strangely, this happened around the time you saw the *Auggy.* As you know, in the late seventies, we stole most of the Americans' bionics plans. Unfortunately, we didn't get everything. Despite our scientists' best efforts, we could never get the small nuclear cells to stabilize when not in use. We scrapped the program in the 80s and we thought the Americans did too. Three days ago, one of the U.S. government's servers was accessed with a hospital computer using an outdated encryption protocol. Our monitoring intercepted it and broke the old encryption easily. It was some doctor named Cynthia Moore. Her research showed interest in some bionic technology files from nearly half a century ago. Perhaps she was repairing an old *Auggy*. Bottom-line, we finally got the solution for the power cells!"

Katya examined the paperwork, her left arm, and then GIP. "You want to replace my arm?"

"We can have you augmented and mobile in two days' time with our current healing technology. Think of what you can do with that on your missions."

"General, I'm willing to do anything for Mother Russia and for you, but your doctors lack the necessary experience."

"I've had them working around the clock to be ready. They assure me they are. They can start tonight."

"What about Estonia?" says Katya.

"The timing couldn't be any more perfect. The trains should reach their final destination in four days. I want you there to make sure nothing goes wrong with the takeover."

"Can I ask, sir, why is it called OP91?"

"Excellent question, dear. The Soviet Union dissolved in December 1991. This operation is our second step closer to forming the new Red Union. Our friends to the west were step one—albeit taking longer than we expected to finish."

Katya got up from her chair and walked over to the bay window. It provided a serene view of the frozen habitat behind the general's mansion. She believed she spotted movement among the trees, possibly caused by the strong winter wind. She enjoyed using her body to cripple her opponents much more than guns and knives. It was the reason she kept it in superior shape. While artificial, the bionic arm would be part of her body and give her an advantage that no one could match, except maybe another *Auggy*. However, most of them had faulty components. This new surgery was a risk, but a risk worth taking to become the ultimate killing machine. She turned back toward the general.

"Can your chef whip up some Plov? I'd like to have a decent meal before I go under the knife."

CHAPTER
THIRTY-SIX

GUANTANAMO BAY, CUBA

The golden-brown sedan pulled off to the side of Sherman Avenue about a hundred yards behind Jasmine's taxi. As her driver made the turn to approach the guard gate at the Naval Station, she regretted her visit to Playa Tortuguilla to get some sun and solitude. That creepy feeling of being spied on rattled her nerves. She expected it in the States, but the general's reach was much farther than expected if he had operatives in Cuba.

The guard's jaw dropped when he saw Jasmine through the back window wearing a see-through bikini cover-up. His eyebrows raised as he scanned Jasmine's military ID, then immediately his body stiffened with a salute while motioning to the guard controlling the entry.

That never gets old, she thought with a smile.

Michael's helicopter from Havana should have arrived by now. Feeling gritty, she had the driver drop her off at her barracks for a cold shower. It was unseasonably warm that day and even the Caribbean beach water didn't help. A text with Michael confirmed his arrival and they would meet at the ferry dock in two hours. As she walked past some open-door rooms filled with enlisted personnel, the whistling echoed in the hallway. Jasmine didn't mind. The station had few women working there, and she was likely the object of their lonely gazes.

She recalled having to share a community bathroom with about 20 other men during boot camp. It was basically just one big, tiled room with shower stations in the middle. Each station had four shower heads in a circular configuration. The first time she walked in, she was naked, while half the squad was cleaning themselves. Time stood still for every male in her presence. Some of them quickly became embarrassed covering their privates, while others turned away. One creep, named Phil, watched every drop of water and soap glide over her silky tanned skin. Eventually, honorable men dealt with Phil. After that awkward day, the soldiers patiently waited for Jasmine to finish before entering the shower. Now an officer, she often got her own room and private bathroom—a reward for her hard work.

"Streeter's G7 is waiting for us across the bay, at Leeward Field," says Jasmine.

"G7? You mean, like a private jet?" asked Michael.

"Well, you're his golden boy. Only the best for you. I had to take a stinky Seahawk to the island last time. It smelled like someone died in it."

"Someone probably did," Michael says, grinning as he receives a slap on the shoulder.

"Are you enjoying being invincible?"

"First, I'm not invincible and second, no. The reason I'm going to the island is because these parts are malfunctioning."

"Poor baby, did your super hand mess up one of your jerk-off sessions?"

"Is that anyway to talk to your commanding officer?"

"Technically, you're not anymore. Now that you're an agent, I work under Captain Chase."

"What?" says Michael, wrinkling his forehead.

"The Navy has released you full-time to SIX. I'm telling you, Streeter's money talks."

"I guess I expected that, but not so soon."

Jasmine put her hand on Michael's knee. "Don't worry, doesn't affect any of your benefits and the condition was that the Navy could use you on missions as deemed necessary."

"They better still call me 'Commander'. I worked hard to get to that position."

The ferry ride across the bay was short. Although Jasmine had been to the airstrip before, the sheer number of armed men stationed today was unprecedented. A military jeep transported them to the runway where the jet was being refueled. From afar, the vessel shined brightly in the sun as the paint color was a metallic silver with red accent stripes. A blonde flight attendant, who looked like a New York model, stood at the top of the aircraft's stairs. She smiled at Michael as he walked up, but he paid no attention. As they sat across from each other in the luxurious leather seats, each behind a large marble table, the busty attendant approached. She carried a serving tray with two highball glasses filled with a clear mixture and floating green leaves.

"Would either of you care for a Cuban mojito? Mr. Streeter uses a special rum from Havana and if you're wondering, yes, they're real," she says.

Jasmine and Michael glanced at each other with furrowed brows while accepting the drink. Upon closer inspection, each drink had a clear glass stirrer adorned with a princess-cut diamond that was at least one carat. They exchanged glances again, this time with a gentle smile. In unison, they said, "She meant the diamonds." They raised their glasses toward each other for an air toast.

After taking a sip, Michael says, "What's wrong?"

"There's a greasy mark on the outside of my glass," replied Jasmine.

"So?"

"You know me and my OCD."

"Ugh, that again! I don't know how you do it—especially being a SEAL. You serve your country from the armpits of the world."

"Trust me, it's a constant battle in my head. It's exhausting!"

"Well, I admire you for it. Mental illnesses are so misunderstood. You have excelled higher than any woman in the Navy, even with a debilitating condition."

"Thanks, Commander, I appreciate those words," as she motioned to the attendant to replace her glass.

The plane moved forward. The jet engines emitted a low rumble that gradually increased in pitch as they reached the maximum thrust required for lift. Jasmine enjoyed the wide view of the azure, glowing Caribbean Sea below. It would be a quick trip to Tortola, the biggest of the British Virgin Islands. A helicopter would then transport them to Necker Island.

"Have you ever thought about settling down?" says Jasmine.

"You mean like raise some rug rats with an old lady?"

"Well, she doesn't have to be old, ya know."

Michael chuckled.

"Maybe … someday … I don't know. What do I know about being a father when I never had one?" says Michael.

"I'll let you in on a little secret. Most new fathers or parents know nothing about parenting. It's sort of like on-the-job training."

Michael laughed. "And you know this how?"

"I read a lot. You should pick up a book sometime."

"I like to read magazines and stuff."

"Yeah, I've seen the magazines you boys keep in the barracks. Illustrations fill 90% of the pages, usually of women."

"Not true, Ensign. Captain Donnelly's magazines have men," smirks Michael.

"No! Really?"

"Yep."

"That makes a lot of sense now. Wish he wouldn't try to hide it. The world is more accepting than ever now."

"Yeah, but there are still some crusty old generals living in the past," says Michael.

"Back to my earlier question, I think you'd make a

noble father because you know all the things not to do. By the way, have you heard from your dad?"

"No, why?"

"Well, to be honest, I saw him."

"What? When?" Michael's eyebrows angled upward.

"If it wasn't for your dad, your mom may not be alive today. He was at her house dealing with the intruder before I arrived. Matter of fact, I don't think that Russian operative will be in active duty for a while. Your father literally threw her body out of the house like she was a small bag of trash."

"With his bionics?"

"Yeah, and you shouldn't be so hard on him," says Jasmine.

"Why? Because he finally did the right thing for once in his life?"

"Because the reason he distanced himself from you and your mom is because his bionics are leaking radiation that could endanger both of you. That's why he hasn't been around your whole life."

Michael's mouth opened wide, and his gaze pierced Jasmine's eyes. He turned away and looked out the window, downing the rest of his glass in one gulp.

CHAPTER
THIRTY-SEVEN

WARSAW, POLAND

Kristap's stomach was in knots as the stolen ambulance approached Warszawa Wschodnia, the east station. The freight arrived in less than five hours. The mission's success was predicated on him coming up with a plan to stop it. After stealing two ambulances from the hospital, they drove through the night from Riga. One of them was easy as they nabbed it during a shift change, but the other had to be taken by force as it was approaching the hospital. With weapons aimed at the driver, they removed the three medics and the gurney holding an elderly patient on oxygen and left them by the side of the road. Kristap wouldn't have felt as bad if the patient hadn't looked almost identical to one of his foster parents. The one other person in his whole life, besides his twin brother, who took a genuine interest in Kristap's well-being. These childhood memories reflected his only experience of being loved by anyone other than

Kaspars. His brother started flicking his lighter to ignite a cigarette drooping from his lips in the passenger seat.

"What are doing, idiot?" Kristap smacked the lighter to the floor.

His brother's eyes furrowed. "What the fuck, bro?"

"How safe do you think it is to light a cigarette in an ambulance carrying oxygen tanks? Do you want to kill us before we even start our mission?"

"Uh, the tanks are in the back with the other cadets—not here."

Kristap frowned. "Isn't it possible for lit ashes to travel backward through the air? Use your head. You're trying my patience, especially since you were supposed to drive four hours ago while I slept. Now I'm exhausted."

"Why didn't you wake me?"

"I would've if you didn't down an entire bottle of gin last night."

"Sorry, Kris," says Kaspars.

The second ambulance was following theirs about 100 yards back, and he figured everyone was hungry by now. Some coffee and a solid meal would help him think more clearly. Besides his brother, there were 10 other cadets and two tank mechanics between the two vehicles. Initially, there were 11 cadets, but one had to stay in Riga because of a childish dispute. There was no tolerance for personal vendettas or hatred on this mission. To succeed, they had to work together. He put one mechanic in charge of driving the other ambulance.

The GPS on his phone found a diner in a shady part of town that would suffice. He preferred to stay away from crowded places and law enforcement. He worried the local police had noticed the ambulance plates. The diner came into view. It was two old, converted train box cars that were sitting on top of an isolated railway strip. It was near one of the industrial train yards for Warsaw and aptly named, "The Last Stop". Besides a couple of cars, the parking lot was empty. Kristap phoned the mechanic to drive past it and follow him to what looked like an abandoned building a couple of blocks away. Even in this crappy neighborhood, Latvian writing on some ambulances parked in the open would raise suspicion.

They found parking inside the building that had more broken windows than intact ones, and the graffiti on the walls inside explained why. As Kristap exited the ambulance, he got a text from General Petrovsky.

"Why the hell are you in Poland?!?!?!? I can track your phone."

FUCK!

Kristap motioned with his index finger showing his phone and walked away from the crew to make a call.

"I tried calling you last night," says Kristap.

He heard clicking and grumbling on the other end of the call.

"I noticed that. Explain, please. Who is watching the crew in Riga?" says GIP.

"They're with me here."

The general swore in three different languages.

"—we got the list of repairs for the Leopards. The mechanics insisted those repairs were impossible to finish on a six-hour trip to Estonia. Some repairs were minor and wouldn't impact the tank's functionality, but several would impair the tanks from moving. I figured you wouldn't want that, so we have to board much earlier."

Kristap's stomach twisted again as there was an uncomfortable silence on the call.

"How will you board the train without a scheduled stop in Warsaw?" asks GIP.

"Still figuring that out, but I've got a few ideas. Don't worry—if we have to board by horseback, like in the old west while it's moving, we will. We'll be on that train."

"You better, or I'll kill you and your brother slowly. I'll do it while you're facing each other, so you can experience each other's pain. Mace won't be joining you till you get closer to Estonia. We had a minor setback with her, but she will be there."

"Affirmative, General. I will send you an encrypted text with the plan as soon as possible. The train will be here shortly after lunch, Warsaw time," says Kristap.

The call cut off in Kristap's ear. He realized the back of his neck was sweating even though the temperature was below freezing. His sole focus now was getting a plate of eggs and sausage, with a cup of black coffee. Walking back to the crew, his brother started approaching.

"Everything, okay, bro? You look a little pale."

Kristap put his hand on the back of his neck and rotated his head to crack it. He observed the thirteen men looking back at him.

"Who's hungry?"

THIRTY-EIGHT

NECKER ISLAND

"They're called AI hallucinations, which means you may receive outputs that are nonsensical, irrelevant, or incorrect in the context of a given prompt. I'm adjusting your LLM to a new state-of-the-art version that even our own government doesn't have," says Dr. Bell.

"LLM? In English, Doc?" says Michael.

"Large Language Model,"

Michael rolled his eyes. "How about a dumb man's English?"

"Sorry. I work on this tech so much I think it's common knowledge for others. Large Language Models, or LLMs, are the AI backbone technology for taking natural human language requests for information and generating results such as the make and models of cars, in your mission instance. Only, instead of you typing the request out on a computer, your brain asks the AI generative pre-trained transformers we placed there for a response. In a nutshell, sometimes the AI makes mistakes, just like the human brain does when it remembers a memory incorrectly. This new LLM upload that our scientists just finished developing should help reduce the hallucinations significantly."

Michael looked up at Jasmine with his eyebrows raised. She shook her head.

"Okay, Doc, that helps ... I think. Should my forearms be itching right now?"

The doctor examined one arm. "Yes, the microscopic Convalescytes are hard at work. They're rapidly connecting the new skin to your old. Should stop in an hour or two. I'm extremely impressed at how well the borophene layers have held up. I see no damage ... you said bullets hit your back?"

"Yes, barely felt them."

Sofia rubbed the back of Michael's bare shoulder. "Is there anything I can do to make you more comfortable?"

Jasmine rolled her eyes.

Michael looked up and smiled. "Can you remove this wire conduit from the back of my skull? I feel like a dog with a leash."

"Let me just check a couple AI readings," says the doctor, walking over to the large monitors behind Michael.

Sophia caressed Michael's back with her long, manicured nails. "The island weather is perfect today. There's not a cloud in the sky and the winds are light. Want to get some rays before you have to run off on a dangerous mission again?" Sofia smiled.

Michael mumbled. "Can this artificial skin even tan?" He raised his voice. "Hey, Doc, can this skin tan?"

The doctor had an intense focus. "Huh? Oh, no, not yet,

but we're working on ways to invoke melanin pigment production."

"Well, maybe you can just keep me company then and protect me from strangers. I'm losing my color." Sofia pulled one side of her skirt down several inches, revealing her pelvis tan lines.

"There's a lot of riffraff on the luxurious beaches of Necker these days?" he asks.

She laughs. "No, but my suits seem to draw unwanted attention."

Michael looked up at Jasmine, who had a soured face with her arms folded.

"Want to join us, Jasmine? When was the last time you treated yourself to a pina colada on the beach?"

"No, thanks, you guys have fun. I already have technical briefings to catch up on after my leave to see my family. Also, Captain Chase said they're getting some odd intel coming out of Eastern Europe that I want to check out."

As Sofia and Michael strolled out to the sand, they had their pick of a spot that was semi-private. Apart from SIX's operation facility disguised as a rehab center, the island only offered one high-end resort with rooms starting at $5000 per night. Seldom did the beach have more than a dozen visitors at a time. It was as close as someone could get to a private island experience. If someone desired exclusive use, the whole resort had a nightly rental fee of just over six figures.

The sky was an open blue canvas. Only a few puffy clouds were visible, as if they lost their way. Turtle Beach's white sand was soft and warm under Michael's feet. Something bothered him about wearing flip-flops or sandals on a beach. Perhaps it was the occasional annoying, gritty sand particles that made their way between the soles and his skin, or maybe it just felt better connecting with Mother Earth directly to a part of his body. Despite the AIonic limbs, he was happy to feel the same sensations under his feet.

"Check out that cute Tiki hut over there. Perhaps they're serving some island drinks. Can you get me one?" asks Sofia.

"Sure, what's your poison?"

Sofia's eyes looked upwards. "Think it's called a Bahama Mama."

SIXAI: Bahama Mama (origin early 1950s, Tiki-style cocktail)

•1/2 fluid oz each of dark rum, coconut rum, and grenadine

•1 fluid oz each of orange and pineapple juice

•Blend ingredients and dash of lime together with ice until smooth, for a frosty, fruity cocktail with a tropical flavor profile. (Optional) pineapple or orange garnish, then serve in a chilled glass.

That's new, they named my AI now?

"Thanks, AI," mumbles Michael.

"What did you say?"

"Oh nothing! Sometimes weird noises come out of my mouth."

Michael, a bourbon enthusiast, longed for a fine whiskey. There are many types of whiskeys, like bourbon, Scotch, or Irish, but he favored the sweet and robust flavor profile of bourbons. He realized this tiny wooden bar shack wouldn't have any brand worth drinking, so settled on a Modelo with a lime and salted rim. The bartender was very young and didn't know Sofia's drink, but luckily, Michael recited its ingredients to perfection.

As he started back to their beach spot, Sofia began spreading oil all over her body. No wonder she gets lots of attention. Her hot pink bikini barely left anything to the imagination. Michael appreciated bikinis like any guy but preferred some mystery in a woman's attire. Sofia's body, athletic and curvy in all the right places, was arousing. Her golden skin was glistening in the sun as he walked up.

"That looks yummy!" She smiled widely. "You want to taste?"

"No, thanks." He took a sip of his Modelo and surveyed the coastline.

"Take off your shirt and stay a while, sailor."

"Why? I can't tan."

She giggles. "That's right ... it's more of a selfish reason for me."

"Do you mind applying this oil to my back? I can't reach."

Sofia laid down on the beach blanket face down, pulled her long brown hair to the side and untied her bikini top's strap. Michael forcefully exhaled and kneeled. He bit his bottom lip as his hands spread the oil over her supple skin.

"I was wondering something," she says.

"What's that?"

"Are the sensations of touch in your fake hands the same as your old hands?"

Michael stopped briefly. "Actually, somehow it's better. It's as if the sensations travel to my brain faster. It's hard to explain."

"I see. Do you mind getting it under my bottoms too? Sometimes the material moves around. I don't want to burn —especially down there."

As Michael moved his hands south, his AI told him his heart rate was increasing. He soon realized he wouldn't be able to stand up in his flimsy board shorts without being embarrassed. He heard her moan, then heard something alarming. Turning his head, he looked toward the water. As his AIonic eye scanned, they focused in on some small arms thrashing above the waves. Two seconds later, he was in the water, swimming toward the danger.

"Shark!"

It was Michael's first time using his augmented eye submerged, and its line of sight was as clear as if he was wearing a scuba mask. He saw three ominous creature outlines circling the kicking legs underwater in the distance.

SIXAI: Time to target: 3 seconds

. . .

The velocity of his body approaching like a speedboat scared away two of the sharks. The third scattered as well, but, unfortunately, it returned. Michael placed himself between the kids and the predator. He motioned to the kids to stop screaming before submerging again.

SIXAI: Tiger Shark (Galeocerdo cuvier).
   •Second most dangerous shark species
   •Average shark bites per year worldwide: 83
   •Unprovoked bites that are fatal: 28%
   •Recommended action: Remain calm, reach out arm, and push down gently on nose

Reluctantly taking the AI's advice, Michael stretched out his arm. The 12-foot-long fish complied and headed for deeper waters. Michael grabbed one kid in each arm and, with his stomach to the sky, kicked quickly toward shore. The parents were already waist high in the water waiting to help. As they settled onto the dry sand, Michael noticed a 2-inch bloody cut on one of the boy's arms.

"Keep this one beachside," he says, pointing to the boy's forearm. "Sharks can smell blood from several miles away."

The boy says, "Sorry, Mom, I cut it on the rocks when we were body surfing earlier."

The fathers each took turns shaking Michael's hand emphatically with gratitude, offering him food or drink and to join them. Michael declined graciously and turned around to meet Sofia, who was just now approaching.

"Damn, you made it there fast, they must have been 200 yards out," Sofia says putting her hand around his upper arm.

"241 yards."

She got closer to Michael now with two hands around his muscular arm. "Did you rip those sharks apart with your AIonic claws?"

"Ha, no I respect all of earth's creatures. The boy's bloody arm tempted them. They just needed a little redirection."

Her body purposely bumped into his and she gazed into his blue eyes as they walked back to their beach spot.

"But you could've, you know. That's hot!"

"Violence is a last resort for me. Only if negotiations fail," Michael says.

"Oh, so now you're negotiating with these ocean beasts, are you?"

"Wait … are you telling me you never saw Aquaman?"

CHAPTER
THIRTY-NINE

SECRET RESEARCH FACILITY NEAR KAZAN, RUSSIA

The underground medical facility was clearly past its prime. Black smudges and small pieces of garbage riddled the white walls and tiled floors. Several fluorescent lights in the ceiling were missing, others were flickering. The air had a staleness to it, almost a moldy smell. Even the male nurse pushing Katya's gurney had a lab coat with a torn pocket. As they wheeled her from her recovery room back to the lab for evaluation, she hoped that the run-down conditions didn't mean that her operation would take place under contaminated conditions. She feared very few things, but the microscopic invaders were unbeatable.

My country never spends a dime more than they need to on anything!

As the front of the gurney pushed the double doors open, Katya saw General Petrovsky smiling widely. White lab coats filled the room along with medical hardware connected to computers.

"The doctors tell me everything went just fine, except for a minor infection that they already took care of," says GIP.

Katya grumbled.

"Why can't I move my new arm? And why doesn't the color match my other arm?"

"Patience," says one of the lab coat people, "You're still healing. The neurotransmitters are still adjusting to the artificial interface they communicate with as your brain sends signals from the motor cortex."

GIP interjected, "We had to use the artificial skin we had in stock to get this done in the short time allowed. You're welcome to come back and get it replaced with a suitable match for your skin tone."

"F-ing terrific! And why is my shoulder on fire? I thought we were only replacing my arm?" asks Katya.

"Mace," says GIP, "you can't have a bionic arm that can lifts thousands of pounds attached to your human shoulder. We had to augment your shoulder to dampen the load on your skeletal frame."

"Fine. I'm starving. Can I eat something?"

The doctor spoke up. "Nurse, let's give her an IV for now. She won't be able to stomach anything while the medication works through her system."

"What the fuck, General! I never agreed to be on medicine!"

"It's just to help you heal faster, Mace. Trust me, please," says GIP.

The male nurse who wheeled her into the room brought over an IV pole. He began inspecting her regular arm for a vein and poked her twice with the needle.

"What are doing, idiot? Where did you guys find this one?"

The doctor quickly stepped in between them, grabbed the end of the IV, and inserted it within seconds.

One of the lab technicians wheeled over a cart with a machine that had a round metal ball, the size of a tennis ball, attached to a cord. She showed Katya the end of a piece of conduit with a round connector.

"Miss, we're going to simulate your brain signals by attaching this to your augmented arm. It will allow us to control its movement. Do you mind?"

"Sure, thanks for asking nicely."

The technician gently peeled back the artificial skin on Katya's shoulder. She connected the conduit and turned to lock it into place. The doctor began typing on a nearby keyboard and suddenly the arm lifted while the elbow bent. Seconds later, the hand closed and re-opened.

It freaked Katya out a little because she wasn't controlling it, yet it was part of her. She felt this phantom limb sensation, like what an amputee must feel from a missing limb. It was like a warm, tingling sensation.

"We are now going to test your grip strength using this solid steel ball," the doctor says. "It has sensors inside that will measure the pressure and feeds it back to my computer here."

Placing it in the bionic hand, the technician held it until the doctor pressed a button on the keyboard. The hand wrapped tightly around the ball. Fearful that her fingers would be squished, the tech let go quickly. The doctor's gaze lifted in excitement as GIP approached to inspect the monitor.

"I think that's like five times the force of a crocodile's bite," says GIP with eyebrows raised.

After running additional tests for another hour, the medical team departed, leaving only the general and Katya. She could start moving around now, including using her new arm below the elbow.

"Do you think you will feel good enough to travel tomorrow? Need you on that train as soon as possible," says GIP.

"Yes, of course, sir. What now?"

"Now I teach you how to fly a car."

Katya's forehead wrinkled. "Say what?"

GIP directed her out of the testing room. They stopped by the cafeteria area since the doctor gave Katya the green light to eat solids. She was excited to see a loaf of rye bread and cold cuts on the counter. The general made her a sandwich since her augmented fingers were still a little jerky and unpredictable.

They proceeded to the main floor of the building and exited to a maintenance garage on the grounds. The general clicked an older looking remote with a large button that he pulled from his jacket. An unfamiliar object appeared as the metal door creaked up.

The vehicle looked part dune buggy, part drone. Instead of wheels, it had four sets of horizontal propellers with blades 2-3 feet long. The propellers connected to horizontal bars that led to a cockpit compartment with a roll cage on top. The driver's seat had a headrest, seatbelt and maneuvering controls.

"You gotta be kidding me," says Katya.

"Another innovation from our comrade scientists with a

little help from a Swedish aerospace company's stolen design."

"Winter's probably not the best time to be flying around in a wide-open aircraft."

"It's not for leisure, Mace. This is how you're going to get aboard the train."

She shook her head. "Sometimes I wonder if you're actually trying to get me killed."

"Try it! That's why we're here. Even an old, fat man like me got it airborne."

"What's the exact plan?"

The general's eyebrows raised, and he pointed to the oversized drone.

"I have another one of these strategically placed in a field near Jogeva. That's where you'll take off and intercept the railway. The train will be heading north toward Tapa train station, a major hub."

Katya huffed, "I thought I was going to Riga."

"Plans changed because of the extended time needed for repairs. The team is boarding in Poland."

"Why can't I just board at one of the stops?"

"Too risky. They installed new camera systems at all their stops. Video recording is becoming too cheap and easy to set up nowadays. I can't risk anyone identifying my best agent. The rest of the clowns on this mission are expendable. The drone car can fly faster than a train. You will abandon it and check on my crew that is already onboard. But here is the fun part; there is an almost 90-degree turn before you reach Tapa. At the turn is the Tapa Railway Station Yard. Part of the train, including a couple tanks, will not make that turn but abruptly visit the yard."

"Don't you need those tanks?" says Katya.

"Not as much as I need a distraction to keep the Estonia response teams occupied. Also, the tanks being ejected will hopefully curtail any concerns that someone was trying to steal them."

"And if this plan doesn't work?"

"You'll be there to make sure it does," says the general.

Katya smiled, then walked over to the flying vehicle. With just her index finger, she located the midpoint on the roll bar and effortlessly lifted the vehicle. Grinning, she moved it outside of the garage and hopped inside to familiarize herself with the controls. The general pointed out some important switches and dials.

"Alright, you better stand back unless you don't mind having your legs chopped off."

"Wait!" The general raised his hand before she started the craft. "You will definitely need these."

He walked back over and handed her some earplugs and goggles.

CHAPTER
FORTY

WARSZAWA WSCHODNIA TRAIN STATION, POLAND

Kristap clicked on his DMR two-way radio and changed the channel to 452 MHz, which he had pre-programmed to use AES-256 encryption. He hoped Andrei, the tank mechanic, had remembered the frequency they agreed to use. They didn't have time for a second attempt. The train was scheduled to arrive at the station in less than an hour. He went over the plan in his head to make sure he didn't forget anything. As his mind contemplated any unplanned risks, the radio beeped.

"Thomas, this is Percy. Over."

"Percy, this is Thomas. Go ahead. Over," Kristap says.

"I'm in position. Over."

"Great. I have 15 minutes past the hour. Confirm. Over."

"Same. Over."

"We start at 20 past. Over."

"Roger that, Thomas. Thanks. Over."

"Good luck, Percy. Out."

Kristap and Andrei had positioned their ambulances a half of a mile away from the closest gate crossing northeast of the station. Each ambulance was on a different side of the track. As the minute hand reached exactly 20 minutes past the hour, they switched on their sirens and started driving toward the track to their meeting point. Thirty seconds later, the ambulances were on a collision course with each other. The sound of the emergency vehicles helped move the other traffic out of the way. Just as they were about to cross the tracks, Kristap turned his vehicle toward Andrei's and the shrieking sound of metal bending almost deafened the sirens. Andrei's vehicle spun almost 90 degrees and half of it remained on the tracks. Kristap's vehicle now t-boned Andrei's.

Kristap acted dazed as he exited the vehicle, making his way to the driver's side of Andrei's ambulance. He mouthed some words and helped Andrei exit the vehicle. Andrei was faking a leg injury and put one arm around Kristap's shoulders. Before they moved away from the vehicle, Kristap tossed two live M67 grenades onto the floorboard. He dragged Andrei quickly behind his own ambulance, hoping it would shield them from the blast.

A deafening explosion, followed by a searing blast of heat, whipped around Kristap's ambulance. The shockwave reached some cars that had pulled to the side after the accident, shattering several car windows. Debris danced across the top of the ambulance, where Kristap and Andrei were resting, and fell right in front of their feet. Kristap's ears were ringing so much he couldn't hear the siren on his vehicle. He soon realized that the fireball had set his own ambulance cab on fire. They swiftly moved from the back of the emergency vehicle to the sidewalk 30 yards away. Some onlookers approached, asking if they were alright.

Kristap looked back at the scene with satisfaction. The pressurized oxygen tanks in the patient compartment fueled the fire, worsening the damage. Debris spread all over the tracks, including a tire that somehow landed upright. It would take the city hours to clear the tracks, forcing a stop of the incoming freight train. As he finished his thought, two police vehicles approached the tracks but parked far from them.

Kristap motioned to the crowd gathering with his palms raised and open. "Get back! The other vehicle is also on fire. It could go at any second."

One onlooker pointed behind him, "Then what about him?"

Kristap turned and saw a man wearing a wrinkly brown raincoat with long, raggedy hair. He stumbled in various directions while walking along the tracks. The wind blew his jacket back, revealing a body that appeared to have just emerged from a coal mine. He was approaching Kristap's ambulance but seemed to be unaware of the danger.

One police officer exited his vehicle, raising a megaphone to his mouth. Before getting a warning off, the second ambulance violently exploded, sending fragments in all directions and instantly decapitating the man in the brown jacket. His headless body took several seconds to react before it collapsed.

"Oh, my God!" yelled Kristap.

"That's going to delay things a bit," says Andrei.

"Jesus, Andrei, have some compassion."

As the crowd sought better views, Andrei and Kristap managed to avoid the authorities' questions. They both hurried to the nearby buildings to conceal themselves. They were to rendezvous with the rest of their team at Hotel Hetman, a short 10-minute walk from the train station.

"You did well, Andrei," says Kristap, "My brother would have just screwed things up, like usual."

"Thanks, appreciate it, but don't be so hard on your brother. He may not be the sharpest knife in the drawer, but it seems like he'd do anything for you."

"That's true and why I love him ... oh, and we had to hide the sharp knives from him as a child."

Andrei chuckled.

Kristap radioed the team at the hotel and told them the good news. The accident would force the train to stop at the station, giving them a chance to board illegally.

It took almost four hours to make the track safe again for passage. Nightfall was near, which gave them an added advantage since the train still hadn't left the station. By hacking into the train station's main ISP line, Kaspars disabled the cameras recording that day. Kristap could never understand how his brother was so technically savvy but had zero street smarts. They carried the tools they needed for tank repairs in backpacks, hoping that the replacement parts were onboard as the intel from Ukraine suggested. Leveraging a tree line to mask their staging area just northeast of the station, one by one, they boarded the train on various cars.

The tanks were on flatcars that were covered with large tied-down tarps to conceal them. Most repairs, unless it is exterior damage caused by battle, are fixable from inside the tank. This design maximizes protection for the operators when a vehicle breaks down behind enemy lines. General Petrovsky's plan relied on this to ensure the tanks were ready prior to them attempting an overthrow of the Estonian government.

Kristap and Andrei jumped onto the same flatcar and went inside the tank. It was like Christmas all over again. Boxes containing brand-new parts were already inside with a list of needed repairs. They high fived each other, then Kristap radioed the rest of the crew to check in. One by one, they confirmed the same good fortune. Out of the dozen tanks, only one was unrepairable, the one on the last flatcar. One of its tracks was missing, with a replacement in a large crate behind it. Both mechanics began working immediately and the train subsequently began moving. With their boarding going unnoticed and the work started, Kristap figured it was time to give the boss the good news.

CHAPTER
FORTY-ONE

UNDISCLOSED LOCATION, VIRGINIA

"Are the black bags over our heads really necessary?" Michael asks.

"Yes, seems like both of you are on somebody's shit list!" William kept checking the rear-view mirror. "If anybody saw us, they'll just think you two are prisoners. We're not ready to give you the intel on our headquarters here."

"My AIonic eye can see right through this bag."

"What?! I knew I should've read the field test results that Dr. Bell gave me more thoroughly."

The white Sprinter van headed for the end of a dirt path. Beyond it was a rushing creek at the edge of a dense green forest. William stopped the van short of the muddy bank that dropped about six feet. The sound of the water current was soothing to Jasmine.

"You can take them off now," says William. "You'll want to see this."

William took out his phone and entered a six-digit number, followed by the pound sign.

A twelve-foot-wide metal bridge protruded from a leafy bank on the opposite side and stopped right in front of the van. As it finished, trees across the creek started dropping into the ground like the earth was swallowing them up. A forest pathway appeared, extending for a couple hundred yards.

"You gotta be shitting me," says Jasmine.

William looked back. "Right? I was a little worried. That's only the second time I've activated the 'magical forest'."

The van proceeded into the forest as the bridge disappeared. As the van continued driving, the trees miraculously regenerated behind it until they arrived at a wooden shack that resembled a medieval outhouse. They exited the van and entered the small shack, barely fitting inside. A rusty potbelly stove stood in the center of the shack, its pipe extending to the ceiling.

"This is really quaint and all, Mr. Streeter, but couldn't we have just met at Langley?" asks Michael.

"Please, call me William and no. If you don't think the CIA has spies from other countries sharing our secrets, you better get that bionic brain of yours checked again."

"It's AIonic and—"

"Hold on!" William gripped the iron stove with his hands as the floor lowered. Michael and Jasmine caught on quick.

The ride down felt too fast for ASME's elevator standards. It didn't matter. Jasmine knew Streeter's money could buy any inspector's approval. It felt as if they went down five stories. The floor gradually slowed, then a set of double metal doors opened.

Jasmine's expectations were completely reversed. She had been in underground, dingy, dimly lit mines before, but this was the complete opposite. They entered a room three stories tall, resembling a Caribbean resort. Three towering coconut palm trees adorned the center lobby. The left side wall consisted entirely of tiny LEDs, resembling the rooms at the Necker facility but on a much larger scale. It was presenting a nearly perfect rendition of a beach in Thailand with limestone cliffs and rock formations. Jasmine recognized it as Phang Nga Bay, including the famous James Bond Island in the distance. An island scent carried on some sort of fake ocean breeze amused her nostrils.

"That's my tribute to the great double O," says William.

"I have to say, William, this is quite impressive! I've been in Fortune 100 office buildings that weren't this nice," says Jasmine.

"They say don't bring sand to the beach. For my lair, I literally had to. We have a couple of conference rooms that have floors filled with sand, and the ceiling lighting tans you at the same rate as the sun."

"How many people work here?"

"A few right now, but SIX will expand with time. Especially after the government sees what we can do. That's why I'm counting on you, Michael."

Michael huffed, "Hmmm"

"The Situation Room is right over here," William pointed ahead.

Michael whispered to Jasmine, "Situation room? Does this guy think he's the President?"

Upon William's entrance, the room illuminated, revealing a large glass table. The table displayed satellite images from various parts of the world and some notes scrolled on one side, providing localized news and updates on worldly conflicts, like the Russia-Ukraine war. William placed his hand down on the corner of the table. A green light scanned it from beneath the glass, bringing up more options, including a folder icon labeled SIX near Michael's side of the table. Michael pressed the folder, but nothing happened.

"Sorry, it only works with my fingerprints. It's what I like to call 'CA' or continuous authentication. Most secure systems leverage some sort of multi-factor authentication, including biometrics, but then the system is wide open. If you shot me in the head right after I authenticated using those methods, you'd have carte blanche access. My systems are more sophisticated," says William.

Leaning across the table, Michael opened the folder, and a sub-folder called "Warsaw East." Several windows appeared, including satellite footage of a freight train, a train station, and several local emergency response transcripts.

"NSA picked up an unusual amount of commercial radio frequency signals in the Warsaw area about eight hours ago. The signals had strong encryption, so decoding didn't work, but the type of encryption suggests military communication equipment. When we checked in with our contact at the Polish Armed Forces, they confirmed there were no planned or unplanned military exercises in the region. On top of that, a freight train made an unscheduled stop at the Warsaw East Train Station."

Michael's eyebrows furrowed. "Do we know why?"

"An accident caused an explosion, a subsequent fatality, and spread debris all over the tracks."

"A setup?" asks Jasmine.

"Most likely. They're still trying to identify the casualty. Witnesses observed two men leaving the scene of the accident. No one can confirm if they were drivers or passengers. Here's the weird part. The vehicles involved in the accident were two stolen ambulances from Latvia."

"What's the chances of that happening? It's definitely a setup." Michael pointed to the satellite photo tracing his finger over the multiple covered flatcars. "Do we know what the train was transporting?"

"No, but it appears big, and the last stop is the capital of Estonia. Cargo that size requires special equipment only available at the capital."

"So, you want us in Tallinn?" says Jasmine.

William nodded. "My jet is waiting at Williamsburg. Sadly, I can't take credit for being the namesake."

"Just us?" says Michael.

"Yeah, NSA doesn't want us to spook the Baltic state, but we'll have the rest of Silver Squadron on standby in Helsinki once you two report back."

"Ahh ... that's why she's here," Michael glanced at Jasmine, grinning.

Jasmine gave Michael a one-finger salute.

CHAPTER
FORTY-TWO

TALLINN AIRPORT, ESTONIA

A little girl with pigtails in front of Katya kept staring at her over the seat as they waited to disembark from the plane. Her mother was paying no attention to her as she was busy engaging with her phone's social media feed. Katya wore pants made of skin-tight spandex and a form-fitting dark grey V-neck sweater. Her black lipstick was the focus of the little girl's attention.

"What's your name?" asks the girl.

Katya tried to ignore her, but eventually looked up and says, "Semone. What's yours?"

"Alina,"

"You know that name means 'beautiful', right?"

The girl's eyes lit up and her lips curved upward. "Why are you only wearing one glove?"

Katya stared down at her left, augmented hand.

Because my boss is a cheap-ass!

"Looks funny, doesn't it? I recently had surgery on my hand and didn't want the scars to scare anyone."

"Can I see them? I think scars are cool," says the girl.

Katya smiled. She actually liked little people. It was the big people she despised with all their agendas and attitudes.

The best part of only having a carry-on was heading to the taxi line before the masses picked up their bags. She contemplated an Uber but didn't want any evidence of being in the capital, especially since she would revisit the capital in hopefully less than 12 hours. She noticed a white Toyota minivan pull up behind the row of taxis. There was an attendant there assigning passengers to vehicles. He gestured for Katya to choose the small yellow Honda, but she disregarded him and opted for the white one with tinted side windows.

"Hey, Lady. Wait!" The attendant started jogging toward her.

"Jogeva, please," says Katya as she entered the back seat with her travel bag.

"Already making friends, I see," says the taxi driver. "They don't like it much when you go out of order."

"As if it matters." Katya blew a kiss to the attendant, staring at their vehicle as they pulled from the curb.

"I'm Denys. Jogeva is about two hours away. You okay with the fare?"

Katya handed the driver three one-hundred-dollar bills through the small opening in the plexiglass shield that separated the front and back seats.

"Oh … okay … lots of American money, but you don't look American."

"What do I look like?"

"Maybe from my country, Ukraine," says Denys.

"Very close. Do you mind if I change back here? That plane was super crowded and stuffy."

"Uh … um … I can stop at a service station—"

"No time, sorry."

Katya pulled off her sweater and unsnapped her lace bra. Slouching farther down in the seat, she lifted her legs into the air till her toes touched the roof. Getting spandex pants off her moist skin underneath was not a simple task. She loved how the material felt like a second skin, so the short amount of inconvenience now was worth it. The tight pants left no room for underwear, and the cooler air inside the vehicle refreshed her privates.

"Phew! I could have used your help back here," she says.

The driver froze with an intense stare forward on the road.

"Denys, I don't mind if you look. I'm not embarrassed. Why should you be?"

"Okay, Miss—"

"Marek, Semone Marek."

The driver briefly looked back through the rear-view mirror and was visibly sweating. Katya opened her travel bag and pulled out a bag of baby wipes. She began wiping the back of her neck, then under her boobs and armpits. She caught Denys glancing back as she wiped her genitals, and the car began drifting out of its lane.

Katya smiled. "Watch the road, Denys."

"Sorry, Miss."

"Do you have garbage up there?"

"You … you can just leave them on the floor," says Denys.

Katya straightened her arms together, grabbing the edge of the seat, which pushed up her round breasts. The ambient air made her small nipples perk.

"Have you ever been with a Russian?" Her eyes piercing his face.

"No Miss, my wife just passed from cancer a year ago. With the war and all, I felt it was best to leave my home-land. That's when I explored jobs here. To answer your question, no."

He didn't even appear to notice the different skin color on her augmented arm. After a little more flirting, Katya got into a clean pair of pants and a similar material top adding a black leather combat-looking vest. She asked the driver to take her to the Kassinurme Fort. She convinced him she was a researcher doing a thesis on historic ruins in the Baltic States. An electric vertical takeoff and landing vehicle would be waiting there in the forest area nearby. One of GIP's cadets was guarding the area to make sure visitors did not wander near it and see the eVTOL. It took almost two hours to reach the ancient area.

"Here we are," says Denys. "You know, I hear it's much more beautiful in the summer. You're visiting during one of the coldest months."

"Yeah, well, my boss has me on a tight schedule. Do you mind taking me to the fort?"

Denys concentrated for a few seconds. "Sure, why not? My chances of finding a fare way out here are slim, plus yours was so generous."

The snow-laden path crumpled under their shoes as

they approached the sacred grove. All the trees' branches were baring the load of white powder. Katya saw a wooden tipi in the distance and then a large two-story log-cabin fort. The area appeared perfectly preserved from centuries ago. Deserted in winter, this tourist site served mostly as a summer destination. They entered the fort.

"Wouldn't it be hot to have sex right here? In a fort that has been standing for nearly 2000 years?" says Katya.

Denys was blushing more than the cold temperatures would cause. "Um … I guess, but it's freezing right now."

"Let's build a fire."

"Inside an ancient wooden fort, don't you think that's a little dangerous?"

"Sure, but haven't you ever taken risks in your life?"

"Not really."

"Come on, live a little," Katya smiled wide.

There were several firepit areas on the grounds with left over wood. They gathered some to use inside the fort. Katya opened her bag and pulled out a small flare, igniting it, then setting it under the pile of wood.

"Where did you get those?" says Denys.

"There was a camping store conveniently located in the airport. I guess visitors enjoy exploring the wilderness here."

Katya pretended to take some notes as she walked inside the fort, touching the logs in a couple of places. The fire burned strong and heated the interior nicely.

Katya turned around toward Denys, biting her thumbnail. "Now let me see the merchandise."

"Huh?"

"Get undressed, dummy. I have certain standards, you know."

Denys moved closer to the fire for warmth as he began peeling off layers of clothes down to his tighty-whities.

"Those too," she said, circling with her finger pointed at his pelvis.

Katya was impressed with his body, given his non-active profession. She licked her lips with her tongue as she approached him, staring directly into his eyes.

"Now ... close your eyes."

With her right hand, she seized his cock and with her left; she gripped the back of his neck. Moving her lips within inches of his, she let out a long breath and then snapped his neck easily with her bionic hand. His body fell into the fire, unable to move, unable to breathe or control his heart. The smell of burning skin irritated Katya's nostrils, and she exited the fort. Denys' eyes blinked, watching his killer leave as he slowly died.

CHAPTER
FORTY-THREE

SOMEWHERE OVER THE BALTIC SEA

Michael was admiring how peaceful Jasmine looked as she slept. Velvety skin accentuated each contour of her face, from her high cheekbones to the elegant line of her jaw. She had a natural radiance with an ethereal glow, complemented by full lips presently curved upward, a sign she was happily dreaming. He sometimes struggled to fathom how a stunning woman like her could be part of such grim tasks, yet she managed it with resilience and grace.

Sleep eluded him on planes, despite his efforts. On this private jet with spacious leather seats and generous legroom, his only accomplishment was a brief nap. This was after consuming half of a labeled bottle, bearing William's last name, but it wasn't enough to relax him. The bourbon offered a complex and rich taste that deeply satisfied Michael, but also made him envious. *This guy has his own brand of whiskey, too?*

"We should touch down in less than 20 minutes, Commander."

The pilot made the announcement over the cabin speakers, which woke Jasmine. She smiled at Michael as she straightened the back of her seat. She sipped some water from the bottle on the table next to her.

"Did you get any sleep?"

"A little," says Michael.

"What's the plan—"

Loud sirens sounded at the plane's front and back. The overhead lights turned from soft white to bright red. Michael and Jasmine's eyebrows scrunched, shifting their gaze from each other to the front. Michael unbuckled his seat belt and headed to the cockpit. He opened the door as the plane swerved left, nearly causing him to rip off the door with his body's momentum.

"Get back in your seat, Commander! We're under attack!"

"What?" says Michael, closing the door and heading back to his seat.

He glanced over at Jasmine, who was expecting an answer upon his return.

"Buckle-in tight, Ensign."

The plane started speeding up in a different direction and climbing. Michael pointed his super hearing to inside the cockpit.

"Tallinn Approach, our MAWS picked up an incoming threat, taking evasive action maneuvers," says the pilot on his headset.

Missile Approach Warning System? This plane has that?

Michael could feel his stomach drop as the plane changed direction again and dove. He had flown in an F/A-18 fighter jet before during practice maneuvers, but this private plane put it to shame. The leather seat's transformation impressed him as it went from wide to hugging his body tight while the plane was in duress.

He overheard, "Approach, deploying countermeasures."

"What did the pilot say?" asks Jasmine in a shrilled voice. "I know you're listening. Are we gonna die?"

"This bucket of bolts has countermeasures!"

"Countermeasures on a private jet?" asks Jasmine.

Intense brightness illuminated the cabin, followed by a thunderous explosion from behind the plane on the port side. A half a second after, shrapnel knocked out several windows behind Michael. As the plane straightened out, Michael looked out the window with disgust. The wing had large holes from the near-miss and was vibrating excessively due to its compromised integrity.

The pilot announced. "Commander, we just dodged a missile and need to land ASAP. The computer up here says the wing is oscillating ten times more than normal. If that wing shears off, we're dead."

What do you want me to do about it? Michael thought. *I don't even know how to pray for our survival.* Then he had an idea. Getting out of his seat, he scanned through the plane's fuselage and punched a hole to the outside near the floor. His hands widened the composite materials until the hole was about three feet high by three feet wide. He was about to stick his head into the hole when Jasmine yelled.

"What are you doing, Michael? Are you crazy?"

"Doing what has to be done."

He stuck his torso out of the plane to his waist and grabbed the wing with his left hand while holding the open hole in the fuselage with his right. The vibration slowed on the wing.

SIXAI: *Move to the left 12 inches to reduce the vibration by 11% more*

Michael shook his head. *Sure, I'm only halfway out of the plane. What's another foot going to hurt?* Squatting, Michael balanced on the wing with one foot and one hand, while gripping the fuselage with the other pair. The air was frigid as he tried to fight the air forces pushing his body off the wing. Suddenly, his body did not feel cold anymore. *That's odd*, he thought. He heard the pilot report they could touch down in three minutes. *If I can just surf this wing for a little longer, we might make it out of this.* He lifted with his outstretched hand and pressed down with his leg to reduce the wing vibration. His AI told him that the chances of this working was 89.254%.

Finally, the airport came into view. His night vision noticed a large lake before the runway. He immediately thought about the questions and media attention he would get if the emergency landing party saw him hanging out of a plane. Jasmine watched him with a look of horror from the window. As the plane dropped to 100 feet over the lake, Michael saluted Jasmine with a smile then jumped.

The water's impact resembled a plunge into a frozen lake. He swam fast towards the airport, only realizing the water's icy temperature when splashes hit his face. It was as if his body had sensed the extreme temperatures and turned on internal heaters. *That's a neat trick*, he thought. Steam rose off his clothes as he walked up the embankment. His augmented eye scanned the runway. There were emergency firetrucks and ambulances near the plane and its port-side wing was drooping onto the ground.

He checked his G-Shock watch and figured the train would arrive in probably six to seven hours. Jasmine and he planned to stay at a hotel called the Nordic during the mission. Their billionaire benefactor made the reservation for them when they were visiting his underground lair. He contemplated calling William and giving him a piece of his mind. Someone on the wrong side knew they were traveling to Estonia. Everything, including their hotel, could be compromised. All of Streeter's fancy and expensive building security was clearly not living up to the billionaire's expectations, but Michael was thankful that his jet was at least super high-tech. He pulled out his phone to send an encrypted text to Jasmine.

"Hotel is likely compromised. Meet me at Taanilinna Hotel."

CHAPTER
FORTY-FOUR

JOGEVA, ESTONIA

Katya drank a steaming cup of black coffee, the morning wind biting through her thin clothes. The countryside was quite majestic and while solid white now would be solid green in a matter of months. The previous night, she located the cadet's camp guarding the eVTOL. His sappy look made her think he hadn't talked to anyone in a couple days. While he wanted to stay with her, she forced him to leave. Her only desire was a serene night alone in the wilderness, devoid of chit-chat, advances, or companionship. An encrypted call came in.

"Mace, are you in position?"

"Good morning to you, too, General. Yes, since last evening. Do you have an E.T.A. for the train's arrival? Using my binoculars, I've spotted the station and estimated that descending the hillside will take 10-15 minutes. This gives me 10 minutes to get aboard before the battery dies."

"Excellent! The authorities are already skittish.

Someone burned down a sacred fort close to your position," says GIP.

"Really? I wondered about all that thick black smoke but was glad I wasn't downwind from it."

"We estimate an 8:20 a.m. arrival time at Jogeva and remember, the freight train will not stop. It made its scheduled stop in Riga for an inspection, and the team onboard remained incognito. Everything is going as planned. It's up to you now. Oh … and one more strange thing, but I took care of it."

"Why do I think that involves some kind of slaughter?" says Katya.

"We paid $5000 American dollars for a dark web tip that checked out. Some woman's sister who worked as a maid for an American billionaire overhead a conversation about a secret mission to Estonia. Last night, a private jet, owned by this billionaire, was scheduled to fly from Virginia to arrive in Tallinn earlier this morning. One of our patrol ships in the Baltic Sea identified it and eliminated it."

"Are you sure?" Katya's brow wrinkled.

"There's not a commercial or private plane on the planet that can outrun one of our SAMs. Our men reported a massive explosion in the night sky."

"That could have been *her*!"

"The Navy chick? Probably." says GIP.

"Too bad. I've been wanting to fight her since I saw her snide face back at the ranch in California."

"Did you see my upgrade to the flying car?"

"You mean the windshield? Yes, at least my face won't freeze."

"Well … if you dressed for the weather instead of a nightclub," snickered GIP.

"You're not my dad, no offense, General. When you use your body as a weapon, a big puffy jacket will not do!"

"Got it. Check in with me when you're aboard." With no pleasantries, the general ended the call.

At 0800 hours, Katya waited strapped inside the eVTOL and had already double-checked everything was operating nominally. She turned the vehicle towards the hillside to ensure a direct line of sight to the tracks by the station. To keep clear of the station so travelers would not spot the flying vehicle, she planned to wait until the train passed the station to start her descent. The diesel engine let out a distinctive series of long and short horn blasts as it approached. It penetrated and echoed through the hilly valley for miles.

Katya started the vehicle's eight propeller system. The snow on the ground danced in circles around her like a magic plume. As she ascended, the propeller noise amplified, and it scared a family of Skylark birds out of a nearby evergreen.

This was only the second time she flew this vehicle, but it felt comfortable. The controls were very responsive and a gauge on the small dashboard gave her continual battery readings, altitude, direction and speed. Animals scattered in all directions, disturbed by the sound that disrupted the usually tranquil meadow, as Katya's flight path approached them. The windshield helped reduce the cold air entering the cockpit, but it didn't matter much as the adrenaline rush warmed Katya's senses.

As she came within 100 yards of the track, the battery indicator warned it was at less than 25% capacity. *What the hell, it's only been 12 minutes since liftoff? Why do I continually trust Russian engineering?* She remembered researching the Swedish brand that this was a knock-off of. It claimed to have at least 30 minutes of airtime. She figured she had less than five minutes.

The eVTOL easily kept up with the train speed, but Katya knew that would also drain the battery faster. She saw a man waving from a Gondola car. It was Kristap. Gravel filled the car, which wouldn't make for the softest landing, but adequate. Only a few yards above the train, she realized it was the perfect time to evacuate. She caught up to the railcar, and Kristap ran towards the front as gravel started spewing dangerously in multiple directions from the nearby propellers. Unbuckling herself, she used a bungee cord to steady the directional joystick. Climbing out of the cockpit caused a weight shift, making the vehicle turn right and veer off the track. The battery gauge started flashing red slowly.

"SHIT! Damn you, GIP!"

She got herself on top of the rollbar near the center to level the vehicle and reached down to move the control, so it was at least flying parallel to the track. Her mind raced, searching for an escape plan to avoid being sliced up like deli meat. The battery gauge was now flashing quickly. Steading herself with one foot on each rollbar, she leaned to the left. The drone dipped and started turning toward the Gondola car. With a calculated leap, she landed feet first on the gravel, but the momentum caused her to fall onto her hands.

The eVTOL ascended a few feet, then its back propellers stopped, sending it into an uncontrolled descent right toward a herd of cows. The front propellers sliced right through two unsuspecting brown ones and knocked hard into three other black cattle, sending them rolling on their sides as the vehicle came to a rest in the farm.

"Jesus, Mace, are you alright?" says Kristap, trying not to fall as his boots slid on gravel as he approached.

"Better than those cows."

Kristap's eyes were wide open. "That was insane. I think you killed like four of them!"

"I didn't. The damn drone did. And the world should eat less red meat, anyway."

Kristap brought her to the flatcar, where men had gathered under the railcar's tarp and inside the tank. Katya requested Kristap instruct the men to exit the tank for a brief mission briefing.

"Team," she says, "we have less than an hour before we reach the turn to Tapa. The general wants us ready by then. Are all the repairs done?"

Andrei, the lead mechanic, spoke up. "We completed them in order from front to back, as instructed. We're currently working on the second to last one. As our last check-in reported, the ninth tank has a missing track and cannot be repaired without special equipment."

"Perfect, great job. Can you finish the last one before Tapa?"

"That should be just enough time."

"I need the rest of you inside the other tanks and ready

to roll them on my mark. Has anyone not had experience in a Leopard before?"

One cadet raised his hand, "I've driven a Bradley IFV, but not a Leopard."

Katya scanned the faces staring back at her. "Then you're a gunner, and you will drive with him," she pointed to a cadet she recognized as a driver in the mission briefing.

"Gentlemen, these tanks typically require a crew of four. We'll accomplish this mission with two operators, except for the trailing vehicles that will only have drivers. Cadets, pair up in the first five tanks and radio me when you have completed your prep work. Kristap, Kaspars and I'll drive the last three. Mechanics, get to work on tank eight. Latvia boys, I want all our extra weapons under the unrepairable tank nine. Can you handle that?"

"Why?" asked Kaspars. Kristap stared sternly at him.

"Do you normally question a superior's orders?"

"No ... I ... I'm just c-c-curious."

"If the mission goes south, we have a supply of weapons to fall back on and defend ourselves. Does that answer your question?"

"Yeah, but—"

Kaspars quickly grabbed his brother's arm to lead him to the flatcar transporting the last tank.

CHAPTER
FORTY-FIVE

TALLINN CITY CENTER, ESTONIA

Jasmine checked her Luminox watch. They had approximately two hours prior to the train's arrival. Despite Michael's advice, she stayed at their original hotel to freshen up. She hoped whoever attempted the attack on the plane would be there and she could practice some of her new judo moves on them. Before they noticed her, she was confident she would notice them. She possessed heightened awareness compared to most. Even at a young age, she remembered when her sisters would try to sneak up on her, but she always knew they were coming. It was like a sixth sense. They received new intel from Langley that the train's last stop was a train yard in the Ulemiste sub-district, so they planned a trip there. If there was a welcoming party waiting, they wanted to pass on the intel. She was outside Michael's hotel with the rental van and plenty of ammo.

"Did you catch any fish?" Jasmine asks as Michael got in the passenger seat.

"Is that really all you have to say after I risked my life to save yours?"

"It looked more like wind surfing to me. Isn't that a fun sport?"

"How about this? On the way home, I'll put you out on the wing."

"Well … we're gonna have to find an alternate way home. Streeter's $100 million jet ain't flying anytime soon," says Jasmine.

"Damn, that means we have to go back to economy class or worst, military class."

Jasmine chuckled, "Boo hoo! By the way, why didn't we stay near the airport?"

"The terminal is only 10 minutes away, besides you got to see the city."

"For a whole five minutes, while I pick your AIonic ass up. Can't you just jump from here to there with those fancy new legs?"

Michael's face soured. "Please don't speak of my technology in vain. It's hurtful. And no, it would probably take me a half dozen jumps."

"Back to business. I noticed a large police presence at the airport, and I bet they were preparing to receive the shipment. The train yard for cargo transfers is just north of the terminals. Let's see if the area looks secure."

It took nine minutes to reach T1 Center, a shopping mall in Tallinn near the Ulemiste train yard. They parked in an adjacent lot near a tram stop. This gave them direct access to the back of the yard. As Michael moved to the back of the van, his eyes widened.

"Where did you get all this? You've only been here, what, four hours?"

Rifles, machine guns, grenades, and pistols lined one wall inside the van. It also included two rocket-propelled grenade launchers. The Heckler & Koch USP handgun caught Michael's eye, but he picked up one of the RPGs first.

"Let's leave those. We don't want to draw any attention just yet. Just take what you can carry," says Jasmine.

"So now you're giving *me* orders, because I'm technically not part of the Navy anymore?"

"Just saying what you were thinking, Commander," she says, smiling. "In my mind, you're a double agent, providing intelligence for SIX, but loyal to the Navy."

"Uh … that's not the real meaning of a double agent."

They double-timed it to the yard. It had warmed up unseasonably and the snow on the ground was melting, making the ground soggy. This softened their steps which slowed their progress. They stayed out of sight, leveraging some of the construction areas and trees at the terminal. The train yard was still, except for the activity near a switch that redirected the main track to the yard. Michael recognized the uniforms as the Estonian Defence Forces mixed in with some local police. The uniform's camouflage pattern, known as ESTDCU, showcases a blend of green, brown and black, reflecting the temperate forests and woodlands of the country. They were congregating around a large crane, like the ones found in coastal shipyards. It appeared to be a temporary fixture placed there just to remove the expected cargo. Next to the crane was a line of heavy-duty trailer trucks. More were arriving as they observed.

"Okay, so we know the train wasn't just transporting commercial equipment. This looks like a military operation," says Michael.

"And we found out this train load originated in the Ukraine." Jasmine pulled out her binoculars for a closer look.

"Seems like the President is providing military aid to Estonia, but why?"

SIXAI: Estonian Defence Forces (Led by Major General Siim Nurk).

•Approximately 7000 active personnel

•Branches include Army (Maavägi), Navy (Merevägi), Air Force (Õhuvägi)

•Strengths: Member of NATO, highly trained, rapid response

•Weaknesses: border with Russia, no fighter jets, few MBTs (main battle tanks)

Michael grabbed Jasmine's arm to get her full attention. She jerked it back.

"Geez, Michael, you need to be careful with that super grip of yours."

"I think the train is carrying tanks. Estonia doesn't have any MBTs in their arsenal. Not sure why Ukraine is providing them, but I bet that's what's hiding under the covered train cars. It all makes sense now. That's why the

Defence Forces are here, along with the crane and cargo vehicles."

"Okay, so we flew 5000 miles here to witness a transaction between two European countries. Why is our government spooked?"

"Maybe we're just some glorified babysitters. Who knows? Let's ensure the rest of the grounds are clear—just a moment. I'll be right back. I hear something," says Michael.

Before Jasmine could even say anything, Michael was running along the property line, taking cover behind some trees and heading to the area where they parked. When she looked over her right shoulder to locate him, he had vanished. Jasmine shook her head. "I knew we should have taken the IEMs to communicate."

Michael found a little girl in pigtails crying in front of the nearby Hansa Apartment complex. He slowed down not to scare her. She was speaking in Estonian, which Michael didn't know, but his AI translated it for him.

"Come on Frisky, come down … come down boy," she says.

"I'll get him," says Michael.

Michael leaped 25 feet into the air, landing on a tree branch below the one that held a medium-sized, golden orange Bengal cat frozen into a crouched pose with his tail tucked close to his body. He slowly raised both hands.

"Come here, I got you."

With that, the kitty relaxed, and Michael could gently take him off the branch. He jumped slightly away from the tree and landed about six feet from the girl.

"Here you go."

"Thank you, mister," she says, "he's always getting himself into trouble."

"Oh, don't be too hard on him. Everyone gets scared of heights sometimes."

The girl's eyes dried up as she kissed the feline. As she looked up again, a breeze swept her hair back, and the person who saved Frisky disappeared.

"You wanted these," says Michael, handing an earpiece to Jasmine.

"Okay, we're going to have to improve our communication here. You can't keep vanishing and reappearing. Where did you go?"

"Oh, it's not important. Can you finish checking the perimeters? I need to report back to SIX to give them our update. I'll monitor you just in case."

Michael pulled out his satellite phone and called William via a secure uplink. Waiting for his benefactor to pick up, he watched as Jasmine ran in a low-profile posture to the other end of the train yard.

"Is Estonia nice this time of year? I've never been," inquired William.

"Hilarious, it's dead of winter. At least it's warmer today. My body is self-adjusting."

"Uh-huh, I finally got to that part of Dr. Bell's feature report. It only works for raising your temperature, not lowering it. So don't go throwing my investment into a pit of molten steel."

His investment? Does he think he owns me?

"I called to give you a report. We think the train is carrying tanks as the receiving party here is military. Can you check in with our friends in the Ukraine?"

Streeter sighed. "I already did. They didn't want to volunteer any information. Maybe they were worried it would leak out. Now that I have better intel to go on, I'll bug them again."

"Jasmine and I'll monitor the premises for any unwelcomed guests. The train should arrive in an hour or less."

"Stay safe. Will check back with you soon. Keep your phone linked."

Michael quickly scanned the entire train yard with his AIonic eye and found Jasmine near some buildings on the east end of the yard. He moved quickly but carefully along the concrete wall enclosing the yard to avoid detection by the Estonian personnel. Jasmine waved him over to an enclosure she was hiding behind that was used for the building's waste receptacles. Her gaze remained fixed south of the yard at a distant parking lot.

"Streeter's checking on our tank theory. Notice anything unusual?" says Michael.

"See that parking lot north of the road, but parallel to the yard? It has two silver sedans with their engines running. I know this because it's cold, and I see the water vapor steaming off the exhaust."

"Anybody get out or come in them?"

"Negative. And the tinted windows make my binoculars useless," says Jasmine.

"I might be able to help with that."

Michael poked his head out from behind the wall in front of them. Using his x-ray vision, Michael tried to penetrate the metal and tinted glass. The distance impacted the efficacy of his vision.

Jasmine's pulse skipped as she watched Michael retreat

back quickly, falling on his ass. His face turned white, and his stare was ominous.

"What? What did you see?" she exclaimed.

Michael kept staring at the wall. "It's GIP."

"Who?"

Michael turned his head to her slowly. "General Ivan Petrovsky."

CHAPTER
FORTY-SIX

The warmer temperature melted the remaining snow that hadn't blown off the top of the train cars. Katya's trip to the engine became even more menacing. Her right boot slipped off the top of the boxcar, but luckily her bionic hand was able to grip into the slippery metal roof, nearly piercing through it to catch herself. She steadied herself again and checked her watch. Their arrival at the turn in Tapa was in less than 25 minutes.

Now crouching above the engine, she contemplated her next move as the cold air pushed on her body. Typically, two crew members operated a freight train—an engineer and a conductor. She needed the train to make it to Tallinn, but she didn't want them to warn anyone. She needed to keep at least one of the crew alive. Despite her new arm's ability to break through the cab door easily, she chose not to do so to avoid being detected by the external cameras. The side windows were too small for a surprise entrance, so she opted for the rectangular front ones. She hoped the metal handlebar above the window would support her weight.

Pulling out her Makarov, she fired into the front window, shattering most of it. With an acrobatic move, she grabbed the top bar and slung her body inside, boots first. The men had already retreated backward into the cab from the blown-out window. One man bravely approached her, and Katya whipped her body around until her long braid was flying horizontal. The mace ball at the end dug deeply into his face, ripping off most of his mouth. He fell in agony. The second man raised his hands. She approached him and swiftly put an end to the first man's misery with a shot to his temple.

"Tell me you're the engineer," she says.

"What d-d-do you w-w-want?" he stutters.

"For you to operate this train."

"But you just killed the engineer." The man's raised hands were shaking.

Darn, I had a 50-50 chance. Maybe I should ask before I act, thought Katya.

"Well, you may be the conductor, but I'm sure you've learned a thing or two working with him. Now, your life depends on it. Give me your phone and show me where the radio is."

The conductor slowly grabbed his phone from his back pocket, keeping his other hand in the air. He handed it over and pointed to a panel on the wall. Katya walked over and punched the panel with her left hand. Sparks flew in every direction. She then reached inside and yanked hard on some wiring.

Glancing back at the conductor, "Are you left-handed or right-handed?"

"What?" he asks.

"Simple question, dude."

"Rr-ri-right."

With a quick, uncaring motion, Katya jerked his arm and secured his left hand with handcuffs to a metal handlebar on the wall.

"Can you operate the train from here?"

"I guess."

"Don't stop this train under any circumstances till we get to Ulemiste, got it?"

"Yes, Ma'am."

"Not that old, darling."

"Apologies, miss."

Katya searched the dead engineer for his personal phone and then, putting one phone on top of the other, placed them in her left hand. She closed her grip slowly and watched as they crumbled like aluminum foil. Smiling, she opened the cab's exterior door and started back to her team.

To shield some of the wind noise, she stopped between two boxcars and pulled out her walkie talkie.

"Mace to Kristap, do you copy? Over."

"Kristap here. Over."

"Are the weapons in place? Over."

"Yes. Mechanics are just about finished with tank eight. It required repairs inside to some of the control levers. Over."

"Meet me at the Gondola car in front of tank eight's flatcar and bring me an RPG. Over."

"Copy that, Mace. Anything else? Over," says Kristap.

"Negative. Mace out."

As Katya reached the car, she waved to Kristap to join her on top of the flatcar connected in front of the Gondola car. As he treaded toward her position, she checked her watch. Less than 10 minutes to Tapa. She glanced toward the front of the train, extending her neck to view the right side. She could see the train yard in the distance. As Kristap got to her end of the car, she reached for the RPG.

"Pass me that and come over," she says.

Kristap made his way over the front edge of the Gondola and gingerly walked across the coupling area to join Katya.

Raising her voice in the brisk wind, "I need you to tell me when you think that train yard is three football pitches away or like 300 meters, okay? Yell the word 'Now', got it?"

Kristap's eyebrows furrowed with deep vertical lines between them, but he nodded. With his back to Katya, she positioned herself on the flatcar's buffer beam so she could reach the coupler's locking pin. She disengaged the locking pin and ripped off the pneumatic braking tube. She purposely chose the lighter car because she knew her arm had no chance of lifting a flatcar with a 60-ton tank on it. With her bionic arm, she grabbed the bottom of the knuckle coupler that was connected to the Gondola car. She tried to lift it, but it didn't budge.

Crap! Plan B.

She grabbed the hinge pin as tightly as she could with her augmented fingers.

"Now!" yelled Kristap.

Katya pulled on the hinge pin with her mechanical hand

until the force caused the cast steel to succumb. The pin's removal caused the spring-loaded knuckle jaw to open, separating the two train cars. Katya climbed back up to Kristap.

"What are you doing?" exclaimed Kristap. "Those cars will derail on the turn!"

"What must be done."

Kristap grabbed Katya at both shoulders with his hands. "My brother is still in tank eight with the mechanics!"

"Oh, well ... too late now," she says.

As the freed back cars approached the 90-degree turn of the track, the momentum and weight behind the Gondola car caused it to derail and head toward the nearby train yard. The flatcars holding the heavy tanks maintained their velocity.

As Kristap watched intently, a smoke-filled trail passed by his left ear, causing him to jerk right. With a deafening roar, the weapon supply ignited in a blinding flash of orange and white as the RPG landed under tank nine. The explosion propelled the tank off the flatcar and toward a stationary line of engines in the yard. The rest of the cars started tumbling and rolling to join the tank.

"No!!!" Kristap reacted, putting his hands behind his head.

The thunderous cacophony of metal ripping through metal got softer as the front of the train kept moving down the track toward Tallinn. Katya lost track of the cars from their train as the flames surged higher, engulfing the train yard and sending billowing plumes of thick black smoke skyward. The scene was one of apocalyptic grandeur and she felt satisfied with her work.

As the chaotic scene blurred from vision, Kristap turned around to Katya, his mouth curved downward, his eyes red and glassy.

"Why?" he says.

"The general needed a distraction."

"Why didn't you let me in on the plan?"

"Would you really have gone for it? In the short time I've been here, I've noticed how friendly you and your brother are with those mechanics. The general doesn't like any loose ends, no matter the cost. Unfortunately, your brother got caught in the crossfire. Is this going to impair your work going forward? If it is, I'll toss you off this train right now."

"My brother was all I had." Kristap looked down at his feet.

"Need an answer, Kristap! We'll be at our final destination in less than an hour."

Kristap paused for a minute and appeared to clench his fingers deep into his palms. He gazed for several seconds at the now distant train yard. He looked back at Katya to respond, tears welling up at the corner of his eyes.

"Don't worry about me." He turned and walked toward the end of the railcar while whispering, "Russia will pay for this."

CHAPTER
FORTY-SEVEN

ULEMISTE TRAIN YARD

"I know you want to run over there and rip his head off, but he's just a puppet," says Jasmine.

"How do you know? The paramilitary is unpredictable and has been known to act independently." Michael peered around the structure for a second look.

"We don't even know what's happening here. Let's wait for more intel."

Michael's AIonic eye caught the darkened smoke in the far distance to the east. SIXAI quickly analyzed that based on its formation, color hues and density, it wasn't from a factory.

"What the hell is that?" Michael pointed to the horizon.

Jasmine looked over. The overcast skies masked the smoke, but it looked darker.

"I can't see like you can. Is that a fire?"

. . .

SIXAI: *Petrodiesel fire origin near town of Tapa (88.7% probability)*
   •Distance as the crow flies: 67.75 KM
   •Distance by land transport: 92.46 KM

"A big one near the town of Tapa," says Michael.

The satellite phone blipped. It was William Streeter. Michael answered with the speaker phone setting.

"Michael here. Do you have an update?"

"Yes, and then some. We just got reports of several enormous explosions at a train yard about 70 clicks southeast of you."

"Yes, Jasmine and I were just discussing—"

As if the Estonia personnel at the train yard were listening in on their encrypted call, they started scrambling. Michael observed an authoritative figure directing and pointing men in different directions.

"The local police are mobilizing. They're splitting up the team here. What about the train cargo? Any update on that?"

Streeter cleared his throat. "Yes, we confirmed Ukraine is giving nine tanks that need repair to Estonia. We aren't sure what they're getting in return. Seems like we sent you both on a wild goose chase."

"Maybe not," says Michael. "Guess who is here observing the transaction?"

"Russia?"

"General Petrovsky."

"Not good," says Streeter. "Maybe he's just a distraction from the chaos east of you."

"What are the satellites showing?"

"We won't have one in range for another hour."

"I get can there faster than that," says Michael.

"Okay but leave Jasmine there. Report in once you get there."

"Affirmative. Out."

Jasmine smiled. "Taking orders from the playboy billionaire now?"

"I did some research on him. Did you know he spent nearly ten years in the Marines when he was younger? He actually made it to the rank of major before going into software development."

"Interesting."

Michael handed Jasmine the phone.

"Keep your earpiece in. I'll update you when I get there. Even at my speed, it'll be difficult to reach the smoking train yard and return before the shipment arrives."

"Don't worry, Commander. Remember, our squadron is nearby across the Gulf of Finland. We have backup," says Jasmine.

Michael, unfamiliar with the country, relied on his heightened senses to find a discreet and low-profile path east. By sensing the noise vibrations, he chose the less crowded countryside. Sometimes, instead of changing direction, like when he came upon a busy highway, he opted to leap over it. It was like playing hopscotch as a kid, but instead of one-foot squares, his jumps were city block squares. While fun, his unfamiliarity with the ability ended up in several bad landings, causing him to tumble head over heels. Luckily it happened in most of the grassy fielded areas. The billowing smoke made his target easy to redirect to, and he reached it in a mere 25 minutes.

The local Tapa police were already onsite, along with some fire engines that were trying to prevent the fire from spreading. It appears a fiery ball, the size of a house, had rolled through the train yard. Some engines and cars were displaced from their tracks, while others remained ablaze. The local responders' priority appeared to focus on the site's personnel and assets, but Michael had a different objective.

Why did part of the train derail? And why does this smell like military-grade explosives?

He kept out of sight by dashing to the ultimate resting place of the charred tanks. Nobody onsite was focused on the tanks, given the impeding disruption this would cause to the rail freight transportation business. Even through the crackling sound of the existing fires and hissing roar of the rescue water as it whooshed upon overheated surfaces, Michael overheard that no workers in the yard sustained injuries.

That's a relief.

Tank one was missing a track and upside down. The underbelly had a hole in it at least six feet in diameter. The tank's bottom was vulnerable, but the scale of destruction showed an extraordinary force. Nothing appeared to be inside except small fires that lingered as they pulled oxygen in from the air outside.

Charred black, the second tank lay on its right side amidst debris and smoke. Michael started choking and lifted his undershirt to cover his mouth and nose.

That's weird! I can't see through it.

It was as if his x-ray vision automatically turned off. He

knew the vision's effectiveness decreased with distance, but anything nearby was fair game until now.

SIXAI: *Composite NERA (non-explosive reactive armour)*
•600 mm (24 in) RHAe (rolled homogeneous armour equivalency)
•Steel and ceramics composite, hardened by a heat-treatment process

Okay ... noted ... two feet of metal, BAD news for my x-ray eyes!

He moved over to the driver's hatch at the front of the hull and easily ripped it open from its locked position. The next thing he saw was gruesome.

Three bodies lay there in various positions, their skin charred and shrunken around their muscles. The epidermis layer appeared like a dried apricot, only black, not orange. Their white teeth protruded out of their heads more than normal. Their grisly faces appeared to have all the volume sucked out of them. Michael quickly made the sign of the cross.

Despite its grotesque appearance, one face had sufficient features for his AI to generate a potential victim's name.

SIXAI: *Victim's name: Andrei Zinchenko (91.8% accuracy)*
•Born February 24th, 1980 in Kharkiv, Ukraine

•Married to Olena Zinchenko with two kids, 5 and 8 years old

•Address: Unknown

•Political Affiliation: Opposition Platform - For Life (secret)

•Religious Affiliation: Unknown

•Occupation: Mechanic - Armed Forces of Ukraine

•Awards: Medal "For Impeccable Service"

Mechanic? Oh, shit!

"Jasmine, do you copy?"

Nothing but a blip returned.

"Dammit, Ensign, do you copy?"

"Ensign here. Over."

"We have a serious situation here. I think all those tanks are operational. Over."

"Did you say operational? But—"

"Yes, alert the Silver Squadron. Tell them to bring ATMs. I'll get there as fast as I can. Over."

"Fuck!" replied Jasmine.

"What?"

"The freight train is arriving, and those tanks are no longer covered with tarps!"

CHAPTER
FORTY-EIGHT

5HRS EARLIER AT MARCH AIR RESERVE BASE, CALIFORNIA

Martha slid her fingers over the scabs on her right arm from her hostage ordeal. The temporary skin was so thick it felt like raised lettering on one of her scrapbooks back home. It was a beautiful evening in the center courtyard as she sipped some iced tea that one of the MPs had brought to her from the kitchen. A gentle breeze brought on a chill to her skin, and she grabbed the sweater that was wrapped around the back of her chair. As she did, she got the attention of the guard behind her.

"How much longer before my ride gets here?"

"Sorry, Ma'am, he's on the way. Captain Donnelly specifically requested that only he drives you to ensure your safety," says the guard.

"But my prayer group starts in a half hour, and it takes a half hour to get there."

"I'm sorry, Ma'am, orders are orders. He should be here soon."

About five more minutes passed by when Captain Donnelly entered the courtyard frantically.

"Sorry, Ms. Cooling. The 215 was jammed at this hour. Are you ready to go?"

"Son, sorry ... Captain, I was ready 15 minutes ago. I thought the Navy taught you boys about time management."

"My mistake, Ma'am, here. Let me help you."

Martha was still not moving at full speed after her ordeal and her left arm had bandages wrapped around it. The captain helped her out of the patio chair and walked with her, interlocking his arm with hers until he could open his car's passenger door. Martha thanked him before he shut the door.

"Do you have the address?" asks the captain.

Martha handed him a piece of paper that he recognized being from the base's stationary.

Martha knew the captain from several events she attended while her son Michael reported to him. He would often discuss insignificant matters, such as a kid leaving chewing gum on a gasoline handle that eventually ended up on the captain's hand. On another occasion, he shared his online dating attempt, where women showed interest only when he promised a full dinner for the first date. Today, he was uncannily quiet. In addition, Martha noticed sweat dripping down his sideburns even though the evening was now below 60 degrees.

"Is something troubling you, Captain Donnelly?"

"Why do you ask?"

"Just woman's intuition—oh! ... you missed the exit for my church."

"Sorry, Ma'am. I'll get off at the next one and turn back."

The captain drove the car onto the off-ramp, which lacked any street lighting. He smacked his phone connected to a dashboard phone holder twice.

"Come on GPS! Is there any provider with reliable coverage these days?" he says.

The captain parked on the side of a road with industrial buildings and empty lots because of the late hour.

"Just one second, Ma'am. Let me fix this phone. We have to be close."

Martha slid the arm of her sweater back to check the time on her watch. Her grandmother had handed down this special watch to her. Despite the worn gold plating and the need for daily hand-winding, Martha loved it. She figured it kept her mind sharper by having to remember to wind it. She didn't enjoy being late to her group, and the captain's lack of urgency was getting on her nerves.

"Do you mind if I pull into one of these open lots?" he asks. "I think I'll get a better signal than near this concrete freeway."

"You know you can download an entire Google map of an area to your phone in case your signal gets lost, right?" Martha smiled with a head tilt.

"Wow, how do you know more about tech than me?"

"Michael is a protective son," she proudly responded with a smile.

"Can I use your phone instead?"

Martha searched through her purse, "I turned it off, so I'm not disturbed during reflection, but, sure, here you go."

The captain handed it back. "Sorry, can you unlock it?"

Martha typed in her 6-digit code since her facial recognition didn't work after a fresh phone boot. She handed it back to the captain, who was already pulling into the middle of a semi-lit parking lot. As he configured the GPS, Martha's door opened abruptly.

Everything went dark for Martha as she felt a fibrous bag cover her head. It had a chemical and earthy combined smell. Four hands forcefully removed her body before she could even scream for help.

"Captain! Help!"

Her hands were zip-tied behind her just before she felt the slippery and cold plushy feel of leather. The sound of a large car door closing was startling. Outside the vehicle, she heard mumbling, but no attempt to rescue.

Dear Lord! My son's old boss has given me up. But why? Jesus, Michael, what on earth did you do to piss off these people so badly?

The sound of a door slightly further from Martha opened. She could hear the traitor's car drive away on the asphalt. Two guys with thick European accents were saying something to each other.

One of them spoke broken English, "Don't worry, lady, we aren't going to kill you … yet!" The man burst out with a diabolical laugh.

"Don't scare her," says the other man. "She'll lose bladder control on my Corinthian leather. Do you know how long it took me to get the blood out last week?"

"Maybe you shouldn't drive such a fancy SUV."

"Shut-up, Leonid. I have a reputation to uphold with the ladies."

"You mean the horse-face one you were with last week?"

The SUV pulled out of the parking lot.

"Can I get buckled in, please?" Martha asks. "Your boss might be unhappy if you lose your prize too early in the game."

Leonid grunted. "Stop the car!"

The car slowed, one door opened, followed by another on Martha's right side. The heavy breathing man repositioned Martha, and she felt the belt pull across her body. As soon as she heard the click, she pressed down hard on the floor with her right foot and sent her left knee flying upward. It caught Leonid right in the nose, instantly causing it to gush blood.

"You bitch!"

CHAPTER
FORTY-NINE

ULEMISTE TRAIN YARD

Jasmine tried ringing her commanding officer, but there was no response. She had to alert the Silver Squadron as soon as possible. The train was getting ready to move backward into the receiving track, where the military presence and large crane were located. She made a call to her Vice Admiral.

"Vice Admiral Jackson here, this is a surprise."

"No time for pleasantries, Vice Admiral. Are you in Helsinki, sir?"

"No, but Captain Donnelly should be. Everything okay?"

"We have reason to believe the Russians are attempting to steal a Ukrainian tank shipment that just arrived here in Tallinn. The captain is not answering. Michael and I need support now!"

"Affirmative."

"Please have them bring anti-tank missiles. There are

over a half-dozen Leopard 2s that were delivered. Mr. Streeter said they needed repair per the bill of lading, but Michael just found a dead mechanic at the site of the explosion near Tapa. Seems like the Russians are already cleaning up loose ends."

"Not good, Ensign. We have a carrier in the North Sea. I'll also alert them to the situation. Give me a SITREP in 30 minutes."

As Jasmine went to end the call, she noticed a missed text message from Martha. When she opened the app, it read, *Hi Jasmine, I'm staying with a church friend. Had to get away from that boring base. Hope all is well.* She tucked her phone away. Jasmine thought it was odd that it came in at midnight. She knew Martha was one of those early to bed, early to rise people.

She glanced back over at the train. Estonian military led more trailer trucks into the area, while others chatted and smoked cigarettes, waiting for the slow-moving train to back up. Suddenly, two of the tanks' turrets rotated. No one noticed but Jasmine.

Oh no!

She got up from her hidden position and started running as fast as she could, waving her arms at anyone who would notice while yelling, "Hey! Hey!"

As a few of the men noticed her quickly moving toward them, she pointed both hands at the tanks. The turrets stopped turning as their guns locked on target. The 120mm cannons fired two HE-frag rounds that exited the muzzle at 850 m/s. The rounds were set to air burst mode and, as they exploded, sent 2500 flaming fragments into the crowd of men and line of trucks. Jasmine went diving into the dirt to escape being shredded.

As she glanced up, she watched in horror as some men ran around on fire before eventually collapsing. The nearest trailer truck exploded, ejecting its driver into the flames engulfing the crane. The tanks' right tracks reversed as dirt and smoke hindered Jasmine's view. As each tank left their flatcars, they formed a two-by-two formation, assembling on the northern side of the train track. The surviving soldiers of the Estonian Defence Forces began firing their rifles at the tanks, which made a repeating ricocheting sound but only caused the turrets to fire a second round in their direction.

The seventh tank broke from formation and headed straight at the men, who bravely stood their ground. Unlike tanks in old movies, the newer ones had no windows or portholes. They used cameras and laser rangefinders for accurate target detection. Two men who dropped their rifles to escape appeared to be deliberately run over by the tank.

"Michael, come in. Over." Jasmine pulled out her Glock and crouched down.

"Please tell me that smoke isn't where you are. Over." he says.

"Yes, and it's worse. The tanks are on the move."

"Which way are they headed? Is the Squadron on its way?"

"Northwest. All of this is happening so fast. Command is probably just getting the message. How far away are you?"

"10 minutes, tops, but wait—"

Jasmine heard a strong wind noise then what she thought sounded like a cow.

"Sorry, had to dodge a farm. I freaking almost ran right through a herd of cows," says Michael. "Tanks going northwest might target the Prime Minister's residence. Shit … that's just a few miles from the train yard."

Jasmine swallowed hard. "They're planning a coup! At the speed these tanks can travel, they'll be there in less than five mikes."

"I'll meet you there. Be careful. Alert the squadron. I can't run that fast and dodge things while talking. I've gotta concentrate on what's ahead of me at these speeds. Out."

Jasmine watched as the tanks easily broke through the concrete wall at the back of the train yard. She couldn't keep pace, with their 40-mph speed, on foot. Her best bet was to follow their path of destruction by car and hopefully not get noticed. It had only been 10 minutes, but she called into the vice admiral again.

"Situation has deteriorated, Admiral. The tanks are mobile and on their way to the Stenbock House. If they follow a direct path line, it could be minutes before they reach Toompea Hill. Over."

"Good grief. I'll redirect the squadron there. Reaching out to the Prime Minister now. Satellite coming in range shortly, after which we'll send out a few drones from the aircraft carrier."

"Careful, Admiral, from my research, historic buildings and landmarks populate the area. Not to mention the civilian residences because of the beautiful views from the hill. We don't want to start a war in the capital."

Admiral Jackson responded with a sigh. "The Russians already did."

CHAPTER
FIFTY

SOMEWHERE NEAR SAN BERNARDINO, CALIFORNIA

Martha realized they hadn't traveled far because the drive was short, and the constant noise of airplanes indicated she was near an airport. She was glad they took off the nasty smelling bag and wrist bindings, but they locked her in a dingy storage room. There were shelves of small automobile parts that permeated the air with an oily metallic stench. There was only one tiny, frosted window in the corner that wasn't meant to open. She thought about breaking the window for fresh air, but it wouldn't help. It wasn't large enough to even consider an escape. The door unlocked.

It was Captain Donnelly. She lunged at him.

"Easy, woman!" Chase says.

The thugs that kidnapped her quickly moved around Chase and restrained her.

"How could you betray your own country?" Martha asks.

"We just need an insurance policy in case your wonder boy tries to foil the general's plans in Estonia. This will be all over soon enough. I believe they're raiding the capital as we speak."

"What general?"

"General Ivan Petrovsky and his elite Russian paramilitary."

"So, the oath you took to defend the Constitution means nothing? What reason do you have to do this?" Martha's eyes furrowed.

"I have 25 million reasons why I'm helping them. I'm retiring early," says Chase.

"That's blood money. Many will die, including Americans."

"When you've been in the military as long as I have, you experience so much death and destruction, it calluses your senses. Nothing phases me anymore, but I would like to live out the rest of my life surfing in the Caribbean and getting daily massages from hunks."

Upon hearing this, both Martha and the SUV driver's nose crinkled up. Leonid smiled widely.

Chase continued. "We thought we got rid of Michael over the Baltic Sea but later found out they somehow landed a plane with only one wing. His AIonics have proved quite useful. Too bad, the billions spent on him are for naught."

Martha pulled forcefully away from the henchmen but could not escape their grip.

"What else have you done?" Martha shouted.

"I just gave the general some important details about Michael's hardware."

Martha's eyes filled with tears. "How could you, Captain? My son has followed your orders for over five years. Has he ever disrespected you?"

Chase began pacing around the room, picking up a shock absorber from the shelf. He smacked the part on his other hand as he paced like he was holding a baseball bat.

"You're right, Mother Martha. Michael has been the perfect soldier, but therein lies the problem. He can do nothing wrong in the eyes of leadership. Do you think the Vice Admiral would nominate me, even once, for a medal? I commanded all of Michael's recent successful missions. The Medal of Honor he received recently, that was my planned incursion! He would never have reached those paramilitary cadets in time if it weren't for the intel I provided on the Ukrainian President's whereabouts. To make matters worse, they transformed him into a super soldier, even though I have at least six more years of experience."

The corners of Martha's mouth turned downward as her lips pursed. "You sound like a sulking child."

With a wide-eyed, crazed look, the captain leaped in front of Martha and stuck the end of the shock absorber into her nose. "Yes, Mother, but now I'll be a spoiled child. I've had enough of this petty conversation. Let's go, boys."

"I have to use the bathroom," says Martha.

Chase grabbed an empty gasoline tank from the bottom of a nearby shelf.

"Here! Use this."

He pushed the can into her chest, forcing her to grab it with both hands.

As he headed toward the door, he turned back.

"Oh, yeah … here's your phone back."

The captain tossed the phone at her feet. Its shattered appearance made it look like it went through a meat grinder. He threw her plastic phone case next as it slid next to the phone.

"Sorry about its condition. We wouldn't want the GPS antenna inside to alert anybody, but at least you can reuse that fancy flowery case." Chase's laugh echoed through the room as he exited.

CHAPTER
FIFTY-ONE

ULEMISTE TRAIN YARD

Sirens pierced the air from multiple directions as emergency vehicles converged on the fire in the train yard. Jasmine retreated toward the van they parked outside of the train yard. She observed the sedans, one transporting GIP, pull out of the parking lot. She deduced he was there to oversee the proper execution of his plan. Taking him out was an option, but the Squadron required ground surveillance and help in case the tanks breached the government building. As she ran out of the train yard, a loud metallic creaking noise filled the air. The giant crane collapsed on top of two of the trailer trucks. It sliced their beds in half like it was going through warm butter.

The tanks' track marks showed them passing by the Skywheel of Tallinn attraction and heading through the back parking lot of a business complex, which included a Kia automobile dealer. The tanks crushed several of the new cars for no reason. Despite not having a visual on the tanks, Jasmine knew their priority was finding a paved road for maximum speed. She headed toward Route 2, which led northwest toward the government buildings. With the Leopard tank's maximum speed at just over 40 miles per hour, it wouldn't be long before she caught up to them.

She spotted the convoy as it turned left on Liivalaia road. GIP's sedans were keeping their distance behind the tanks. Jasmine kept them in sight but didn't want them to make their tail. She kept passing cars that had the good sense to look in their rear-view mirrors and allow the convoy to pass. Seconds later, a massive fiery explosion happens ahead of the lead tank. She approaches the smoke-filled area to find a grain trailer truck on fire and upside down in the opposing lane. One of the tanks must have used their main gun. Jasmine gasped when she saw a flattened station wagon under the flaming truck.

These fuckers are evil.

She input directions to the Stenbock House in her van's GPS and rang the Admiral.

"Ensign Pham, I have two UH-60s enroute to Stenbock. Over."

"Copy that, Admiral. I'm tailing them and it looks like they'll be at Toompea hill in three minutes. What is the squadron's ETA? Over."

"10 at most. Over."

Jasmine sighed. "Affirmative. Out."

She knew the admiral would order the use of Hellfire missiles against the tanks if they breached the building. She was hoping Michael had enough time to use his AI and figure out a best-case scenario here. The last thing they needed was a firefight in Toompea, a beautiful historic district in Estonia.

Jasmine took a side street to see the tanks' intended route. When she looked down the street and saw the blockade setup by the Estonian Defence Force, her stomach dropped. Typically, it would be adequate for a minor civil war, but this convoy included the planet's most sophisticated tanks. She recognized some Marder 1A3 infantry fighting vehicles blocking the road, but their light armor stood no chance against a Leopard's firepower. Luckily, the streets were relatively empty. They must have some sort of early warning system for the district's occupants.

The convoy appeared from behind the 19th century cathedral and rounds of ammunition started flying toward them from the blockade. Jasmine's vehicle was now subject to friendly fire as red streaks zoomed past her driver's side window. She immediately pulled into a perpendicular side street and exited the vehicle. Stenbock House was less than 200 yards away now.

The local military was ineffective, as expected, against the tanks. The narrow streets surrounding the historic buildings were their only tactical advantage. They had erected blockades in front of one street requiring the tanks to pass through them single-filed. The lead tank could have rammed through a building to clear an alternate path, but the Russians were short on time. Additionally, if the buildings had basements, the building incursion could cause them to end up there. Suddenly, the formation stopped moving.

Jasmine had never been part of an actual tank fight, but she had studied strategies. One of them being the distance between the target and the lead tank's main gun. They were preparing to fire.

As she said a quick prayer hoping the Estonian forces would not play sitting duck, a body fell from the building on the right landing like a superhero on the tank. It was Michael. She watched as he bent the main gun backward like it was a Styrofoam pool noodle. The gun backfired into the hull, which caused the top hatch to blow off, releasing a plume of black smoke.

The Estonian force stopped firing, and Michael moved to the second tank. A man appeared from one of the tanks behind Michael and began prepping the external machine gun. Just as he started aiming it toward Michael, Jasmine took aim with her Glock at the back of the tank cadet's head. Amid pulling the trigger, a body swiftly approached her periphery.

"Finally!" the attacker yelled.

Jasmine turned her body to face her attacker and take aim, but a black boot was faster, kicking the gun out of her grasp. As the attacker's body spun around, Jasmine noticed a long braid of hair with something shiny at the end of it rapidly approaching her left temple. She ducked just in time. A second later, the attacker sent a front kick at Jasmine that knocked the wind out of her while pushing her hard into the limestone wall of a nearby building. As Jasmine regained her breath, hands pinned her shoulders to the building. The intense pressure on her right shoulder felt like a dislocated socket.

"You're a crafty one, but don't think I'll have any mercy because you're the first female Navy Seal."

The attacker's sadistic grin and black eyes made Jasmine realize there was hatred inside, even jealousy. Using her left hand, she pinned the attacker's right hand to the wall and delivered a powerful palm strike to the opponent's nose, following up with a knee strike to their groin area. Jasmine slipped away from the wall as the attacker became disoriented.

"Nice to meet you, Mace. I expected more based on your savage reputation." Jasmine moved out into the open street and into a fighting stance.

Mace's eyes turned narrow, and her teeth clenched. She lunges at Jasmine, but Jasmine counters with a swift roundhouse kick. Mace's left arm halts the progress of Jasmine's leg. There is a surge of pain as if her leg hit a brick wall knocking Jasmine to the ground.

What the hell?

Mace straddles Jasmine while sending her left fist barreling toward Jasmine's jaw. Jasmine barely misses her fist, and the cobblestones shatter loudly next to her right ear. A few fragments rip into Jasmine's neck.

What is her fist made of?

Jasmine rolls quickly away and stands back up, staring at Mace's arm as she also stands.

"Maybe my new name should be Southpaw." Mace holds her arm up and rotates it at the wrist. "I have the good ol' US of A to thank for making this possible."

Happy for the chance to catch her breath, "You're bionic?"

"I prefer to be called an Auggy." Mace's mouth curves upward, and she runs toward Jasmine.

Jasmine retreats to a nearby building, kicking in the door. Just before entering, she sees Michael move from one tank to the next out of the corner of her eye. He stops what he's doing and looks in her direction. While running up the stairs, she clicks her earpiece.

"Commander, just keep going. I've got this."

Mace entered the building, glancing up at Jasmine at the top of the staircase.

"You two may have spoiled our plans, but that's doesn't mean I can't still have fun."

Jasmine keeps climbing, eager to get on the rooftop and wave down the approaching squadron. Luckily, the steel door to the roof is unsecured, and she looks around to get her directional bearing. As she hurries to the rooftop's edge where the tanks are attacking on the street below, the steel door she just went through flies past her.

Jasmine snaps her head back to see Mace rushing toward her. She grabs two of her six-inch throwing knives from her thigh holster. One after another, she hurls them at Mace's head. Instinctively, Mace uses her left arm to shield her face, and both blades lodge deep into her forearm. White sparks start spewing from the second blade's entry point, followed by a flare-up, as if her arm was a gas grill burner that was just doused with grease. Mace stops and grabs her left forearm with her right hand, only to pull it away quickly, shaking her hand. She looks up at Jasmine.

"Bitch! You broke my arm!"

An explosion on the street distracts Jasmine, causing her to look over the roof's edge. As she turns back to Mace, a black multi-directional tread pattern of the bottom of a boot darkens her vision. She loses her balance and subsequently feels a sensation of weightlessness and disorientation. As her body falls helplessly off the building, her thoughts focus on a fond memory with her younger sisters.

CHAPTER
FIFTY-TWO

5 MINUTES EARLIER

While Michael moved to the next tank, he could hear the Navy's air support approaching from a couple of miles away. His thoughts focused on the safety of the people in the historic town and hoped he could prevent a massive fire fight. While gripping the metal commander hatch with his fingers, his head jerked right from an impact that felt like several judo chops. Ammunition ricocheted off the metal, causing him to seek cover in front of the tank. Another stream of bullets started coming from a different direction. The Estonian Defence returned fire to assist, but he was pinned down. Movement at the back of the convoy caught his attention. Jasmine was engaging with a figure. He zoomed his eye in and captured a facial scan of an individual who looked to be an assailant dressed like Catwoman.

. . .

SIXAI: *Assailant's name: Katya Morozov (100% accuracy)*

•Ties to Eurasian Organized Crime

•Political Affiliation: Cossack groups

•Known Associates: General Ivan Petrovsky, Sokolov Syndicate

•Callsign: Mace

•Known Aliases: Semone Marek (most recent), Natalya Volkov

Michael wanted to help Jasmine, but he knew she would tell him to stay focused on the mission. Peering over the tank's tracks, he searched for the gunfire's source. It was coming from the fourth and fifth tanks' external machine guns. To operate these, the cadets must open the commander's hatch. It exposes the operator slightly but is more effective if the tank cameras' view is blocked. Michael figured this was the case given the tight formation, otherwise they would fire the turret machine gun from inside the tank. With his augmented eye, he could line up the sight easily for a shot with his SIG at the man on the fourth tank, but the fifth tank was at a slight angle that prevented a direct line of sight. He wondered how his borophene endoskeleton would hold up to the nearly 15 rounds per second that would come from tank five as he tried to reach it.

Michael avoided the risk.

He lined up his gun's sight to the man on the fourth tank. His AIonic eye zoomed in through the gun's sight to see the exact inch where the bullet would hit. It would travel 91.4 feet and just graze the man's right ear. Among the chaos, Michael chuckled inside, realizing his head had its own built in rifle scope with what appeared to be unlimited magnification. He adjusted his gun slightly right and fired. The hollow point bullet hit the tank operator right at the top of his nose, forcing his head back before he fell back inside the tank's hull.

Right after the kill, the enemy machine gun fire stopped briefly, then restarted.

Michael contemplated his next move and wondered how many cadets were in each tank. It would have been nice if his x-ray vision worked through the composite metal. He was pretty sure all the occupants of tank one were dead, though, after the misfiring of their main gun. Usually, four troops crewed these tanks, but two could suffice. Just then, his AI gave him an important update.

SIXAI: *Tank five will need to reload in 48 rounds or 3-4 seconds*

Brilliant, thought Michael. *That's very helpful.*

As soon as the firing stopped, Michael grabbed an M67 grenade from his tactical vest and stood up. His augmented eye noticed the fifth tank's commander hatch was open. He made a practice throw maneuver, like how a quarterback pumps before he sends the ball to a receiver. Michael hoped that would give his AI a second to make the proper adjustments to his arm's strength. He pulled the safety pin and sent the grenade sailing into the air. His AIonic eye followed the trajectory and confirmed it hit the mark, as there was no evidence of a bounce.

A muffled explosion followed by a series of louder detonations as Michael watched the tank explode from the inside, sending the entire turret 15 feet into the air before it landed on tank six, crushing its main gun.

"BINGO!" Michael fist pumped, but then his stomach knotted up from a faint scream. His eyes darted toward the sound's origin. Jasmine was falling off the building.

Without thinking, Michael lunged, intercepting her body mid-air but with too much velocity. Their momentum carried them past the tank convoy and toward a garden nearby Tallitor's Tower. Michael held Jasmine's head with his hand close to his chest and did his best to wrap his legs around her body, as he had no control of their flight. Garden onlookers scattered, fearing what appeared to be a meteor strike. The flailing bodies scraped a few leafless tree branches before they hit the grass hard and started rolling. Michael was lying on top of Jasmine and her eyes were closed.

"Jasmine! Jasmine, are you okay?"

Jasmine's big brown eyes opened slowly, and she stared intently into Michael's. She kissed his lips, and it sent shivers down Michael's spine. He momentarily lost track of his location and mission objectives. She smiled widely.

"Now, I am. But I think your enormous body is collapsing my lungs."

"Oh, sorry," Michael released her and stood up while reaching out his hand to help Jasmine stand.

Their ear radios blipped, "Triple-S here. We're ready to intercept. Hellfire missiles are hot. Over."

Michael says, "Commander Cooling, here. No need, we have this under control. We don't want the Navy unnecessarily involved at this point. NATO will think we have declared war against the Russians. Over."

Jasmine's eyebrows furrowed at Michael.

"Affirmative. Are you sure? We see some tank damage, but the Estonian military is still present. Over."

Michael winked at Jasmine and mouthed, "Trust me."

"Send one chopper back, have the other one land at Stenbock House, just in case. Over."

"Affirmative. Triple-S Out."

Jasmine swiped at Michael's arm, that was loaded with dirt and grass debris. "I don't think it's a good idea. These Russians seem hell-bent on succeeding."

"Stay behind in case they retreat. Give me five minutes," says Michael.

Michael started running back toward the convoy. Tank seven was not moving, but tanks two, three and four were encroaching on the Estonian Defence by pushing the damaged lead tank aside. As he got closer, he had to crouch down to avoid getting hit by friendly fire from the locals. Despite the hindrance, he reached tank two's right back side. Using both hands, he pulled hard on the track's drive sprocket and pushed with his right leg against the skirt for leverage. It ripped off and the tank immediately started turning a hard right, crashing into the concrete building. He repeated this for the remaining two tanks in-motion.

The damaged building wall crumbled onto the tank's top hatches, preventing an exit, but Michael knew they could get out via the driver's hatch in the hull's front. He waited with his SIG raised.

A couple of cadets climbed over the rubble and aimed at Michael with AK-74s. He dropped them with one shot each. Bullets started reigning out, temporarily lighting the darkness behind the building rubble. Michael took cover behind tank five.

A second later, an arm was around his neck, and he felt the cold steel of a barrel on his left temple. Instinctively, he used a Krav Maga move to lower his center of gravity and then pivoted to face the attacker as the gun fired. Michael noted it didn't cause the ringing effect as it would with normal ears. With his attacker off-balance, Michael grabbed one of the cadet's arms with both hands and started swinging the attacker's body around in circles like he was holding a heavy sling. He released the body, launching it over a nearby building like a cannonball.

The firing stopped, and Michael observed some uniformed men running away in the distance. He gave Jasmine a heads up over the radio that she might see them coming.

He inspected the tanks systematically to ensure they all were neutralized. As he appeared out of tank seven, an Estonian colonel greeted him.

"Who or what are you?" asked the colonel with raised eyebrows in broken English.

"Just a friend," says Michael. "Are your men alright?"

"A couple of casualties, but it would've been much worse if it weren't for you. Thank you. Can I ask your name to tell the Prime Minister?"

"No. But please return to her quarters just in case this isn't over."

The men shook hands, then Michael slowly walked towards Jasmine at the park.

"Come in, Triple-S," Michael says.

"Triple-S here. Over."

"Targets neutralized. Defence Forces are going back to your position. Over."

"Affirmative. Do you need a pickup? Over."

"Standby. Rendezvousing with Ensign Pham." says Michael.

"Ensign here. No sign of enemy retreaters. What's your position, Commander? Over."

"Heading—"

A purple and gray explosion of smoke suddenly permeates the air in front of Michael's face. Vertigo overcomes him as he falls on the cobblestone near the Aleksander cathedral as everything goes dark.

Two sedans with tinted windows pull up next to Michael's still body. Men emerge from the front car, pull him inside the rear seat, and both vehicles depart the historic area.

CHAPTER
FIFTY-THREE

SOUTHERN CALIFORNIA

Martha couldn't sleep. Her stomach was grumbling, and she could not get comfortable. She checked her gold watch, and it was well after midnight. The guards provided her with a tiny pouch of tuna for dinner but didn't leave a blanket for her to sleep with. Using old tires, she crafted a mattress and used paint-ridden drop cloths as a makeshift bedsheet. She tore a part of her shirt off to make a mask to help with the rubber and oil smell that permeated the air.

She heard a vehicle approaching quickly followed by a sliding stop on the gravel outside. A door opened and closed. Martha could hear mumbling in a Russian dialect outside her room, as if the henchmen were arguing. She heard one walk away as the door to the storage closet was unlocked.

The dim moonlight coming through the sole window in the room revealed a hulking figure that stumbled menacingly inside, holding a bottle. Leonid's accomplice stood at nearly six and a half feet tall, had broad shoulders and bulging muscles coming out of a poorly chosen nightclub button-down shirt design. The shadows on his face high-lighted his square, scarred jaw that had an unkept short beard. His massive hand raised the bottle to his lips and most of the liquid missed his mouth. He was slurring in Russian. As he got closer to Martha, his cold, steel-gray eyes pierced through her.

Martha sat up on her makeshift bed as a horrible combination of cheap cologne mixed with alcohol stung her nostrils. His narrowed eyes and wolfish grin caused Martha to shiver as she tried to avoid direct eye contact. The man grabbed her chin with his index finger and thumb and lifted it in his direction slowly.

"These American women play hard to get. Can you guess how many drinks I bought tonight?" he says.

Martha didn't respond and tried to look away.

"Okay, I tell you … six. Do you know how many numbers I get?"

The man's face moved within a couple of inches of Martha's.

"None!"

Martha hoped Leonid would return from his break, so she tried to appease the man.

"Maybe you used too much cologne."

The man stepped back and smelled his armpits oddly.

"Nyet, I don't think so," he says.

"Listen. Could I get a blanket and maybe something else to eat?"

The man ripped off his shirt and threw the alcohol and sweat soaked material on Martha's face.

"There you go!" His laugh was sinister.

Martha threw it onto the concrete and struggled to stand as the thug's hands seized her shoulders. His grip felt like she was in a human vise.

"Sweet Martha, you're my date tonight."

His eyes darkened, and he was able to restrain her with only one hand as he unbuckled his belt. Martha started whimpering as he wrapped the belt around her struggling wrists. Despite her efforts to free herself, his grip was over-powering. He undid his pants with the other hand. Martha tried to free herself again, but he pulled her in closer to him.

While grinning, he whispers. "Would you prefer I knock you out? I don't mind doing you unconscious."

As his pants dropped, he flipped Martha around and onto the tire bed with her backside facing him. As he lifted her summer dress, a rush of wind pushed against her hind legs. Suddenly, the man's body sailed past Martha's head and crashed into the small window. Looking up, she saw the body fall with arms severed and blood gushing. She twisted around.

"I guess he didn't fit," says Michael Sr.

Martha jumped into his arms and Michael held his right arm above her head so as not to touch her with his hand.

"You seem to make a habit of being a hostage," Michael says.

"And you of saving me. I was so scared, Michael. Thank you … you're an angel."

Martha noticed his right hand floating in the air. "Did you hurt yourself?"

His forehead crinkled and lower lip protruded. "Ah …

no … but that hard shove might've pushed my hand too far under his briefs. If you know what I mean?"

"Ewww!"

"You wouldn't know where the bathroom is, would you?"

Martha laughed. "No, that was mine." She pointed to the gas can.

Michael's nose crinkled.

"Wait!" she says, grasping his arm. "There was another guy."

"Oh yeah, the guy who was outside smoking? The last thing he heard was 'You know those things will kill you, right?'"

Martha smiled and hastened down the hallway.

"Here you go," she pointed to a door leading to a bathroom.

As Michael cleaned up, Martha couldn't stop staring at him.

"How did you find me? They smashed my phone," she says.

"Remember that hydrangea flower phone cover I got you as a get-well gift when you were in the hospital?"

Martha frowned. "Yeah, it would have been nice if you delivered it in-person."

"Sorry. I don't do hospitals. Well … that phone case has a low energy Bluetooth tracker embedded in it. It works with other phones' location tracking. Don't worry, the data stays encrypted. So, technically, your captors' phones actually helped me find you anonymously."

"The tech sounds cool, but that was a little creepy of you, especially not telling me."

"Sorry. I was worried about your safety after the first encounter." Michael dried his hands.

"This is one time I'm glad you were a creep. That reminds me, my case is back in the storage room. Can you get it for me? I don't want another look at that ghastly man."

Michael Sr. walked into the room. Blood pooled on the floor near the window. After grabbing her case, he spotted the bottle on the floor. He raised the mouth of the bottle to his nose for a second, then downed the last of the vodka.

Martha dusted off the case that Michael handed her. "Have you heard from Michael or Jasmine?"

"No, but some of my military sources say the Silver Squadron headed to northern Europe, not sure exactly where. Perhaps they're there," says Michael.

"Can I use your phone to call them?"

"Sure, can we leave this place before someone discovers us and the two dead Russians? It's late and I have a splitting headache. The last thing I wanna do is answer police questions."

Martha realized they were in a junkyard when they exited the building. Just outside the door sat Leonid, with his back leaning against the outside wall. An old metal hubcap was separating his head from his shoulders. It looked like his head was on a silver dinner charger. A cigarette was in his mouth, still smoldering.

Michael opened the passenger door of his F-150 and helped Martha into it. They drove out of the junkyard with the headlights off onto they hit the main road.

"Why don't you stay with me tonight, Martha?"

"I would like that," she smiled. "But can we stop to eat first? I'm starving."

"Sure. My fridge only has beer, and I'm a lousy cook."

They arrived at an all-night diner conveniently located just five minutes from Michael's residence. He wanted a couple of beers and picked this place to avoid a long drive home afterward. Young adults gathered in a corner booth, laughing, while enjoying their shakes and fries. An older man sat on a counter stool, appearing as though he may drift into slumber while sipping his coffee. Michael and Martha opted for a booth by the window.

"Breakfast sounds perfect. I can eat breakfast at any time of the day." Martha gleefully read the menu up and down.

"Well … the roosters are about to crow, so technically, breakfast is the suitable option."

"Right you are," Martha put down her menu and stared into Michael's piercing blue-gray eyes. "You know, you really are something special." Her eyes welled up.

Michael blushed. "Ya know, I'd do anything for you, right?"

"Jasmine shared why you purposely avoided me and Michael. Must have been tough on you."

"It was." Michael paused. "I might have good news, but I don't want to raise your hopes."

Martha's eyebrows lifted.

"I've been testing myself weekly and in the last couple months, the leakage has dropped significantly. It's still leaking, but if my calculations are correct, the exposure per day is no more than what a medical professional in radiology typically encounters. I plan to validate this by visiting a radiation specialist, but if it checks out—"

"You can see us more regularly," Martha's eyes widened, and a tear dripped down her right cheek.

Michael gently embraced Martha's hands into his as the server stopped at their table.

"Are you lovebirds ready to order?"

CHAPTER
FIFTY-FOUR

PÄRNU RIVER, ESTONIA

A woody, leather scent filled Michael's nostrils. His head felt intoxicated, even though he hadn't recently consumed alcohol. He opened his eyes as the focus became clearer on the black material in front of him. He realized he was staring at his underwear. His head felt heavy to lift, but even worse, he couldn't move his arms or legs.

You gotta be fucking kidding me.

His ankles had thick steel shackle bands around them. The bands had exterior holes fit with large screws, at least two inches wide. This secured the shackles to the wooden floor below his bare feet. The coldness around his wrists behind him made him surmise a similar type of bonding. His skull itched, as if something clung to the back of it.

The room felt empty beside the gentle humming of some sort of machines behind him. Large, layered logs formed the surrounding walls, just like a nineteenth century cabin, but the windows were modern. One of them was slightly open, which was pulling in the cigar scent he smelled earlier. Using x-ray vision, he tried to see who was on the porch, but the thick logs hindered his view. He reminded himself to read his body's operator manual more carefully, if he got out of there alive. He heard the men's entire discussion, but it was in an unfamiliar Russian dialect, and for some unknown reason, his AI didn't interpret it. Outside his room's window, he could see a dense forest of evergreen trees dusted with old snow. There was the sound of a river flowing nearby, indicating he was somewhere in the countryside.

The room's door opens and Captain Donnelly strolls in grinning, carrying a large silver suitcase. GIP and another cadet walk in behind him. Michael's eyes narrow and his brow furrows.

"Captain, are you here to negotiate my release?" says Michael.

"No, I negotiated your capture ... oh ... and your mother's again. Just in case you got any crazy ideas. Sorry to disappoint you."

"You fucking traitor. They will court-martial you for this."

Chase's mouth drooped. "And miss out on that fat government pension ... hmm." He cocks his head left and looks up. "No, I think I made the right decision. My Roy Stuart surfboard just shipped from Zealand."

A cadet enters the room, immediately whispering to the general. Michael's super hearing picks up two Russian words he recognizes, "mother" and "escaped". The general grimaces.

Michael says, "You might want to ask the general what he thinks of your service so far."

Chase turns around to the general, whose face is flushed.

"What happened, sir?"

The general points and gestures for Chase to hand over the briefcase. He walks over to a table behind Michael and empties half of the contents.

"What the hell!" says Chase.

"The woman escaped, again. You did half the job, so you get half the pay. Take this and leave before I change my mind."

The general pushes the briefcase forcefully into Chase's chest, causing him to have to hold it with both arms. His face pales as he scans around the room. He makes his way to the door and looks back at Michael.

"It was nice working with you, Commander. You might get a medal for your heroics today. Too bad they'll have to pin it on the inside of your coffin."

"It's a good thing my hands are bound. Don't forget to check that money for counterfeit. That's one of his little operations back home," Michael motions to GIP.

Chase's eyes and jaw tense and his skin shade lightens even more before he disappears.

The general stood in front of Michael with his hands on his hips. The gold buttons on his black tweed military uniform were barely keeping his large abdomen from bursting out of the jacket. Michael couldn't help but notice a white piece of food lodged deep in the general's peppered beard.

GIP says, "So you Americans spend millions, maybe

billions, on this body and here we are back at, how do you say? Square one? All you have to show for it is a pair of BVD underwear keeping your ass from sticking to the cold metal chair."

"What do you have me hooked up to?"

"Oh, that's thanks to the Captain, or should I say Chase's last present to me, since his discharge now is inevitable. Anyway, he provided the encryption key to unlock the programming interface to your artificial intelligence. He also shared a little secret."

The general leaned into Michael's ear.

"Your low-power mode setting, which we have activated."

Jeez, brush your teeth, man. Michael pulled his head back. *That's what the "LPM" means.*

Like a microwave with no one to open the door, SIXAI continuously reminded Michael of the power setting.

A woman Michael recognized entered the room, dressed in a nearly transparent white bandage dress with high heels, as if she had planned later to visit a nightclub.

"Where have you been?" asks GIP.

"Finishing my make-up. I have a TikTok broadcast right after this," says Irina.

The general rolls his eyes and moves aside.

"Remember me, Honey?"

Michael slowly turns his head from looking out the window.

"Yeah, you're kind of hard to forget," Michael smiles widely.

"Awe, that's sweet." Irina runs her fingers along Michael's broad shoulder and under his muscular pectoral.

"They did a good job on your body. I heard from our captain friend that there is one place they left all natural."

She pulls at the top of his underwear to look inside.

"Too bad. Maybe they could have given you one that works," she says.

"Oh, it works," replies Michael, "just not on hussies!"

Irina let the elastic slap back on Michael's lower abdomen and slaps him hard across the face, shaking her hand in pain.

"Ow. God damn you! What the hell's your face made of? Father, give me the gun!"

GIP cocks his Makarov and hands it to Irina. Black tears start running down Irina's cheek from her mascara. She points the barrel of the gun point blank at Michael's privates. Michael suddenly has an epiphany and smiles while activating his warming ability, but just on his hands behind him. This reaction irritates Irina even more.

"Why are you smiling and what is that smell?" she says.

One cadet says, "He's probably shitting in his pants."

Everyone laughs, except Irina and Michael.

Irina repoints the gun at Michael's crotch. "This is for my dead fiancé."

She fires two rounds at Michael's briefs, but he shows no reaction. She notices two bullets laying on the floor at Michael's feet.

"What the hell?" Irina looks back at her father, who appeared just as surprised as she was.

"Borophene Valuables Defense," says Michael. "That's what the 'BVD' stands for on my underwear. Oh … and General … it seems as if our mutual friend Chase forgot to read the manual that came with this tech. Low-Power Mode can only be activated if I confirm the request with multi-factor authentication ... using my brain wave. Incidentally, I just told my AI to cancel the request."

Michael noticed the cadets in the room were from the tank convoy. They started backing up a few inches at a time to leave the room. Michael twisted his wrists and the super-heated steel around them snapped apart. Quickly bracing his body with his hands on the edges of the chair, he lifted his feet with such force the 8-inch-long screws holding his shackles ripped out of the solid wood floor. Splinters flew toward Irina as she stepped back. Michael eyed Irina as he stood and she screamed with her hands in the air, retreating from the room. The general followed her but didn't get far. Michael grabbed his neck and tossed him over his shoulder. Just in time, the Russian scientist operating the equipment behind Michael moved as GIP's body smashed into the technical equipment. The general slid to the floor, knocked out cold. The scientist beelines for the cabin's exit.

As Michael left the room, he heard two vehicles kick up gravel as they hastily departed the property. He grabbed a fur coat from the living room couch as he walked out to the patio. A pine scent filled the clean, crisp winter air. The background sound of a rushing river moving over its rocky bed was soothing to Michael after an exceptionally violent day. His peripheral vision glimpsed a metal ashtray on the ground next to the exterior wall of the cabin. A half-smoked cigar was lying in it with a book of matches beside it.

This must be my lucky day!

CHAPTER
FIFTY-FIVE

Michael was slowly spinning a ring around his finger when the general came to. He was brushing off some dirt on his pants and picking at something stuck on his leg. The general sat in the same chair and room where Michael had been an hour earlier. His entire body was duct-taped to the chair, looking like a silver mummy. His head, hands, and bare feet were the only parts exposed. Michael looked up as he caught movement.

"Oh … good evening, General. Sorry about the tape. I destroyed the shackles getting out of them and I couldn't find any rope anywhere. What kind of log cabin doesn't have rope?"

"You son-of-a-bitch! Where are my men and my daughter?"

"First off, don't talk about my mom that way. Second, I don't know, they ran like frightened deer when I stood up."

"Do you think what you did today will stop my plan?"

"And what plan is that, General? To keep invading countries until Russia becomes the Soviet Union again?"

"It'll be called the Red Union. I'm just one general in a line of leaders that will make it a reality. You can't stop us all."

"Not all at once." Michael flicked off the final bit of gum stuck to his pants. "But I'm sure Congress will help me find the resources I need. By the way ... was it really necessary to throw my fatigues in the trash? Does nobody honor the uniform anymore?"

"We don't consider the United States to be honorable. You think you can police the world, but you know nothing about war. Your President is weak," says GIP.

"So much hostility. Did you have a rough childhood? Did someone take away your Russian nesting dolls before you were done with them?"

"You won't think Russia is so funny when we control your country using the very thing your country thinks will advance your Information Age, *Artificial Intelligence*. How will your government know if it's artificial or real, when the responses are natural language generated? Social media misinformation is just the beginning."

Michael stood up and paced the room in front of the general.

"Yeah, yeah, you're getting way too technical for me. We should probably focus on the here and now. I couldn't find any fireworks, but the Navy provided me with an incendiary grenade. That's what you're probably feeling inside your butt cheeks right now. It took me 10 minutes to tape it just perfectly."

The general squirmed in the chair.

"You probably know, being a general and all, that those grenades burn at almost 4000 degrees, wait ... you're on the metric system, 2200 degrees Celsius, sorry. One must wonder what happens to your insides after a controlled burn for 30-40 seconds. While you were out, I did a minor operation on it and added a wick to light it. But I'm not an animal like you. I'll give you a chance to get out of this."

"By me giving up all of those involved in the Red Union movement, right?"

Michael says, "That'd be a good start."

"Do you think I'm like your weakling Crap-tain and would turn on my country for selfish reasons?"

"I guess not. That's very honorable." Michael started patting his pockets. "Now, where did I put those matches? Ah, here they are," reaching into his leg pocket.

"Wait …" says GIP. "You said you would give me a chance to get out of this."

"I thought I just did."

Michael walked over to the table behind the general. He picked up a phone, swiped it, and held it in front of the general's face.

"If you can call someone to save you in the next …" Michael looks at the long wick lying on the floor while scratching his chin, "10 minutes, you'll be free to terrorize Europe. At least until we meet again. Good luck!"

Michael gently placed the general's hand around the phone. He moved to the room's rear, struck a match, and lit the lengthy wick. He turned his earpiece to send-only mode before dropping it behind a binder on the table. The general searched anxiously for a number one-handed.

Before Michael left the room, he turned with a smile. "I'll give you a tip. Use Siri, it's much faster."

It took Michael a couple of high jumps to get his bearings and figure out a northern direction. He figured his team would rendezvous in Helsinki after the tank incursion. His thinking was completely different now. In the past, he would head to the closest airport and charter a plane to reach his desired location. Having the ability to move fast and not tire gave him a quicker option.

SIXAI: *GPS information*
  •Distance to Estonia northern coast: 80 miles
  •Helsinki: 50 miles via the Gulf of Finland

His enhanced body could do that in less than two hours. The gravel stones beneath Michael's boots emitted a sharp staccato as he dashed away, accompanied by desperate cries for help from inside the cabin.

CHAPTER
FIFTY-SIX

NECKER ISLAND

The water's color changed as the helicopter approached the shoreline and flew above the reefs. The deep blue gradually transitioned into lighter shades of azure and turquoise, signaling the shallower depths. The vivid blues mesmerized Jasmine as it reflected the sandy bottoms and the clear, sunlit waters. The peaceful water and her recent near-death experience made her yearn to visit her mother's home island in the Philippines. The single time she'd been there as a teenager left an unforgettable impression. Camiguin, known as "the island born of fire" because of its volcanic origins, had gorgeous waterfalls and hot springs. The place had to be hard to leave, but when her mother met her father while she was on a missionary trip to Vietnam, island beauty came second to love. They ended up in the United States after her father's siblings moved there for various reasons.

"Are you daydreaming again?" asked Michael.

Jasmine turned to him and gently smiled.

"It's been a rough week, to say the least. Then you disappear, hours pass, and the first thing I hear on our secure channel is a man screaming. He sounded like he was being burned alive."

Michael says, "Technically, he was burning from the inside out, but who cares? He deserved worse."

Jasmine scoffs, "No, I meant you could have given me a heads up you were escaping. I thought that man was you!"

"Right. Sorry. How about I make it up to you after our visit to SIX? Does dinner on the beach sound intriguing?"

"Maybe, if I forgive you by that time."

The UH-60's pilot radioed for a landing, instantly receiving confirmation. Two of Jasmine's least favorite people were waiting near the roof's landing pad, Sofia, the nurse, and William Streeter. She gagged every time Streeter spoke with his pompous, chauvinistic tone, but tolerated him since he saved Michael's life. Sofia was just annoying. When Michael was around, it was like no one else existed. It's fine to be attracted to someone, but don't be rude to others.

"Good to see you both!" says Streeter. "Don't worry about my plane. I already have another being built."

Umm, we weren't and who cares?

"That plane's tech saved our behinds," says Michael.

"From what I hear, it was *your* tech that did the saving." Sofia wasted no time wrapping both of her hands around Michael's arm while leading him to the roof elevator. Jasmine and Streeter followed behind.

Streeter looked down at Jasmine. "So, I heard you met the infamous Mace."

"Yeah, she is as bitchy as everyone says she is. But I have to admit, she has a mean front kick, and she had some sort of augmented robotic arm."

"Really?" says William. "We knew the Russians had always tried to develop bionics, but we never thought they had succeeded. Intel never confirmed."

"Don't worry, my knives took it out quickly, so they need to work on its resilience. Did you know there are about a dozen bionic individuals nationwide who lack healthcare? The old organization just abandoned them, and many are having maintenance issues."

William sighed. "I assumed there were, but I didn't know the exact number. The ancient technology is so outdated that I wouldn't be able to help them, even if I tried."

"What about replacing them with your tech?"

"Maybe. I can't solve everyone's problems, Ensign."

"Then how about just one person, Michael's father?"

"I'll think about it. We need to get Michael to my office. The NSA wants a full briefing on Estonia. After that, he has a checkup with Dr. Bell."

After the call, Michael met Jasmine at the underground research lab. Dr. Bell was scratching his head in front of a computer, writing with his pencil, and then immediately erasing what he wrote.

"Dr. Bell!" says Michael.

The doctor rose, smiled, and offered his hand to shake Michael's. He approached Jasmine for a hug, but she withdrew and offered her hand instead.

"Let's get you over to the examination table. I know you may feel fine, but I want to run some diagnostics, especially after they tampered with your AI interface," says Dr. Bell.

"Yeah, how did they do that, Doc? I thought Streeter only bought the best security."

The doctor sighed. "That was my fault. The encryption keys were supposed to rotate every four hours, but the code had an infinite loop. Fixing that today."

Sofia emerged from the adjacent glass-walled room. Jasmine could have sworn she saw her unbutton her blouse at the top before she entered. Her eyes pierced Michael's face and grabbed his forearm to lead him into the examination room. The doctor started asking Jasmine some questions, but she wasn't listening. Jasmine overheard Sofia tell the Commander to undress then to cover himself with a towel. Sofia stood there, making no attempt to leave, as Michael removed his shirt.

"Ahem, Nurse Sofia," says Jasmine.

Sofia turned.

"Can I talk to you for a moment out here?" asks Jasmine.

Sofia scowled and walked out of the room while Michael finished undressing.

"Can you get Michael something to eat and a gallon of water, please? We have been going non-stop since leaving the aircraft carrier in the Atlantic. Michael forgets to eat sometimes and his AIonics need water."

"Certainly, but—"

Jasmine looked her right in the eyes. "Please!"

Upon Sofia's departure, Jasmine and Dr. Wells entered the room to find Michael on the examination bed.

Dr. Bell says, "Give me a second to hook up to the

interface behind your skull. By the way, how are the hallucinations?"

"Improved, Doc, barely had any, but I was disappointed to find out a knock-out gas can so easily disable this billion-dollar body."

"I read that in your report before you got here. I have a few solutions for that. First, I can have AI recognize your unconsciousness and program it to take over your body's control, meaning the artificial limbs. Alternatively, we can program the Convalescytes to develop immunity to all known airborne and injectable toxins. That will take several weeks with minimal exposure, similar to how your body becomes immune to viruses by introducing vaccines to it."

"I opt for the second option. I want to be in control of this body, not AI."

The doctor smiled. "I figured you would say that, so I prepared some of the nastiest toxins."

Michael stared at Jasmine. "How long will this take, Doc?"

"Why, Commander? Do you have a hot date?"

Michael curled his lips up to the left. "Yes, I do actually."

CHAPTER
FIFTY-SEVEN

HIGHLAND, CALIFORNIA

"They did a marvelous job on this sliding glass door," says Michael.

He opened the large glass doors, exposing the patio and outside air and the moonlit hills behind her property. A warmer than usual breeze swept across Michael's face.

Martha says, "I figured it was time to replace those thirty-year-old single-pane doors. That evil Russian woman was just the catalyst. These allow me to open the room to the entire patio, one benefit of living in California where the bugs are minimal. Can you help me open the wine?"

"I'll take care of it," a darkened figure appeared from the shadowed hallway to the front entrance.

"Michael!" says Martha. "I see you're letting yourself in now?"

"To be fair, you showed me where the hidden key was. Given the recent circumstances, it might be better to just discard the keys. I can put a lock on there that requires a fingerprint to open," says Michael Sr.

"Nonsense, that's too technical for me."

Jasmine left Michael's side and immediately ran up to greet the guest and hug him. Michael hadn't seen his dad for years, and their last meeting was unpleasant. He noticed the affection that his mom and Jasmine showed him, but something inside of him was holding him back. After a moment of contemplation, he approached and offered his hand.

"Thank you for saving my mom ... twice."

Michael Sr. batted Michael's hand away and hugged him tightly. It went from awkward to comforting for Michael, and he noticed his mom's eyes watering up.

"Can I help with anything?" Jasmine asked, hoping to give the men some time alone.

Martha took the hint and motioned for her to help at the stove.

Michael Sr. eyes pierced his son's. He held onto both of his shoulders.

"I can't even tell your real eye apart from your augmented one. It can't be easy to match that azure tone."

Michael says, "Yeah, they did an awesome job, but sometimes I feel guilty."

"Why?"

"They spent billions on research and enhancing me but could have given countless others with disabilities a chance at a better life."

"You have always been selfless, son, something you definitely didn't get from me. Probably the reason they picked you. You know, Abraham Lincoln once said, 'Nearly all men can stand adversity, but if you want to test a man's character, give him power.' You're one of the few men who can handle all this power."

"Thanks, Dad, but I still don't understand why you didn't just tell Mom and me up front about your radiation problem. We would have understood—"

"You both wouldn't have let it interfere, and I couldn't risk contaminating the two people I love."

Michael's eyes teared up. He looked over at Jasmine helping his mom, and his pulse quickened. Michael Sr. turned back toward the kitchen.

"I can tell she's special to you. Definitely a keeper."

Michael sighed. "Yeah, but now I've got more to worry about. She's not one to back down from a dangerous mission."

"Then make the most of the time you have together. That's all we can do with the important people in our lives. At least until fate has other ideas."

Martha carried a large bowl to the dining table near the men. It had heaps of spaghetti covered with tennis ball size meatballs with flecks of green in them. Michael Sr. went over to the kitchen island to open the wine.

"Mom, this looks great, but how many people are we feeding tonight?" says Michael with a grin.

"Honey, I know this is one of your favorites. Besides, spaghetti leftovers are perfect. I want you and Jasmine to take the extra pasta back to the base. You both look too skinny."

Jasmine laughed. "They gave us some time off, Ms. Cooling. We might take a little R&R."

"Good! You both deserve it after what you've been

through the last several weeks. Are you planning to visit your parents again?"

Michael Sr. interrupted, "Actually, if you don't mind, I have something important that I could use both of your help with. Can we talk about it after dinner?"

Martha scoffed. "No more secrets, Michael."

"Not a secret, some military research that I don't have access to."

"Well, technically, not sure if Michael has access either anymore," says Jasmine.

Martha looked up while putting the delicious smelling garlic bread on the table. "I was wondering about that. Do they still consider you a commander in the Navy?"

"Of course, Mom, I wasn't court-martialed, but technically I report to SIX," says Michael.

Jasmine spoke up. "He's kind of like a double agent, but one who works for the same side. Should I call you Agent Cooling from now on or, better yet, A.C.?"

Michael shook his head. "Commander or Michael is fine. Can we eat? I'm starving."

It was hard for Michael to keep swallowing as fast as he wanted to. The laughing prevented that. Michael and Jasmine swapped stories about their childhood experiences. Michael Sr. recalled a harder childhood, when knowledge meant mastering library research and using encyclopedias. He was trying for sympathy, but even Martha was calling his bluff. Turned out Michael and Jasmine were classmates for a week in high school. Jasmine stood up for a bullied girl and was expelled. It turned out that the bully's parents were the principal contributors to the school's fundraisers.

Martha pushed a third helping, but Michael couldn't fit another morsel in. Jasmine commented how there was a second stomach, just for desserts, so Michael indulged in a piece of his mother's homemade blueberry pie. Michael couldn't remember the last time he had such a wonderful evening.

Michael Sr. went over to his jacket and pulled out a leather case. He walked over to the table and opened it. Inside were two highly illegal Cohiba cigars due to the trade embargo with Cuba.

"Man, you're really trying to get on my good side tonight," says Michael. "How the hell did you get these?"

Michael Sr. grinned, "I have high friends in low places. Let's take these outside. Jasmine, could you join us?"

"Sure, sure, I'll clean up the table. It's not like I cooked the entire dinner or anything." Martha shook her head but smiled.

The rest laughed and headed to the patio outside. The nearly full moon was casting a silvery glow over the rugged Highland mountainside, painting it in shades of pale luminescence.

As Michael lit his father's cigar first, then his, the flame temporarily lit up the dark porch. Taking his first puff, he tasted sweet undertones of honey and caramel.

"Do you guys inhale those?" asked Jasmine.

"I do," said Michael Sr. "but it's not like cancer is gonna kill me."

Michael rolled his eyes. "Stop that, Dad. What did you want to talk to us about?"

"The traitor."

Michael and Jasmine looked at each other.

Michael Sr. says, "Your mom told me he was boasting about retiring somewhere in the Caribbean during her kidnap."

"Interesting," said Michael. "He also mentioned just purchasing one of those top-of-the-line surfboards, trying to remember—"

SIXAI: Roy Stuart (New Zealand-based surfboard shaper).

•High Quality Materials: paulownia wood, balsa wood

•Signature Models: The Baron, The Makaha, The Pipeline

•Price range: $5000 - $20,000+ depending on materials

"It was a Roy Stuart surfboard which, by the way, has a lifetime warranty. Perhaps he left a forwarding address or email we can trace with the company."

"I've heard of those," says Jasmine. "A few folks have them in Orange County. They travel worldwide in search of massive waves."

Michael Sr. says, "Good info. I'll check that out. You know what's considered the surfing capital of the Caribbean?"

Jasmine and Michael shook their head. Before Michael's AI revealed it, his father gave the answer.

"Barbados."

Jasmine smiled and looked at Michael. "Guess I should

start looking for some new bikinis. Sounds like we know where we're taking our leave."

The three of them clinked their wine glasses together before heading back into the house.

The End

*** Michael Cooling (Artificial Agent) will return ***

PLEASE LEAVE A REVIEW AND/OR A RATING

If you enjoyed this book, it would be tremendously helpful to me if you're able to leave a review or, at least, a star rating on Amazon or wherever you picked up this book. **Star Ratings and Reviews help me gain visibility**, and they can bring my books to the attention of other interested readers. Thank you!

A Message from J.W. Jarvis

Building a relationship with my readers is the very best thing about writing. **Join my VIP Reader Club** for exclusive information on new books and discounts. As a gift for joining, you can download one of my fantasy novellas, *The Phantom Firefighter*, for **FREE** below.

Just visit
https://BookHip.com/DTHFNNR
or scan the QR code below with your phone

ABOUT THE AUTHOR

J.W. Jarvis lives in sunny California but is originally from the
suburbs of the Windy City.
When he's not thinking of ways
to create inspiring characters
and nonstop action stories, you
can find him reading, golfing,
traveling, or just sipping a hot
vanilla latte. Visit J.W. Jarvis at
www.authorjwjarvis.com

facebook.com/authorjwjarvis

x.com/authorjwjarvis

instagram.com/authorjwjarvis

Made in the USA
Coppell, TX
29 October 2024

39355237R00225